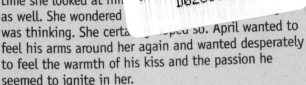

April couldn't keep he
time she looked at hin
as well. She wondered
was thinking. She certa__ __ped so. April wanted to
feel his arms around her again and wanted desperately
to feel the warmth of his kiss and the passion he
seemed to ignite in her.

Her throat became dry thinking about the kiss they'd
shared earlier, and she became eager to share more
than a kiss. She laughed to herself as she thought
about the old Betty Wright song, "Tonight is The
Night." She thought back to her seventies party and
how they'd danced to the song. She could feel his
growing excitement as they literally did a bump and
grind during the song. It seemed the song had the
same effect on everyone else at the party, so nobody
noticed they were drenched with sweat afterward.

It took all the control she had to send him home that
night. She wanted to tackle him and make love on the
living room floor. Her desire had been magnified to
the tenth power since then, but she'd managed to keep
it in check. They needed to take their time and get to
know each other before their passion claimed them.
Passion had a way of clouding judgment; she wanted
her mind clear when it came to Marcus.

CAROLYN NEAL

At Last

AT LAST

An Arabesque novel

ISBN 1-58314-478-1

www.kimanipress.com

Printed in U.S.A.

Acknowledgments

To my husband, Michael, who always finds the right words to encourage and support all that I do. To my beloved son, Michael, the answer to my prayers. You are truly God's greatest gift to me. My sister, Rita Ford, who is absolutely a phenomenal woman. Thanks for being the best sister and friend anyone could have. Your tireless efforts and salesmanship were second to none when it came time to get the word out about my first book. To Tracy Brown, Annette Wright, Carolyn Smith and David Brown. I love you all more than you'll ever know. I would like to express my thanks and gratitude to the many friends and family who supported my previous novel, *Flawless*. A special thanks to the wonderful women of *True Learners, Knowledge Yearners* reading club of St. Louis, for graciously supporting me. Thanks to Cathy Fraser for selecting the book for the club and hosting a welcome for me in her beautiful home. That invitation will always be close to my heart. Thanks, Sally Byars, for the introduction. With girlfriends like Cynthia Hill, Dorothy Dandridge and Kim Smith, who needs a PR team? Thanks for your loyal support.

Chapter 1

April had barely entered her home when the phone rang. She ignored it to make sure she did what she did every evening when she first got home. Her dogs ran to greet her, wagging their tails, eyes pleading for pats and playtime, her usual way of greeting them. "Hey boys, you miss your mommy?" She bent down, but didn't have to go far to pet her two large German Shepherds, Preston and Jimmy. They each weighed over one hundred pounds and were loyal protectors of April. She rewarded them with playtime, treats and lots of love. Since she didn't have any children, she doted on her pets.

The two bigger dogs squeezed out the little mixed-breed dog that a friend had brought her when it was near death from abuse. Despite his diminutive size he ran as enthusiastically and greeted April with the two larger dogs, and eagerly waited for her touch and special greeting. She had nursed the puppy back to health and named him Champ. Secretly, he was her favorite because of having been through so much abuse and having survived. Like her, he was a survivor.

Her finicky cat Midnight lay on the sofa in the family room nonchalantly watching the commotion, which caused April to smile. She knew later that evening the cat would at some point jump onto her lap expecting to be stroked.

After feeding the dogs, birds and cat she took a long, hot, leisurely soak in the bathtub. Looking at the flashing light on the answering machine around ten that evening, she finally pushed the Play button. She'd gotten a glass of ice and filled it with water, her favorite drink. She sipped while listening to her messages. She had several messages from friends and colleagues inviting her to various functions, but she listened intently to the one message she knew she'd return that evening.

"Hey baby, it's me. I just called to see how you were, I hadn't talked to you in a few days. I'm leaving for Seattle and hope to see you before I go. I miss you already. Call me." She immediately picked up the phone to return the call.

"Good evening, April." Donald had anticipated her call and he smiled broadly when her name flashed across his caller ID.

"How's it going?" April asked.

"Now that I'm talking to you, it's going good, very good." Donald couldn't hide the pleasure in his voice even when he tried.

"Hmmm, that's quite a nice thing to hear after the day I've had." April purred in the phone. She sat in her favorite recliner stroking Midnight.

"Feel like talking? I can come over." Donald's voice was low, seductive and hard to resist. April pictured his smoldering, intense brown eyes and reached over for her glass, taking a sip of water as her throat grew dry and tight.

"I'd like that very much. When can you get here?" Her voice mirrored his seductive invitation.

"I'm on the way."

Donald and April had shared the titles of lovers and friends, but his intentions had always been to make her his permanent lover. He made no effort to hide his feelings for her. They'd taken many vacations together, they dined together and had great times together, but she would never commit to elevating the relationship above the title of friendship.

Anytime she needed something done around the house, he was there. She'd gone through a very difficult time trying to overcome some childhood secrets, and his was the shoulder she'd cried on. That made their relationship special, but hadn't elevated it to lovers like he wanted. They'd made love, but they were still not lovers. Neither dated anyone else, but still they weren't lovers. Sometimes it frustrated him that she could be so uncommitted, knowing how he adored her. He knew April always withheld a part of herself, she never gave herself to him totally.

April thought at times she wanted to elevate the friendship but had a thriving veterinarian practice, a political agenda that was filled with meetings and a family that always seemed in peril. On the surface, she didn't seem to have the time to cultivate the relationship. She didn't want to try to dissect why she never tried to develop a relationship with any man, even a good man like Donald.

She knew it was her lack of willingness to commit because, had it been up to Donald, they'd be married with two-point-three children and a house that he'd designed for them the first month they'd met.

Donald Perrault was sexy and charming. His confident manner commanded attention wherever he went. His broad shoulders and six-feet-two stature made it difficult not to notice him. He wore his hair cut short and had a smile that could melt the polar caps. He was a successful architect. April had tried explaining to him that she loved him, but she wasn't in love with him. Her love was brotherly, it was that of a dear friend.

The two had met when he brought his niece's poodle into her office with glass stuck in its paw. Donald's architectural business kept him busy, and left little time for dating. The one Saturday he had a date, he'd agreed to watch his niece's dog while the family was on vacation. But somehow the animal had gotten out of his yard and when he finally found it, it was limping with blood coming from the right paw. The poor thing was shaking with fright.

He knew that his niece would be upset if he let anything happen to the dog and since she'd trusted it with her favorite uncle, he made sure to get it the best treatment possible. He didn't want to take the animal to just any vet or animal hospital. His date didn't appreciate the time he'd taken to look for the animal and had left in a huff. Donald called one of his friends that had pets and the friend recommended Dr. April Nelson. The friend made the call for him and had arranged for them to meet at April's office.

Donald was amazed that he could find a vet that would open an office at ten o'clock in the evening on a Saturday. Then, when he saw her, the attraction couldn't be denied or fought. April was five feet seven inches tall, with a slim but curvaceous figure that begged for hugging. Her long, dark brown curly hair called for his hands, and he found it difficult not to caress it. Even though she didn't have on any makeup she was beautiful. Her thick dark eyelashes framed the most beautiful brown eyes he'd ever seen.

Her smile radiated warmth as she explained the care of the dog's bandaged foot to him. Even the blue terry cloth hooded jogging suit she wore couldn't hide her curves. Their styles seemed in contrast at that time. He was dressed in a black Hugo Boss suit. Not having changed from his date, he felt overdressed but found April unpretentious and easy to talk to.

Her degrees and many awards were hung in her office, but otherwise there was nothing ostentatious about her.

She obviously took pride in her work, and that impressed him. He wondered what she looked like when she dressed to go out, but somehow knew her style was unassuming and comfortable. He never thought he'd envy an article of clothing but at that time he yearned to trade places with that blue jogging suit. He desperately wanted to caress every curve.

Before he left that evening they shared a cup of coffee and good conversation. The chemistry between the two couldn't be denied and April had given him her personal phone number without his asking. Her casual, easygoing style captivated him from that moment, and hadn't released him.

He smiled as she handed it to him. "What's this?" he asked.

She smiled easily and replied, "My phone number if you'd like to share another cup of coffee." He liked her direct style. On some women it may have seemed forward or too aggressive, but somehow it seemed natural for April. She'd had his heart ever since. They started out being lovers and now had become very close friends, but he wanted more.

"That sure didn't take long." April greeted Donald at the door with a smile. He greeted her with a light kiss on her cheek.

"I was anxious. I haven't seen you all week." His eyes slid down to the pink silk pajamas she wore. On any other woman the pajamas would have been just that, pajamas, but on April they were more. She gave them feminine appeal with her shapely figure and long legs. The lace down the front seemed to bring attention to the swell of her breast making Donald take a deep breath. He wanted to make love, but knew April couldn't be rushed. She wasn't the kind of woman that you could seduce quickly and leave. She never gave her time or emotions easily or quickly to anyone.

"You look awfully good." He barely seemed to whisper. Their eyes met and flirted briefly.

"Thank you." She took in the smell of his sandalwood-scented cologne and smiled as he leisurely strolled into the living room. The room glowed softly from candlelight. He sat on the sofa and listened briefly to the music that had suddenly filled the room. Looking around, he noticed the quiet. The cat, Midnight, lay quietly in a corner, obviously sleeping.

"Where are the dogs?" he inquired softly.

"They're in the basement. Thought I'd make some uninterrupted time for us for a change." The seductive cadence of her voice made him want to take her into his arms. They hadn't had time for each other in months because of her intense schedule and personal life, and now she'd made time for them to spend time together, alone.

The soft music and quiet made him relax as he motioned for her. "Come here." He patted the space next to him. She walked over, sat down. He wrapped his arms around her and gently brushed her hair away from her face. "Looks like you've had a hard day."

April said, "It was. I'm short staffed, I need to hire a temp until Nia comes back from maternity leave. Poor Bridget is about to go insane. Would you like something to drink? I've got some…"

Not allowing her to finish, he interrupted her. "And you'll get it together, you always do. Stop working so hard. You should work that office part-time."

She stood. "I couldn't. I have too many people who rely on me. My patient base has grown so much over the past two years." He pulled her back down.

"Well, rest for a few minutes. I can get me something to drink later."

She sat down and placed her head on his shoulder. They

sat quietly and she began to think about what it was about him that brought such comfort to her. It was a comfort she enjoyed, a comfort that she'd grown to depend on. April didn't have to think about it, didn't have to plan for it, it simply happened whenever she needed it, and tonight she needed it.

She became totally relaxed for the first time in weeks and after several minutes drifted off to sleep. Looking down at her nestled against him, he slowly stroked her hair. She looked so peaceful in the glow of the candlelight, he let her sleep for several more minutes.

Donald eventually lifted her from the sofa and carried her into the bedroom. He experienced mixed feelings because his body ached from desire as he watched her several more minutes. The rise and fall of her breast made him want to wake her, but he felt obligated to be considerate and let her sleep. April didn't always get a good night's sleep so he let her sleep undisturbed. Besides, since their status had changed back to friends, sex was out of the question, but that didn't stop him from wanting her.

Donald knew that she didn't have time for much else or anyone else so he felt honored when she made time for him. His patience was wearing thin, however, and he wanted more from her. If only she could let go of her community involvement, he thought as he watched her sleep. The neighborhood was already a lost cause and there was nothing this beautiful woman could do to save it. Donald looked across the room at April's planner on her nightstand and quietly laughed. Even from where he sat he could see the many notes and items paper-clipped to it. If only he could get her to agree to let go of some of her extracurricular activities, there would be time for them. He sighed heavily and turned off the light.

The next morning found the two in bed side by side. April slowly opened her eyes and looked at the clock on the nightstand as it flashed 5:42. She looked over at Donald sleeping peacefully and felt embarrassed that she'd fallen asleep. She watched him as he slept and wished she could love him the way that he deserved. Her thoughts were interrupted by the dogs in the basement barking. She got out of bed to see what was causing them so much excitement. She could tell from their excited barking that something was wrong. She grabbed her robe and raced to the kitchen window. Although the early sun was covered by a thin layer of clouds, it was light enough outside for her to see two men trying to pry open the door of her neighbors' garage.

She heard police sirens in the distance and immediately walked over to the phone, picked it up and dialed 911 to report the suspicious activity. All the while, she took in their general description and clothing. After talking with the police, she called her elderly neighbors and warned them to stay inside and asked them to make sure the doors and windows were locked. She went downstairs and calmed her excited dogs down with a few minutes of playtime and doggy treats.

April made her way back upstairs and was making a pot of coffee when she heard, "What's going on?" Donald appeared, wiping sleep from his eyes. He wore pajama pants that he kept at April's for the occasional times he spent the night. His bare chest flexed and his trim waist made April sigh out loud.

"I think two men are trying to hide in the Andersons' garage. I just called and talked to Sean at the police department. Seems they fit the general description of two perps who robbed a gas station over on Arsenal." Her casual tone didn't keep Donald from becoming excited.

"April, you sound like a policeman or detective. Come back to bed and let the policemen do their job." His words came out more forceful than planned, but he'd grown tired of April putting herself in harm's way. To his way of thinking it was wasted effort to protect a community that was already lost to violence and drug activity. It was a rift that kept them apart as she clearly thought differently.

"Are you crazy? Why would I come to bed when there are two men hiding in the garage right next door? I'm keeping my eye on them." The words barely came out of her mouth when she saw the police car stop suddenly near her garage. The policemen jumped out, guns drawn, yelling for the two men to come out of the garage. After a few minutes of a tense standoff the two men exited the garage and were told to lie on the ground by the officers. While she and Donald stood in the kitchen watching the scene unfold, her front doorbell rang.

April walked past Donald, who had a look of disapproval on his face. The corners of his mouth were turned down and just as he started to speak, April stopped him.

"Don't start with me, Don, I live and work in this community and I refuse to give up." She held up her hands to stop any further discussion of the topic as she headed toward the front door.

She peeped through the frosted glass of the front door and recognized the police officer. She tied her robe tightly around her and then opened the door. "Good morning, Dr. Nelson. Sorry to disturb you, but I knew you'd want to know the situation."

April greeted the officer warmly and invited him inside the foyer. The officer went on to explain to her that the two men were suspects in a robbery that had taken place several blocks away and had led policemen on a high-speed chase nearby. The car struck a tree and the two ran from the vehicle in an attempt to escape the police. Because of her call to the police department, the two were apprehended. The officer thanked her again for helping to keep the neighborhood safe and left. She called her neighbors to make sure the elderly couple were okay. After talking briefly to the Andersons, she went to the kitchen, but Donald wasn't there.

She heard the shower running in the bathroom and went inside. She couldn't help but smile at his silhouette behind the frosted glass, which exposed his naked, well shaped body. Donald spent hours in his home gym and was rewarded with a body that was chiseled almost to perfection. April knew he garnered attention from women everywhere he went and admitted to herself that he was built for loving.

April asked, "Would you like to have breakfast with me?" She was a little embarrassed yet aroused when he turned off the water and slid the door open, exposing himself. Donald reached past her to get a towel from the nearby rack. She blushed at his nude body as if she'd never seen him naked before, but it had been too long ago, much too long.

"Actually, I have to get home. I have to get on a plane for Seattle in a few hours." His voice lacked warmth or interest.

"I'm sorry I fell asleep on you last night. I didn't realize how tired I was." She stroked his arm as he patted himself dry.

"No need to apologize for being *tired*. I can understand *that*." His tone had become firm and his emphasis let her know that wasn't the problem of which he was concerned.

She stopped stroking his arm and looked at him. "What is it that you *can't* understand?"

Taking a deep breath, he looked at her wild hair, which she hadn't bothered to comb but somehow still managed to look beautiful, and his heart softened slightly. "I *can't* understand your need to save this community. You know I have more than enough room for you and your pets at my house. This neighborhood has gotten too dangerous. I worry about you all the time."

"Don, I really do appreciate that, but I can't just give up my home because some thugs decide to participate in illegal activities. My neighbors and I are constantly fighting every day to keep this neighborhood safe. It's important to me."

April searched his eyes for understanding but found them blank. "If you can't understand *that* I don't know what else we have to talk about," she protested.

Donald continued drying himself. "I understand that you use your community activism and your job to hide from me. That's what I understand." The hardness had crept back into his voice. Don hadn't meant for them to argue, but she could be so stubborn at times it made it impossible for them to enjoy what little time they could share.

"Then you don't understand me at all." April turned to walk away, feeling guilty because she wondered if his assessment of her was correct. She sometimes felt like she hid from him, but she also knew there were never enough hours in a day to get done all she needed to get done. If only he could understand that there were things going on in her life that demanded her attention. People needed and counted on her to be there for them. April sat quietly in the kitchen nursing a strong cup of black coffee. It was going to be a long day, she thought.

"Dr. Nelson, Mrs. Collins is on the line, says she's got an emergency. Mitzi is throwing up and becoming dehydrated. I told her we were closing for the day, but to bring her in as soon as possible."

April was just finishing up a golden retriever puppy that had a broken leg. Without looking up at her receptionist she replied, "Thanks, Bridget. I can stay a little later and take care of her. You know how she loves that little dog. It's probably hurting her more than Mitzi to see her dehydrated. Who else is waiting?"

Bridget took a deep sigh, thinking how she was tired of skipping lunches because her boss didn't have the heart to turn anybody down. She took off her latex gloves. "Just Mr.

Howard's two boxers for their shots. You were working like a fiend all day long, I swear I don't know how you do it." She scratched the back of her head between two thick braids. "Since we worked through lunch, would you mind if I leave a little early? I wanted to go and get my hair done tonight."

Bridget knew the request would be granted, she always bragged about having the coolest boss in the world. April worked her like a farm mule, but she also was very generous about giving her paid time off.

"Sure, we should be done by 4:30. If you need to leave sooner than that, just let me know and I can activate the buzzer," April replied without looking up as she continued working.

"That should be fine. Thanks again, Doctor, you're the best." Bridget prepared the paperwork for the golden retriever puppy and then she turned to go and tell its owner the puppy was fine. She checked on the lone remaining customer in the reception area.

Since Nia was on maternity leave, it left only Bridget to work the receptionist area and to assist April when needed. April carried out the puppy who was still sleeping and gave the owner instructions on the care of its leg. She petted the two boxers, who willingly went with her for their shots, along with their owner. They talked about the weather while April went about her work, and then Mr. Howard asked the same question he always asked. "You know, my son is still single, when can you take him off my hands?" His eyes would light up with laughter each time he asked her, and each time her answer was the same. "Oooh, that sounds really inviting, but I think I'll have to pass. Think I'll let you keep your son." She would return his smile and they would spend a few minutes talking about the dogs, what was going on in the community, or any other topic of interest.

April knew she took too much time with Mr. Howard, but

she also knew that he was lonely, that his son spent no time with him. His wife had passed years ago, and he had no one else but his son and his dogs. Mr. Howard came to the community meetings once a month and was an avid member of the group, so April always made extra time for him. He would bring her vegetables he'd grown in his garden, and she often baked goodies for him.

April walked Mr. Howard out, and once he left, she turned to Bridget. "If you get a chance, please call the temp service and see how soon we can interview a few applicants."

Bridget looked up from the computer. "The few they sent last time were pitiful, and undertrained, I might add."

"Don't I know it, but we've got to get some help, even if just a receptionist to check in patients and record basic information. I don't want to burn you out, I'm sorry we worked through lunch."

"Yeah, but you had lunch brought in, so I was fine. But I'll call and see what they can do." Bridget thought and then suddenly stood up. "You know what, my cousin just got laid off. She could do this, she loves animals. She's a customer service representative at a call center, great on the phone. She's used to working crazy hours, so this should be a breeze for her."

April looked at Bridget and smiled. "So, what are you waiting for? Call her, we are in desperate need of help. We needed her, like, two weeks ago."

Bridget laughed, "I'm calling, I'm calling. Can I at least get a glass of water? She won't be home for another half an hour, anyway."

"Call her and leave a message. If she's anything like you, I don't want to lose out. She'll get home and have a job offer waiting for her."

Bridget smiled at the lopsided compliment. "So it shall

be done." She then picked up the telephone and called her cousin, Samantha.

April returned to her office and collapsed in the chair. She still had plenty to do as she looked around her office at the stacks of trade magazines she'd intended to read. There were patient files and various other details calling her attention. It was going to be another late night for her. There were many times when April worked alone at night. She'd had a friend install a security system that included an electronic buzzer that could be heard throughout the office and she could not only communicate with the visitor, but could also buzz them in. The system also had motion detectors. The neighborhood had taken the plight of many inner-city neighborhoods. It was overrun with crime and boarded up buildings that were breeding grounds for illegal drug activity and various other nefarious dealings. It was less than two miles from home, making it accessible, and April had refused to leave the area despite encouragement from well-meaning friends and family.

She loved the energy of the city despite its problems, and South St. Louis had a myriad of problems. She was the president of her community organization and was well-known in the neighborhood as someone always willing to help, with a pet, or with a neighborhood or personal problem. Policemen and politicians knew she could be tough when attending neighborhood meetings. Her passion had forced her to take a stand with many of the local residents and owners who chose to let their houses become run-down, or didn't follow city ordinances by allowing loud music or too many residents living in a house.

She and others had cleaned up their block by calling the police for all kinds of infractions—including loud music, what appeared to be gang activity, public drinking—and had videotaped a drug transaction, which led to a conviction. They researched the books at City Hall and found absent or negligent landowners who'd let their vacant properties get infested with drug activity, or overgrown weeds causing fire hazards, and got the city to take action.

April had formed a group of volunteers whose primary concern were judges who were believed to be too soft on criminals. They sat in courtrooms and observed trials and sentencing of violent criminals. Their main objective, however, was to observe the judges and research their previous history of court decisions. If they had a record of frequently being too lenient with career or violent criminals they would be publicly denounced by the organization April headed. Members of the community were urged not to vote for them, and were encouraged to play more active roles in the selection of judges and local politicians. She was a woman of passion, and anyone who knew her knew better than to stand in her way when it was time to get the job done.

It was this same sense of compassion that made her call Donald later from her office. "Good evening, Don, it's me. Listen, I'm sorry about this morning." A comfortable feeling embraced her as she sat back in her chair.

"It's okay. I try to understand but frankly, April, I don't understand how you can continue to live in the city. It's dangerous, property values are lower because of the crime. But none of that matters to me. Your being safe is the important thing. I hope you understand that."

It was a point of contention that she knew would always divide them, he knew it as well. April moved the conversation to neutral territory. "So, how's Seattle treating you?"

"It's going very well. The company I met with today praised the designs, and I think the bid we made earlier to the city is one of the two that are being seriously considered. If either one of these pans out it will open a whole new avenue for us to pursue. I hope to put some other things into play that may pay off big for me. So, I should wrap things up here tomorrow and be home by Wednesday."

The familiarity in Donald's voiced relaxed her.

"How about you? Everything okay with you?"

"It's going pretty good. It's just been busy today. I'm staying a little later than I planned."

"You know I worry about you working late by yourself. I'll stay on the phone with you until you get safely home."

"That's really not necessary, although I do appreciate your intentions. I grew up in the city and I know how to take care of myself. Besides, Bridget is still here. I have one more appointment left."

"Stop acting like you don't need anybody, April. Call me when you're ready to leave. I'll stay on the phone with you until then."

"Okay, you're right. You know, Don, it's good to have a friend like you. Think you may be free one night this week for dinner at my place?"

Bridget stood at the door to April's office and silently mouthed that Mrs. Collins was waiting with Mitzi. April mouthed back, "Thanks, I'll be there in a minute."

"Woman, you know I'd walk a country mile for one of your home-cooked meals. Name the day and time, I'll be there."

"How about Thursday night?" April was planning a menu in her head. She had looked at her schedule and saw Thursday was her lightest day of the week.

"Sure, that sounds good." Don was almost certain there was more on her mind when he asked, "Are you okay, you sound kinda melancholy. Everything all right?"

"Everything's fine, just doing some thinking, that's all. Listen, I've got an early day tomorrow and I'm running late for a dinner tonight. My appointment's here, I've gotta go, but

I'll call you when I'm leaving the building. And don't forget, I'll see you Thursday."

April listened for a moment to the silence and wondered what had happened. "Don, are you there?"

"Yeah, I'm here. I've been doing some thinking, too. Your friend. Is that all I am to you, April?"

April thought as she unfolded herself from the chair and stood. "I'm not sure what you're asking. Yes, you're more than a good friend, but we tried the lovers part and that didn't work." The phone was silent again, then she asked, "You do remember that, don't you, Don? It almost ruined our friendship. We're much better friends than lovers. I value our friendship, and I value you. Yes, you are important to me and I hope you know that. It was difficult coming back from being lovers to being friends."

"I do remember our friendship almost being ruined, but we weren't where we are now. We both had other things going on. You may not believe this, April, but I love you in ways I've never loved another woman. What I feel for you is much bigger than friendship. I think we should try again."

April was stunned by the revelation. Donald had always seemed comfortable with the relationship as it was. There were sparks of passion between the two of them and in the past they'd occasionally acted on it. Their kisses were always of the friend-greeting-friend nature. She didn't want to jeopardize their friendship again. Surely he wanted and deserved a woman that would love him the way he wanted to be loved.

Their love affair had been disastrous; ending it was something they'd both agreed to. They also had agreed to remain friends, but found it difficult without bringing up hurts from the past. It seemed as if time was on their side, and as time went by they were able to forgive, forget and move on. But that had taken three years, and now he was suggesting that they try it again. She didn't think their friendship would survive another disastrous love affair, but she wasn't sure if the friendship would survive if she told him she didn't think it was a good idea to try again.

"Why now, Don, after all this time?"

"You know how I feel about you, April. I've never tried to hide it. I just think sometimes you are running from something. You hide behind your work and community involvement to keep from making a commitment to me." April could hear the frustration in his voice.

"I've given that a lot of thought since you brought it up. At first I thought maybe there was some truth to it, but you're wrong." She tried to gather her thoughts, she closed her eyes and thought the best approach was to be direct. It was her style.

"Right now I do have a lot going on, and I'm not hiding behind anything. My sister's marriage is falling apart. All of a sudden she's looking for resolution to her problems in a liquor bottle. I work ten and twelve hours a day and am entrenched in a community action program that I love. I've convinced the owner of an empty building to donate it to us so we will have a place to meet monthly. We've taken the time to do repairs and cosmetic work to the building. I'm constantly writing letters asking for donations to our organization. All of that takes a lot of time from my personal life, Don. It is my personal life, and I make no excuses for that. I need someone who respects and supports that, and you and I both know that's not you."

She listened for his protest, but it never came.

"What time is dinner Thursday?" Donald's voice sounded normal.

"Seven okay?"

"Yeah, sounds good to me."

"I've gotta go. Thursday night, dinner, my place."

"You're on. Do I need to bring anything?"

"A good appetite."

She went to greet Mrs. Collins and Mitzi. She told Bridget to go on to her appointment and that she would see her in the morning.

Later that evening she proceeded to make arrangements to close her office for the day and turned the lights off. Tomorrow would be another busy day for her. She called Don to let him know she was leaving her office and was heading home. She reminded him that she was going out for the evening to a fund-raiser. When April got home that evening she was exhausted. After feeding and spending time with her own pets, she showered and got dressed for an evening out. She'd been invited to a fund-raising dinner for the district alderman. On the drive home she'd looked at the beautiful summer sky and yearned to go home and just sit on her porch swing. She could easily sit on her porch with her pets and watch the world go by, but for now she had too much to do. So she headed out for the evening to a fund-raiser.

Walking into the foyer of the downtown hotel April looked around for her friend Dr. Carmen Dubois. Carmen was a psychiatrist and was also active in the community with April. They'd forged a friendship in college and had remained close through the years. April had sought professional help from Carmen years before while trying to cope with the death of her younger sister and other childhood trauma.

The hotel foyer was full of men and women fashionably dressed for the fund-raiser and socializing with drinks in their hands. The overhead lighting sparkled brightly and the red velvet drapes and chairs beautifully accented the room, giving it a formal flair. The crowd was lively and April began having second thoughts about attending. She wasn't in the mood for lively, animated socializing. Her thoughts were on her sister, Summer, and the problems she was having.

"You looking for me?" Carmen's voice caused April to turn around.

"There you are. I was about to leave," April teased.

"What, and not stay for the dry chicken and overcooked vegetables?" Carmen replied teasingly.

"You look beautiful. I love the new hairdo." April lightly touched Carmen's hair.

"Thanks. I must say you look great as always, seems no matter what you put on you're always stunning. I can't stand you." Carmen clicked her tongue and rolled her eyes playfully.

The two laughed and walked into the formal dining hall which was even more decorative than the foyer. The room contained the same type of red drapes and chairs, but the crystal chandelier was multi-tiered, which captured and held the light of hundreds of candle bulbs and added elegance to the room. Around the outer perimeter there was a wall of mirrors which made the room look larger and reflected the light from the chandelier. After making a few stops to talk briefly with associates and members of the community they finally sat down and talked.

"I'm still trying to get my sister Summer in to see you, but she's so resistive. She's from the old school of thought that we don't need to go to psychiatrists." April smiled slightly as she looked at her friend. She had trusted Carmen with secrets she'd never shared with anyone else and the bond the two held caused them to be more candid with each other. April never felt a need to start her conversations with small talk. Carmen understood her.

April continued, "She's having problems at work and it's affecting her marriage. Actually, I think it's probably more that she's found herself trying to drink away her problems."

"Sounds like she needs help immediately." Carmen's attention was focused on April but occasionally she smiled at a passing guest in acknowledgment.

"Not only that, but she never has come to terms with some of our childhood trauma or Autumn's death." April reached for a glass of water on the elaborately decorated table and brought it to her lips. She stopped in midaction as her eyes caught the attention of a tall, strikingly handsome man whose eyes seemed to be boring into hers. April turned her attention back to Carmen after taking a drink of water and setting the glass back on the table.

"So, how are you going to get her to come in? I can come visit her if she's more comfortable with that." Carmen was looking intently at April and looked in the direction of April's wandering eyes. Carmen smiled knowingly in the direction of the tall man and looked back at her friend with a look of mischief that escaped April's usually keen eye.

Despite April's obvious distraction she continued her conversation. "I haven't convinced her to seek therapy yet, but I'm working on it."

April spent the rest of the evening trying in vain not to look at the tall, handsome stranger who had caught her attention. She didn't know why his eyes sought hers out, or if it was the other way around, but he smiled at her whenever their eyes met. Their eyes seemed to meet and do a teasing dance the entire night. His smile reminded her of butter; soft, smooth and sinfully delicious.

At ten-thirty April looked at her watch and jokingly whispered to Carmen, "It's my curfew, I've got to go. Tell the alderman the check is in the mail." The alderman was still talking about the improvements to the community that he'd like to see achieved. April had heard it all before so she knew she could leave without missing anything. She looked at all the food she'd left on her plate and knew that the handsome stranger had consumed her appetite. One more quick glance in his direction confirmed he was indeed tasty looking, she thought. It had been a long time since she'd been so attracted to anyone.

"I've got to stay and talk to a few people, but I'll talk to you later. We can figure out something for Summer. I'll do whatever it takes, she needs help right away whether she admits it or not."

"Thanks, Carmen." April looked in the direction of the tall, strikingly handsome stranger with the killer smile and was disappointed to see his chair was empty. She pushed her chair back and removed the napkin from her lap and placed it on the table.

Carmen smiled and whispered, "Well, well, the good doctor does have a pulse."

April didn't hear Carmen's comment as the alderman's voice resonated throughout the room. She continued to proceed out of the dining hall, stopping occasionally to say good-night to a few people.

She was able to sit on her porch late that night with her pets as she watched the sky turn its purplish blue and fill with stars. Every once in a while a light breeze would gently blow across the porch, causing a slight shudder from her.

Later that night her dreams were of the tall handsome stranger whose name she didn't know, but whose mere presence had caused her so much of a distraction. Even in her sleep, she could still visualize his eyes, and those lips that begged for hers. There was something very commanding about the way he looked at her. Something that caused her to return the look rather than take her usual stance, which was to look away in disinterest.

Chapter 2

Early the next morning April called her sister Summer. April often talked to her while preparing for the workday. She was sitting on the sofa this morning in her slip and pantyhose. Midnight leaped onto her lap. All she needed was to put on her skirt and blouse, everything else was done.

"Hey, Sis, how's it going?" April asked as she sat on the sofa stroking Midnight.

"It's okay, I guess. Cooking breakfast for your favorite brother-in-law and nephew." Despite the attempt at sounding lighthearted, Summer's voice was laced with sadness.

"Summer, I'm sure you don't want to hear this now, but I've been telling you for years to leave that crazy company. You've put your heart and soul into something that you'll never be a part of." Even though the initial shock was over for Summer, hearing it from her sister, the words still stung.

April continued, "How many hours, holidays, weekends

and sacrifices have you made for that company? They couldn't possibly pay you enough! You've worked birthdays, holidays, anniversaries and this is your reward, a demotion. You remember the time they scheduled a hair show on Mother's Day and you had to work? And now they've decided to downsize which means that they want you to do the job of two people." She clicked her tongue in disgust. Midnight looked at her curiously as she made the noise.

Taking a minute to let her sister ruminate on the thought she continued, "Kenneth and Andrew were so disappointed you wouldn't be home for Mother's Day. I couldn't believe they'd do such a thing, scheduling a hair show on Mother's Day. Well, I know you're not going to let them get away with what they're trying to do." April didn't attempt to mask her anger.

Summer was used to her sister's tirades because April was never one to sit back and watch anyone be taken advantage of or tolerate any injustices. Summer knew she had to have some plan of action that would halt the inquisition that April would continue at any minute.

"I'm flying to New York next week to meet with the new management. Hopefully I'll have some time alone with Paige and a few of the other senior reps to discuss what we can do. They claim this downsizing is necessary in order for the company to move forward."

"Do they know the gig's up?" Summer could picture April's perfectly arched left brow going up, and for a moment the thought forced the corners of Summer's mouth to simulate a smile. The conversation was too intense for a genuine smile. How many times had she seen that brow go up when something met with her sister's disapproval?

"I'm sure they all suspect something, but nobody's said anything. I have an appointment to see an attorney in two weeks. I can't see how the company plans to move forward when they're letting go half the staff who built the division. They think we're all going to go away quietly and let them do whatever to us. Well, I've got news for them."

April stood up from the sofa and went into the bedroom for her printed skirt. She removed it from the bed and stepped into it. She took the peach-colored blouse that accented the peach in the printed skirt from the bed and began buttoning it up. "You sure are talking tough for somebody who thought that company could do no wrong. Why the sudden wake-up call?" She began tucking her blouse inside the skirt and zipped it up. She looked in the mirror and liked the image. She applied a light coat of lipstick and fluffed her hair. "I've told you for years to start your own business. You have a master's degree, for goodness sake, you don't have to be their whipping girl."

"April, subtlety is not one of your finer points. What does it matter *why* I'm waking up? The point is I'm awake, and I'm not taking it anymore. Hold on a second." Summer put the phone down and went to the stairs. *"Drew, Drew."*

"You called me?" Andrew yelled from the top of the stairs.

"Please turn that music down. I'm on the phone." Walking back to the kitchen island, she found herself dreading to resume the conversation. It had only been a day and already she was tired of talking about LaFlair and its so-called new structure. The company was downsizing because it had acquired another beauty care company and Summer had been demoted to a district manager. Her previous position as regional manager had taken ten years of hard work, dedication and sacrifice to acquire. It had been taken away without so much as a blink of an eye. Summer was devastated by the news. It had forced her into a deep depression that was not only affecting her, but her family as well. Her fragile mental state caused grave concern to April.

"That doggone rap, hip-hop, or whatever they're calling that music is about to drive me crazy." She liked music and ordinarily it wouldn't have bothered her but her nerves had been a wreck since the letter came delivering the bad news regarding the company's restructuring.

Taking a deep breath, trying to get her nerves under control, Summer glanced out the kitchen window for a moment. Something about looking out into the yard and seeing the burst of flowers and greenery soothed her. She loved her backyard. Kenneth was a wonderful gardener and it showed in the care of their yard. It could have easily been a cover for *Southern Living Magazine.* She promised herself that the next time he asked if she wanted to help in the yard she would help; better yet, she'd volunteer to help in the yard. In the past she'd always been too busy working, or running off to the post office or doing some other work-related task. Somehow things were being put in perspective for her.

"I don't understand children nowadays, guess it's a good thing I don't have any. I don't know what kind of mother I'd be. Seems like all the kids are listening to it." April decided to change earrings and walked over to her jewelry box in search of her large hoops.

April thought back to her teenage years and smiled at how adults didn't understand what teenagers did back then, either. "Now, I will admit I like that Nelly song, the one about being hot. I played it for the kids at the block party and they went wild. I enjoyed watching them dancing and having a good time. I must admit I also like that new group KRT, they're out in your area, I think they're going to be big. But beyond that, these kids can have it." She put the hoops in her ear and smiled at the look they gave her, almost exotic. She knew she wasn't a fashion diva like her sister, but she had learned to love her earthy look. Her upward slanted eyes, high cheekbones and a mane of curly brown hair gave her an exotic look. She was five foot seven with a metabolism that kept her slim despite not having time for a workout regime other than walking her dogs.

"What do you know about KRT? Trying to keep up with hip-hop. But you know, that's not all there is to being a teenager. You would be a good mother, you just don't have patience for them now because you don't have to. As much love and care as you show your nephew and your pets, I know you would've been a wonderful mother. Anyway, it's not too late, you're still young." Thinking she was successful in steering the conversation away from LaFlair, Summer continued. "So tell me what's happening with you."

April thought about telling her sister about the man she'd seen the previous night, but there really was nothing to tell. She didn't even know his name, besides, she wanted to focus her attention on more important matters at hand. Summer had called her previously, crying about the demotion. She had confided in April that she'd started drinking to try and ease the pain. That conversation caused April much concern and sadness. She didn't want to see her sister slip into a familiar pattern that had caused them both so much pain.

"Nothing's really going on other than the usual. I want to know your plans for LaFlair and what you are going to do to get your life back on track. Now's the perfect time for you to develop a business plan for yourself." April was packing her briefcase, preparing for the long day that loomed in front of her.

Summer turned over the bacon on the stove and said, "April, I just said I haven't decided how to proceed. Kenneth and I plan to talk about it this evening, and since you're being nosy, let me return the favor. When are you going to get some personal business of your own so you can stay out of mine?"

Ignoring the question, April asked, "Have you told your son what's going on?"

"No, I haven't, actually. I haven't had time to tell him. Besides, I don't want him to worry about me, or if our life-style will change. He's got enough on his mind trying to get into Morehouse."

"See, that's why I'm glad I don't have any kids, because he should know what's going on with you and Kenneth. He's a responsible, bright seventeen-year-old, you shouldn't keep things from him." April looked around the room to make sure she had everything. She smiled as her dogs gathered around her in anticipation of her leaving for the day.

"No, April, I'm not keeping it from him, just haven't had time to talk to him about it."

Summer took eggs from the refrigerator, cracked them and emptied the insides into a bowl. She began whipping them with a fork as she listened to April.

"You've had time, you just don't know what to say to him. This is a difficult issue to discuss with your child, that's why you haven't talked to him. You know we grew up in a house of secrets and hated every minute of it." April walked back to the living room and was sitting back on her comfortable sofa now, looking through her planner. Her day was heavy with appointments at her office, but she knew her thoughts would continue to focus on her sister.

"I respect your input, sister dear, but I have a little more experience in this area than you do and I believe I know what's best for Andrew. And don't think I've forgotten about you not having any personal business of your own to share. Listen, I need to finish breakfast, I'll talk to you later." Summer chuckled to herself. April was a real pistol and was not one to keep her opinions to herself, but occasionally she'd have the last say. She thought about their childhood briefly and immediately became sad. There was no way her child would ever have to endure the kind of pain she had.

April checked the clock and left for work, but not before writing a note to herself to call Carmen. Summer was hurting, and most of all, she was hiding the hurt. April knew what kind of damage that could do.

Chapter 3

Kenneth Hughes sat looking out of the window of his
office, playing catch with the autographed Lou Brock
baseball his wife had bought him years earlier. It was the
typical office of a publishing executive: cluttered, small and
unpretentious. He was well liked in the small Christian publishing company. Thought to be courteous and affable by all,
he was a dedicated hard worker and was expected to
someday be the CEO of the company.

But today his thoughts were on his problems at home, with
Summer. He'd loved the woman for what seemed liked an
eternity, and thought their lives would always remain the
same until recently. He'd felt comfort in knowing that, he'd
proclaimed his need for sameness while they dated. She was
the one who embraced change like a long-lost friend. That was
one contradiction in their relationship that always worked; opposites attracting and finding harmony in their opposition.

Summer caught his attention at a book signing for one of his authors. Standing in line while waiting for an autographed copy of a book, she was the most beautiful woman he'd ever seen. Her eyes and smile silently invited him over to her, but once he approached her, the words wouldn't pass his lips.

He still remembered the white cashmere sweater and winter white slacks she wore, and an enchanting smile that surely mesmerized anyone who encountered it. Her beautiful, soft brown eyes were full of mischief and wonder. He got so lost in them when she looked at him that he simply couldn't speak.

Kenneth sometimes became shy in certain situations, but he'd never swallowed his tongue as he'd done the first time he tried to talk to her. He was drawn to her like nothing he'd ever experienced. The overwhelming feeling frightened yet entranced him. He had to meet her.

She seemed totally unaware of the impact she had on him as he stood in front of her, saying nothing. "Hello, I'm Summer Nelson." She extended her hand and before long the words finally managed to leave his mouth.

"Nice to meet you. I'm Kenneth Hughes. Did you enjoy the reading?" He could feel beads of sweat forming on his forehead, even though it was a brisk January day.

"Oh, yes, I love his writing. I'm always reading something inspirational and he's one of the best around. What about you?" When she smiled he stared at her sparkling white, even teeth. She had two small dimples just below the corners of her mouth and he thought they were the cutest things he'd ever seen.

"Yes, I always enjoy working with Harrison." He returned her smile nervously.

"You work with him?" Her eyes seemed to illuminate with excitement.

"Yeah, I'm an editor with Sacred Hearts Publishing and he's one of our authors. I'm supposed to be working, but this is one of the best parts of my job. Getting out and seeing the readers respond to an author's work." Standing with his hands in his pockets, he refused to take them out, unsure if he'd be able to control himself. He usually was very much in control, but this woman seemed to subliminally beg for his embrace. He stood there like a shy ten-year-old talking to a girl for the first time.

He always said it was love at first sight, and argued feverishly with anyone who suggested otherwise. He could feel his heart opening up, allowing her to enter. Something he'd always thought only authors embellished in novels. But the feeling was real, it was true and it was urgent.

"I've never met anyone in publishing before. Sounds exciting, how'd you get started?" she'd asked with her head held gently to one side.

He somehow worked up the nerve to invite her for coffee in the bookstore's restaurant and by the end of the evening he knew he was in love. Even though it was years ago, he remembered it like it was yesterday because he valued and trusted their relationship. She was one of the most loving people he'd ever met. Naturally gregarious, Summer could work a crowd like no one he'd ever seen, she was a natural salesperson. She could sell sand to the Arabs, he often teased her. Men and women liked her because of her genuine interest in people and her natural ability to hold a conversation with anyone.

His coworkers were so impressed the first time they met her, they all complimented him on her beauty and sweet disposition. He knew people expected her to be shy because he was, and he took much pleasure in watching her smiling and talking to people at their first office Christmas party.

That enchanting smile could melt the coldest heart. The most amazing part was that it was all genuine, she honestly found interest in everyone she met, and could hold a conver-

sation with anyone about anything; a natural conversation-
alist. He often told her she should write a book on the art of
social communication.

But in the past year, a different Summer had emerged, a
stark contrast to her lively, effervescent personality. She was
now solemn, unapproachable and occasionally cold. He knew
that the changes at work were partly responsible but she'd
taken the demotion too hard. She'd become bitter and spiteful
lately and there were other issues that bothered her. Issues
with her family that she'd never shared with him. Negligent
of him and their son, their family was in peril and somehow,
someway, he was going to get it back to where it should be.
It was too valuable to lose, it was his life, their future together.

His thoughts were interrupted by his telephone ringing. He
looked at the phone and took a deep breath before answering,
"Hello, this is Kenneth Hughes."

"You sound so professional, brother-in-law, I thought I
had the wrong number," April joked. She kept a close eye on
the clock on her desk, she knew her next appointment would
be coming soon. She looked at her planner and wished she
could take some time off.

"Hey April, I was just about to call you." Kenneth swirled
around in his large office chair and faced the window. He
loved looking out the window while he talked on the phone.
He had a view of downtown St. Louis that was breathtaking.
He could see the Arch, the old Courthouse, the ballpark and
various other landmarks.

"About Summer?" April stopped what she was doing and
closed her eyes. She massaged her forehead as she tried to
search for answers to the questions that haunted her sister.

"Yes." Kenneth stood up from the chair and looked toward
downtown St. Louis. His free hand automatically went to his
pocket anytime he was nervous.

"Is she getting any better?" April asked hopefully.

"No, and she won't open up and let me in. She's shutting me out, which is causing problems. It's like she thinks she's in this situation by herself. You know, I would never put you in the middle of a situation, but this is more than a marital disagreement. She needs help, more help than either of us can give her." Kenneth took his hand from his pocket and ran it across his short hair. It was another habit he did whenever he became nervous. Summer had pointed both habits out to him on their second date and he laughed as he marveled at how observant she was.

"Kenneth, you know this isn't just about work. Summer has never dealt with some other issues that she needs to open up to you about." April stopped herself before she betrayed her sister's confidence.

Summer had insisted that April never tell Kenneth about some of the trauma they'd endured during their younger years. Summer felt it was something she'd share with Kenneth, but had told him very little. All Kenneth knew was that their childhood was difficult and unhappy. Their father had left the family when they were very young. Their youngest sister, Autumn, had been killed by her boyfriend years earlier. Summer shut Kenneth out during that time, too. She refused to talk to him about it.

"I know, April, but I can't get her to open up. Have you had any luck with getting her to agree to see your friend?" He sat down again and reared back in the big leather chair.

"Unfortunately no, but I'm going to keep trying. I'll think of something. In the meantime, Kenneth, keep loving her. She needs you now more than ever before, she just doesn't realize it." April got up and put her white coat back on. It was time for her next appointment.

"You don't have to tell me that, April, I can't do otherwise.

I'll love that woman for eternity. I just wish it was enough."
His voice spoke his pain.

"It's plenty, she's just hurting right now. We're going to
help her get through this. I guess you're right, we should start
our search." April tried to sound encouraging, but she knew
it would be an almost impossible task. For her part, she was
to try and locate her aunt and uncle. Kenneth had a more
daunting task.

April's other phone line buzzed and she told Kenneth, "I've
got to get back to work. Carmen has agreed to come to the
house if Summer doesn't want to meet her at the office."

"That may be something she'd agree to, but don't count on
it. Talk to you later. I'll get started on my research right away."
Kenneth felt some relief, but he knew there was much ahead of
them if he and his wife were to work through this difficult time.

April spent the next nine hours working in her office. While
driving home that evening she listened again to a rather vague
message from Carmen saying to expect a call late that
evening, and gave her very few details.

She had settled comfortably in her swing on the front porch
when the phone rang. She picked up the cordless phone and
ushered the dogs and cat inside. She locked the door while
answering the phone.

"Hello."

"Good evening, may I speak with Dr. April Nelson." The
voice was unfamiliar but warm, it was full-bodied and very
male. The voice seemed soothing, mellow, like a spring rain.
She instantly felt comfortable.

"This is April." Not quite sure if she should like what the
voice on the other end was about to say, she sat patiently in
her favorite recliner and waited for the telemarketer to tell her
how she'd been chosen to try a new credit card at an unbeat-
able introductory low rate. *These people pick the worst time*

to call, her mind thought, but somehow she could never bring herself to be rude unless they provoked her.

"Hello, April, this is Marcus Davis. Carmen Dubois gave me your number. She says we seem to have a lot in common and thought perhaps we might want to get to know one another."

If nothing else, this man was direct with a voice so masculine and soothing she automatically smiled. "Yeah, she left a message for me today. Seems she is fairly certain we should meet. She told me you me you specialize in pulmonary disease. Tell me a little about yourself, Dr. Davis." She thought, *As far as us spending time together, I'll be the judge of that.*

April reached for her remote, reared back in her recliner, and anticipated the boredom she was certain was coming her way. A man with a voice like his had to have a seriously inflated ego, but the night was young and there was absolutely nothing on television.

They talked for over an hour and the conversation ended with her agreeing to meet him a week from Saturday night for dinner.

Chapter 4

April couldn't believe how quickly her sister was sinking. Summer had always been the smart one, the pretty one, the successful one. She was the one against whom April measured her own success. There were times when she envied her sister's ability to "have it all," if there was such a thing. Summer was an overachiever in everything she did, a true perfectionist. But somehow she was falling apart, and didn't appear capable of doing anything about her slow descent into the abyss.

They both had grown closer as they got older, not further apart like some sisters. It didn't matter how busy they were, or what was going on in their personal or professional lives, they made time for each other. When her only nephew was born, April spent nearly all of her free time with him. She watched the miracle of his birth. She was there when he took his first steps and said his first words. Andrew was like her own child. She didn't want to imagine what he was going through watching his mother fall apart.

Despite what Summer said, April knew that Andrew was extremely perceptive and bright, he knew what was happening to his mother. April was determined to get her sister to understand the why of her sudden inability to cope with the difficult situation at work. Summer didn't seem to associate her inability to cope with what was happening in her life currently to how she internalized coping with stress as a child. Their mother had always sought relief from any kind of stress in a bottle. She drank to get rid of stress, hurt or anything else that she couldn't cope with.

Prior to seeing a therapist years earlier, April herself had been on a similar destructive pattern, but recognized the symptoms and signs early on and decided almost immediately to seek professional help. She'd kept her struggles to herself and when she finally sought help it amazed her what she learned about herself.

Her confidence had all been a facade, an internal survival mechanism that shielded her from a past that would've kept her on a downward spiral.

She had shared some of her past with Donald, who would hug and hold her during those times as he listened silently. He never judged or asked any questions. He just made her know that he was there for her. Often they'd make love afterwards and April felt that it was more of a release than anything else. She knew it wasn't love, but comfortable intimacy with someone she cared about. Donald certainly never complained. Theirs wasn't fiery, passionate lovemaking, it was comfortable. She found it satisfying, but it certainly wasn't the ardor she wanted from a lover. Her initial attraction to Donald was full of promise, and once they started dating they both agreed they were opposites. They did enjoy spending time together, but there was a missing element, April felt. He simply didn't make her toes curl, and if she was going to have a lover, that was a requirement. Donald only laughed when she tried to break it off after dating a few months. He eventually admitted their differences were insurmountable. There was absolutely no way he could support her community activities, and insisted she could make more money by moving her practice to the county. He did the wrong thing by trying to pressure her, he should have known better. They argued constantly about her working late, going to meetings, not having enough time for him. It got to the point where she wondered if they would even speak to each other again, but after some time they agreed to be friends. Even that was a struggle, because Donald would try to seduce her, and she fought not to allow that to happen. But there were times when her body needed, and she allowed it, so it became a disagreement for them. Their finally becoming friends had been a long, hard struggle, but they made it. Donald had been the only man in her life since. She had little time or interest in casual dating. He escorted her to functions, they dined together, so she didn't see much point to casual dating. Donald, on the other hand, wanted more.

Donald arrived promptly at seven Thursday evening. After greeting him and taking him by the hand into the living room, she became aware of the silence. "Have a seat."

He hadn't said a word since she opened the door. "I've got to check on dinner." She walked into the kitchen and wondered what the silence meant. She took the dinner from the oven and turned to see him leaning against the kitchen door frame, silently watching her.

"What?" Hunching her shoulders, she couldn't read his quiet. She took the lid off one of the pots and stirred the contents.

"Nothing…well yeah, there is something. I want to finish our conversation from the other night on the phone."

An audible sigh slipped from April's throat. She hadn't meant for it to escape, and he immediately knew that she hadn't changed her mind. She put the lid back on the pot and put the ladle she'd used to stir back on the counter.

"Look, Don, we've got a wonderful friendship, there aren't many men and women our age that have what we have." She reached out to take his hand, but he withdrew.

"And what is it exactly that we have, April? Even when we were lovers, we weren't lovers, were we? You always held back, just like you're doing now."

Was this really Don? she thought. His insinuation found its mark and caused April to become quiet and pensive.

He walked over to the kitchen island and sat down on the chair. "Don't you ever wonder why a beautiful, successful woman like you is lonely?"

April felt her stomach tighten and realized she was starting to get aggravated. She tried to remain calm as she explained, "There's a difference between being alone and lonely. I never really view myself as alone, I just don't have a lover at the present time. I have friends that love me, and I thought you were one of those, but I guess not."

She untied the apron she was wearing and put it on the kitchen table. All the while her eyes never left his. He looked down at the island and avoided her gaze.

She cautiously gauged his response. The only giveaway was a quick, slight twitch of his right eye that she wasn't sure was in response to what she'd said or if she'd imagined it.

"You know I love you, April, in ways you may not accept, but I love you just the same. Don't you know I left here after making love to you wondering why I couldn't get next to you? What was it that I wasn't giving you that you needed? What would it take for you to love me? If we're going to just be friends, then okay." His posture had become rigid. The casual air he'd exhibited when he first entered the kitchen was gone.

In the past, she had given him her body but not her heart. She walked over to the island and stood next to him. She looked at him. "I'm truly sorry if I led you to believe otherwise, but our friendship is very important to me. I value it, I count on it. Maybe in the past I've sent mixed signals. I just feel comfortable with you and I thought you felt the same. I told you before I don't have that kind of amorous heart for you. I can't change that. I know you're wonderful, but I simply can't change what my heart feels. You don't want a woman who doesn't feel that way about you." She took his hand, which forced him to look into her eyes.

Donald knew then that he would never again be allowed to hold her in the night again. She had admitted to her feelings to him, but he thought he could change them. He knew she didn't feel the same way about him, and he knew there were times when making love was just a release for her. In some ways it was also a release for him, but he did feel she was the one for him. "Comfortable wasn't really what I was going for, but if that's what you got from it I guess maybe things weren't what I thought they were." The two stood in silence for several seconds, they both realized that their relationship had been changed irrevocably. It was time for some honesty. The kind of honesty that would truly test their friendship.

"I don't feel the kind of passion for you, Donald, that a woman feels for a man she loves. I value the friendship. During difficult times I found some comfort being in your arms, when I should have just let us be friends. I think I tried to love you the way you deserved because you're such a good man. I never meant to hurt you, then or now." April was consumed with guilt as she murmured, "I'm so sorry."

"Well, at least now we are both on the same page, we have

an understanding. Friends, right?" He extended his hand, and she shook it.

"Yes, friends."

"Okay, best buddy, what's for dinner? I'm starving." April patted his back, knowing that he'd let her off easy because sometimes that's what friends do for friends.

"What do you love?"

"Don't tell me you made manicotti?"

"And a wonderful salad, homemade rolls and for dessert, chocolate fudge cake."

"Well, let's get started."

She walked to the refrigerator and took out the salad. "The table is already set. If you would put this on the table, I'll get the manicotti and rolls." She passed the large bowl of salad to him and then turned off the oven.

"What would you like to drink?"

"Tea is good."

April mumbled to herself, "Just like I thought." He could be very predictable at times. After taking the food to the table she poured two glasses of iced tea and carried them to the table. Looking around, everything was finished and she was more than ready to relax and enjoy dinner.

They settled into a nice conversation during dinner, with Donald telling her about Seattle. He enjoyed the city and had taken a trip to the Space Needle. He did confess the weather was more to his liking than the weather in St. Louis. He told her that several of the homes that he'd seen did not have air-conditioning because it didn't usually get very hot in Seattle. He told her about how green everything seemed to be and that it did not seem as though the summer sun burned the grass like it was known to do in St. Louis.

"What, no ninety-plus weather in the summer, along with

humidity so thick you can almost swim in it?" April asked in mock indignation.

"No, just lots of rain in the spring, though." He looked over at her and said, "I remember you once telling me you love a spring rain."

She laughed, "Yes, I do, but not an all-day, everyday rain like they have there." The two talked comfortably about the Midwest weather.

They joked about the really hot summers, the unpredictable mixture of temperatures in the fall, and the cold winters in St. Louis. Donald told April that spring and fall were his favorite seasons of the year, and then confessed, "April is my favorite month."

"You are such a liar, you told me three years ago that October was your favorite month because it usually had the best weather. Not too hot, not too cold, and the change in the season was nice."

"Damn, you remember that? I always say you have a memory like no one I've ever seen."

"Obviously I do. So what were you saying about April?"

"Uh, it's my new favorite month?"

"Yeah, sure it is." April continued to enjoy her manicotti.

Later that night after Donald left, April sat alone looking out the window, thinking about her sister. Although Summer was very demonstrative with her family, she withheld secrets from her husband for too long. They were determined to help her overcome the past and had begun a search they hoped would bring some answers for Summer.

April understood Summer's desire to never see or speak to their mother again. It had taken April a long time and a lot of counseling to pick up the phone and call her mother. Even then it was difficult to talk to Mildred Nelson some days as she was in total denial about the past and even refused to talk about Autumn, as though she'd never existed. April tried to tell Summer that everyone copes with pain differently and even though their mother never appeared to grieve, she had to have been in pain. It was impossible to give birth to a child and know that someone murdered her without feeling pain. It was painful for your husband to abandon you with three children. Their mother's method of coping with any kind of emotion was to get lost in the arms of a man, or by drinking and raising plenty of hell. Mildred Nelson spewed hateful words at her children for months whenever she broke up with any one of their many "uncles." Her drinking binges lasted for days, cursing and neglecting her daughters during that time. A true raging alcoholic, the woman had spent most of her children's formative years emotionally detached and void of any motherly feelings.

Even as adults their mother made no apologies to her children for her past behavior, wouldn't discuss it, denied it if brought up and always yelled about them forgetting the good times, and only wanting to focus on the bad times. Mildred Nelson had sent one child into death without ever being a real mother or saying, "I love you," or doing any of the things a mother does for her children to let them know they are loved.

She made one daughter fearful of ever becoming a mother, not allowing any man to really get close to her. One daughter was happy on the outside, but felt guilty about not deserving all that she truly had. She struggled with the fact that she'd not spoken to her mother in years, that her mother had little interaction with her only grandchild.

Summer rarely mentioned their mother now, and whenever April conveyed any remnants of a recent conversation she'd had with their mother, it was met with stone silence. Unless April mentioned talking to Mildred, her name was never brought up.

April stood up and stretched. It was past her bedtime, but sleep hadn't come. She walked to her bedroom and murmured, "We are our mother's daughters, but we are nothing like our mother," before getting into bed.

April tossed and turned, but still couldn't sleep. For some reason she thought about the last fight she'd had with her mother. April told Carmen about the fight she'd had with her mother during her senior year in college.

It all began when she'd missed her bus after work, and had to wait an additional hour for the next one, which was late because of some minor mechanical problem, the driver had told her when the bus finally arrived. It was after eleven o'clock when she finally got home, and she knew that her mother would either be passed out on the sofa or fussing about her getting in so late.

After a full day of classes and going to work right after, she was worn out. Despite the fact that her mother had an old Chevy and no job, she never allowed anyone to drive it. April was on her own for transportation to and from school and work. She'd been saving for nearly a year for a down payment on a car, but her money had mysteriously disappeared when she went to retrieve it from the jar she kept it in.

Two days later she noticed her mother stepping out in a new dress with matching shoes, but had enough sense not to question her. That made her open a savings account at a bank, with only her and Summer's names on it.

Just as she was putting the key in the lock, the door jerked open. "Where the hell have you been? You know better than to be dragging yourself in here this time of night."

"We couldn't get the register to balance, and I missed my bus. Sorry."

April tried easing past her mother, but she blocked her. "And your dumb ass didn't have sense enough to call."

Tired and not wanting to argue, she mumbled, "The store had closed and I couldn't get to a phone." Just as she managed to walk past her mother, she felt a sharp pain in her back, sending her spiraling forward. Her book bag flew off her arm. She was barely able to break the fall as she caught hold of the recliner before falling to the floor, with excruciating pain.

Tears burned her eyes as she turned to look at her mother, who screamed at her, "Next time, you find a damn phone. You hear me?"

Wiping the tears from her eyes with the back of her hand, she had become more angry than hurt and before she could stop herself, she yelled back, "If you were so concerned, why couldn't you drag yourself away from the television long enough to pick me up?"

Before the final words came out of her mouth, her mother had dived on her and was hitting her with closed fists on her head and anywhere else she could throw a punch. She didn't want to fight her mother, but the heavy punches were too much and there appeared to be no stopping the barrage of blows. April pushed her mother in the chest as hard as she could. Mildred looked as though all the wind had been knocked out of her, then she rolled to her side, holding her chest.

After several deep gasps and finally catching her breath, she spewed, "No, you didn't just hit me. You must have lost your mind hitting me like that. Git outta my house now, before I kill you and don't even think about ever coming back. I don't need another woman in my house. If you grown enough to hit me back, then you grown enough to get your ass out and take care of damn yourself."

April was frozen in fear just looking at her mother's contorted face. Mildred yelled, "Bitch, I said git outta here before

I kill you." Mildred was still taking deep breaths, and April wanted to apologize, but the anger on her mother's face wouldn't allow her. Her lips were squeezed into two thin, tight lines, and her fists were balled up like they would start swinging any minute. April was afraid if she stayed any longer her mother would hit her again.

While it wasn't uncommon for their mother to haul off and slap one of them for some minor infraction, her abuses with April had become more aggressive. April ran to her room, packed a few of her clothes and books. She didn't know where she was going. Summer lived in a dorm at St. Louis University and barely had enough room for herself, it was very late at night and she was in an inner-city, dangerous neighborhood where walking the streets at night could cost a life. Yet she found herself walking the streets after midnight, trying to hail down a taxicab.

She thought she would never forgive her mother for that night, and never told anyone about it except her sisters and Carmen. Autumn had cried and begged her to forgive their mother when April called her at school in Texas.

When she told Carmen the story, April thought the woman was going to leap from her chair as she sat leaning over, taking in every detail. She had never been a crier, but when it was all told, it took her nearly half an hour to stop crying as she thought of how she hadn't in fact returned to her mother's house afterwards. But the years and the visits to Carmen had put the episode into some perspective for April. Without a conversation with her mother, April determined, with Carmen's help, that her mother was an alcoholic, even way back then. Her coming home an hour late from work under most circumstances would be considered innocuous, but because her mother was drinking that night it unleashed aggression toward her daughter. Carmen had helped her to understand that her mother's drinking enhanced her aggressiveness because it reduced her self-awareness and her ability to consider consequences.

Another startling fact that April learned during her time with Carmen was that children of physically aggressive parents tend to use aggression when relating to others, even as adults. Her mother had full parental responsibility of raising them after their father left, which aided to her frustration and dependence on alcohol. Although April made it a point to not drink now, she remembered a time when she did, and now her sister was having a problem with alcohol. She knew the struggle was a difficult one, so she was determined to help her sister in whatever way she could. For herself, childhood had made her ask questions she dared not share with anyone.

Tonight, all April could think was what an old, sad, bitter woman her mother had become, which was just a step away from the bitter, mean, young woman she was the last time the two had fought. She took a deep breath that seemed to require all the energy she had, and feeling quite drained physically and emotionally she drifted off to a fitful sleep. Despite the fact that she'd spent plenty of time with Carmen, she never directly shared those questions that lingered in the recesses of her mind. Those questions were for her to learn the answers to—they were way too personal and invasive.

Saturday arrived and April had agreed to meet Dr. Marcus Davis at a local restaurant for dinner. She made the choice based on the fact that it was close to her home, somewhat elegant and if needed she could dump her date and head over to Ted Drews for ice cream that she knew could make her smile.

He described himself and told her he'd be wearing a gray shirt and slacks. April smiled to herself as she thought, "Sounds boring. Just like a doctor to wear gray." She had told

Summer about her last blind date which had caused her for years to refuse any offers of future blind dates.

A well-meaning friend had introduced April to Lance, an executive producer at one of the local affiliate news stations. They talked on the phone briefly before agreeing to meet for dinner at an upscale restaurant of his choosing. But the night went downhill from the beginning.

The man was full of himself the entire night, constantly mentioning celebrities that he'd met and the inadequacies of the so-called "on-air talent" at the news station. He had bored her to near tears talking about himself, which she politely tolerated with a smile, but then he overstepped his bounds when he stupidly asked her, "Why would an absolutely beautiful woman as intelligent as you appear sabotage her earning potential by being a veterinarian?"

Not even a pretense of understanding or an appreciation that she loved what she did, just as he probably loved what he did. Instead he chose to chastise her. "A beautiful, sexy, smart black female doctor, you could be making megabucks in gynecology, or obstetrics, family practice, anything, even ear, nose and throat. I don't get it, are you a glutton for punishment, why veterinary?"

As he sat stuffing his mouth with the overpriced bloody rare steak he'd ordered, he was shaking his head as if confused the entire time and waited for her reply. It was the only time during the evening he was quiet. She enjoyed the quiet, but was compelled to reply.

Looking him in the eye, she smiled cryptically and said, "I never mistake a dog for anything other than a dog, and I can look at a kitty anytime I want." He was too dense to get her immediate meaning, he just sat with a blank expression, and finally, after she doused him with her drink she told him to "Kiss my animal-loving, underemployed behind." Summer yelped with laughter when April told her the story. No more blind dates for her, she confessed, until tonight.

Carmen had insisted that she meet Marcus despite April's vigorous protest. April decided to meet Marcus at the restaurant rather than have him pick her up at home, at least that way she wouldn't have to tolerate him on the drive to and from the restaurant and she could leave anytime she was ready.

When April got to the restaurant she walked into the lobby area and looked around for a tall man wearing a dull gray shirt and slacks. She was happy to see he hadn't arrived yet and thought about leaving, but was tapped on the shoulder.

"Hello, April, I was expecting to meet you at the hostess station. Somehow you got past me." April turned to meet the voice and was pleasantly surprised. It was the man from the alderman's fund-raiser. Their eyes met and she felt a small catch in her throat as she tried to find her voice. The commanding eyes were taking all of her in and she couldn't help but return the smoldering gaze.

She somehow managed to extend her hand to shake his. The gesture felt totally contradictory to what she was feeling. Her immediate thought was to let her arms go around him and bring him to her. She knew he was watching her at the fundraiser, and she felt the immediate attraction, but up close, he was more attractive and appealing than she remembered.

"Nice to meet you, Marcus." She eyed him appreciatively and added, "I never knew gray could look so good on a man." They both laughed and he took her hand. Instead of shaking it, he gently held it and leaned over to kiss her cheek. April closed her eyes and enjoyed the subtle kiss. She was the cynic as she thought to herself, "Please don't let him say something really stupid."

"I've been begging Carmen for your name and phone number since the night of the fund-raiser, and was happy to hear you finally conceded." He continued holding her hand while he spoke and she could feel the warmth generated from the contact spread down to her toes.

"I'm glad you were persistent." She tried to remain calm as she thought, "Begging her, huh? She certainly never told me that." She allowed a tiny smile to form on her lips as she said, "I'm starving. You ready to eat?"

Marcus looked at her and replied, "Yes, I'm ready to start the evening." His voice was smooth and clear, it resonated with a warmth she liked in a voice. It was soothing, almost like listening to music, she thought.

Marcus could not believe that he was actually out with the beautiful woman who had captured his attention that night. He wanted to know more about her. He'd had attractions before, but none nearly as strong as this one. When Carmen told him she was a doctor he was impressed, and knew he had to find out more. He did not want to be disappointed again, so he was surely going to get to know Dr. April Nelson. One thing was for certain, Dr. Nelson was a well-put-together package. She had the most beautiful, enchanting eyes he'd ever seen.

They waited for the hostess to seat them. April liked the feel of his strong hand on the small of her back as he followed closely behind her. It felt strangely provocative as she felt a rush that ran the length of her body. He pulled out her chair for her and she enjoyed the gesture.

Once they were seated and had discussed the menu, they placed their order with the waiter. They engaged in small talk for several minutes and when dinner was brought to the table April began by asking the first of many questions.

"So, Marcus, you said the other night that you were married for two years? Right after college?" April had set her fork aside as she eyed Marcus, waiting for his response. Her friend had told her very little about him other than he was very busy and enjoyed being active in the community. Carmen thought they had that in common and much more. What Carmen didn't know and what April tried to conceal was that from the moment their eyes had met she'd felt heat rising throughout her body. It was unlike any reaction she'd ever experienced.

She estimated his height to be just over six feet with a body that could drive any woman to distraction. His light gray shirt tucked neatly into dark gray pants were anything but dull. He wore a black belt with silver accents that emphasized a trim waist. Most doctors she knew didn't have time to work out so she was impressed by his hard body.

Marcus held her gaze as he replied, "Yes, it was the dumbest thing I could have done. I was in med school trying to juggle the commitments of that and a new marriage. My wife wasn't very understanding of my schedule and ended up having affairs with some of my fellow students. During the divorce she implied she couldn't understand how they had time for her but I didn't." He almost smiled when he said it, but April could tell it wasn't something he took lightly. April wanted to say, "She must have been some kind of a fool," but she kept that thought to herself.

"People sometimes just don't understand what it's like to work eighteen-hour days and study for six." His voice softened as he looked at her.

"So, why haven't you remarried, surely things have changed now for you?" April was curious. He was too good of a catch to be still available.

Marcus studied her curiously and replied, "Probably for the same reason you haven't. I tend to be a workaholic. Most women are unwilling to put up with my schedule…." He began to chuckle and looked deeply into April's eyes. "Actually, that's just a cop-out. I haven't found the right woman yet. I haven't taken the time to work on relationships outside of work like I should. I don't have time to go to mixers or wherever people go to meet these days. I think I've grown too shy in my old age."

His voice sounded playful and sexy and so were his eyes, she thought as she tried to guess what color they were. They appeared to be gray, but she wasn't sure.

His genuine smile pleased April as she nodded in agreement. "I understand, trust me. My friends seem to think I mind being alone, but actually there are times when I prefer it."

"Well, I certainly hope now isn't one of those times." Marcus peered into her eyes as his eyes flirted with her.

"No, Marcus, I'm having a wonderful time." April was putting the last forkful of her entree in her mouth. She wasn't shy about eating, or her healthy appetite. She enjoyed the dinner more tonight because of her handsome and stimulating dinner companion. This was a combination she hadn't enjoyed in quite some time.

"Well, let's get something good for dessert so we can dish about well-meaning friends who are always trying to fix us up." Marcus pushed his dinner plate aside.

"Sure, I'm game." They both laughed good-naturedly.

They shared a sinful chocolate dessert and continued to talk about work and personal projects.

"Tell me about the community group you're involved with." Marcus leaned forward with curiosity and April took note. She liked that he asked her questions about her rather than monopolizing the time talking about himself. It was a welcoming and refreshing change, but she'd gotten the impression early on that Marcus was different from other men she'd met.

They spent the evening talking about various programs, friends and their jobs. Marcus was also involved in the community, but hadn't devoted as much time as he would have liked. "Have you read any of the books written about the neighborhood?" April asked with curiosity.

"Just one, it was rather informative, but not what I'd call engaging. I thought the community had a richer history, so I just like hearing people talk about it. Why do you ask?"

"I've been toying with the idea of writing a book about it from a different perspective. I don't know now, it's fairly preliminary, but something that would be 'engaging.'"

Marcus laughed and asked for more details. They talked about the idea, and agreed it could be a worthwhile team project. They shared a more-than-common interest in the neighborhoods that made up the South side of St. Louis. April grew up in the area and had lived there all of her life. She loved the area, and Marcus, although he didn't grow up in the area, had moved to the area and fallen in love with it. After dessert, April invited him to follow her home for coffee.

Marcus trailed April in his car. Once they arrived at her house, she was barely out of the car and he was there offering his hand and escorting her out of the car.

"I had a lot of fun tonight, April. I can't remember the last time I felt so relaxed on a date. I think our well-meaning friend was right, we do have a lot in common." He was following her up the stairs to her home and enjoying the view. She turned and responded with a faint smile. He tried not to appear eager, but it was so difficult to read April. She, after all, had invited him home with her, but she remained unreadable. He was going to follow her lead and allow her to set the pace for the evening.

April turned to him. "I have to get things ready first. Just have a seat on the porch for a few minutes and I'll be right back."

She went inside first to put the dogs in the basement because they didn't like strangers. They barked loudly, and Marcus knew exactly what she was doing. It gave him a measure of comfort to know she had such loyal protectors in her home. She returned to the front door, but not before checking herself in the mirror. She fluffed her hair and freshened her lipstick. She opened the door and found Marcus looking more inviting in moonlight than she remembered.

His lush lips invited hers and she felt the heat starting to rise again. His smoky eyes held a hint of mystery and mischief to them. She liked that, liked it a lot. She felt her knees starting to weaken and she thought they'd buckle if she didn't get away from him soon. She purposely avoided looking at him as she waited for him to enter. She locked the door behind him and prayed she'd manage to behave herself. Her resolve weakened when she allowed her eyes to travel down Marcus's tall frame and settle on his backside. April closed her eyes and took a deep breath. Even with his clothes on, she could tell he had one of those bodies that was made for good loving.

Looking around, Marcus said, "You've got a wonderful home," when she pointed him into the living room.

She smiled and nodded. "Thanks, I haven't had time for all the renovations I'd like, but it's very comfortable." April offered him a seat and afterwards went to the kitchen to check what kinds of coffee she could offer him. When she returned he was seated comfortably on the sofa, stroking Midnight.

April laughed, "I'm surprised he let you get that close to him, usually he doesn't take to strangers."

"Animals are usually a good judge of people. He senses I won't hurt him." His eyes made contact with hers and continued to cause her pulse to quicken.

April smiled and said, "I've got green tea, English tea, swiss mocha, regular coffee and decaf, and some fancy stuff I got last time I was in Jamaica." She tilted her head to one side and said, "Name your pleasure." The last part came out sounding more seductive and suggestive than she wanted, but she found it difficult not to flirt with him.

Marcus cleared his throat and forced himself not to respond

like he wanted. It sounded like an invitation to him, but he didn't want to rush her. "I'd prefer some decaf."

"Sure, I'll be right back." She spun around and headed toward the kitchen, glad that he was practicing some self-control as she'd obviously lost hers.

"Let me help you." Marcus sat Midnight on the floor and stood, following April to the kitchen. She could feel him staring at her but it didn't make her feel uncomfortable, it actually made her put just a little more swing in her hips. Before she reached the sink Marcus took her by the arm and turned her around. He looked into her confused eyes and slowly lowered his lips to hers.

His mouth claimed hers as he tried to extinguish the fire that had started the moment his eyes met hers that evening. His tongue tangled with hers in a lovers' dance, and the two leaned into each other trying to satisfy the demands of the kiss. His arms circled her waist and pulled her closer to him as they followed up with another passion-filled kiss. When they finally parted he apologized. "I hope I'm not scaring you away, but I've wanted to do that all night." He was breathless and his smoldering gaze filled her with desire for more. His gaze settled on her lips, and he knew that was a mistake. The demand was more than he could control.

April put her arms around his waist and brought him closer to her again and this time she initiated the passion-filled kiss. When they parted again, she rasped in a voice much deeper than usual, "Me, too."

They both laughed nervously. "This isn't like me," she confessed. "This is a little scary, don't you think?"

"Yes, but in a good way," he acknowledged, but his gaze never left hers and she could tell that he was as consumed as she was. She could tell from the telltale bulge that lightly caressed her leg when they were close.

April was forced to agree. "Listen, I'm not usually so…"

Marcus put his finger to her lips to stop her. Even his finger on her lips felt good. She resisted the temptation to give a seductive lick with her tongue.

"You don't have to explain." He bent down and took her in his arms again and just held her. She laid her head on his chest and it felt as good and as natural as a cool breeze after a summer rain. He couldn't believe how good it felt to just hold her in his arms. It was a feeling he wanted to experience more.

Marcus was the first to pull away as he explained, "I think I'll take a rain check on that decaf, before something else happens between us. I do want to see you again." He looked into her eyes for approval and all she could do was nod her head. Passion hung in the air heavily as they both breathed deeply.

April hadn't met a man who left her speechless, but the good doctor had affected her. He gently massaged her shoulders and asked, "Walk me to the door?" She nodded, once again feeling like such a dunce she wondered where her voice was.

When they reached the door, he took her hands and kissed the palms of each one. "I'll call you." He turned and left and April locked the door. She stood breathlessly with her back against it. Midnight sat in the foyer looking up at her, and only then did she manage to find her voice.

"What are you looking at, you little traitor? Next time I'll let the dogs stay up here and put you in the basement, at least they wouldn't have let me make a fool of myself." Midnight nonchalantly turned and slowly walked away, making April laugh to herself.

"Hello, April." Marcus called April early the next morning as he'd spent a restless night thinking about how much he wanted her. He wanted so much to know more about her and was sure she felt the attraction that hovered between the two of them. Marcus believed the attraction was more than physical, he felt a connection with this woman that he'd only seen twice. It forced him to call her early the next morning.

The first time he saw her he was taken aback by her smoldering dark eyes that slanted slightly upward. Her lips were lush and were the most kissable he'd ever seen. The dress she wore that night emphasized her small waist. Her hips beckoned him as they were dangerous curves. The sway of her hips exuded femininity. He'd watched her from the time she walked into the room until she left. He couldn't contain himself when he finally walked over to Carmen that evening, begging for the woman's name and phone number. He loved the softness of her oval face. Even though she wore little makeup, she wore a quiet, subtle beauty that money couldn't buy.

"Good morning, Marcus. After such a late night I'm surprised you're up so early." April turned over in bed and looked at her clock.

"I can't remember having such a stimulating conversation with someone, and thought maybe we could go for brunch. I wanted to talk to you further about the proposal you had for a book about our South side neighborhood. Figured maybe it's a project we could team up to do."

Marcus liked the idea of the project when she brought it up at dinner, and it was the only excuse he could come up with that would explain his overwhelming need to talk to her at six in the morning. In reality, his arms ached to hold her again, but he knew that it was too soon to tell her that, but he was certain that one day soon he'd share that information with her.

"That sounds good to me. I'm sure my brother-in-law can help direct us in researching the area. There's a bed-and-breakfast that offers a Sunday brunch over near

Arsenal, I've heard it's wonderful. They have live jazz, and they say the food is excellent."

"I know the place, can I pick you up at ten this morning?"

"Yes, do you remember my address?"

"I remember the address. I'll be there at ten." He sounded eager and she had to laugh to herself.

Before ending the conversation April said, "Marcus, about last night… I don't usually rush into things, and I'm not usually so…" April searched for the right word, and finally said, "Forward."

"Okay, but I didn't think you were being 'forward,' I just thought maybe we both got a little caught up. We did have a nice evening." Marcus knew that they were more than "a little caught up," he could feel the pull she had on him. Something that he hadn't felt before, and something in the way she held him told him that she felt the same way. He was good at judging people, and was certain he had not misjudged.

Marcus was ringing her doorbell at ten, trying his best not to appear too anxious. He was dressed casually, and looked forward to seeing and talking to April again. He didn't wait long as she opened the door and they exchanged greetings.

"Good morning, you look very nice." Marcus eyed her appreciatively. The dangerous curves that he'd noticed the first time he'd seen her were more noticeable now with the casual cropped top and shorts she wore. Last night her dress had been less revealing, but one look at her shapely legs in shorts made the man in him antsy, he wanted to see more. Even though the attire was casual, she still looked very well put together. She had a tiny waist and curves in all the right places.

"Thank you, so do you. I just need to get my purse, and we can leave." April turned to get her purse from the table in the foyer and took a deep breath. She mumbled to herself,

"Those damn lips! And those eyes. This is going to be interesting." She let out a little moan as she turned to face Marcus again.

"Did you say something?"

"No, just thinking out loud. Brunch sounds good, huh?"

"Let's go, then. I've heard the place has the best banana pancakes in the area."

When the two arrived the bed-and-breakfast was already packed, they lucked up and got the last available table. The jazz band featured a local singer, and her voice filled the room with a seductive tune. There were even tables set up outside in a beautiful courtyard.

The breakfast selection was massive. It included bacon, ham, sausage, pancakes of different varieties, eggs, homemade biscuits, omelets and potatoes. There was an array of fresh fruits and all kinds of toppings. The two helped themselves to just about everything on the buffet.

They were eating heartily and enjoying the music when a petite, slim, attractive woman stopped at their table. "Are you two enjoying yourselves?"

Marcus, whose mouth was stuffed, looked at April, who nodded and said, "This is lovely, I didn't expect it to be so large. I usually think of a B and B as a small, intimate place."

"That's one of the things that make us so different, it's spacious but our rooms and service are very intimate. We offer some untraditional services, like massages, manicures, girls and boys weekends. We wanted something a little different. That's why we host the Jazz Brunch on Sunday, as kind of an introduction to our new business. We will host it until this fall, with hopes of letting people know there is a B and B right in the city with a bit of city, and lots of intimacy. By the way, I'm the owner, Cozette Nichols."

She extended her hand to April. "It's nice to meet you, I'm April Nelson…."

"Oh, no, you're not, you're Dr. April Nelson, I saw you in action at one of the Police Board meetings. You were something else. I've been meaning to join the neighborhood group. I have become entrenched in the community, and I want to know what's going on." Cozette looked over at Marcus and said, "I'm sorry, I just got caught up. I love talking about this place."

She extended her hand to Marcus, who wiped his hand on a napkin and extended it. "I'm Marcus Davis. Nice to meet you. Forgive me for my manners, but the food is great." Marcus smiled at Cozette and she turned her attention back to April.

"Actually, he's Dr. Marcus Davis, and as you can see he's very modest and he's enjoying the breakfast," April teased, causing Marcus to send her a smile.

Cozette looked from one to the other and asked, "Is there a special occasion or anything you two are celebrating?"

Marcus looked at April and said, "No, we just heard about the place and wanted to give it a try. I think we may become regulars." He winked at April, who sent him a show of approval with a smile and slight tilt of her head.

"Oh, you two make a lovely couple. Please, let me give you a quick tour of some of our rooms when you're done eating. It won't take long." She gave them a pleading look.

April looked at Marcus, who again nodded. "Sure, that sounds delightful."

"And by all means, tell me when the next community meeting is because I will be there. I should be around, but if I'm in the kitchen, just ask the hostess to find me. Thanks so much for coming today." Her smile was genuine as she looked from one to the other.

"We'll do that, and I'll have the date for you."

Cozette excused herself and continued around the room introducing herself.

Finally, April sat listening to the music and tapping her foot when she discovered she couldn't eat another bite of food. Marcus looked over at her and smiled. "You look like you enjoyed yourself."

"I still am, this band and the singer are wonderful. I'm really enjoying this." It had been a while since she had gone out and just sat, ate and enjoyed music. It was a pleasure she promised herself she would have more often.

"How'd you hear about this place?" Marcus looked around, enjoying the ambience of the place. He definitely wanted to return with April.

"My assistant told me about it. She's my social connection, tells me all the newest, coolest places to go. She thinks I need to get out more."

Marcus laughed. He'd also been staying close to home lately, and his well-meaning friends had encouraged him to get out more.

"Well, tell her she was on target with this place. I don't think I'll need to eat the rest of the day." Marcus rubbed his stomach. The two enjoyed a few more songs and then decided to find Cozette for the tour.

"I'm glad you two enjoyed your brunch, but now the treat really starts. I think you'll enjoy the difference in our place. We are targeting a different clientele, those who yearn for something beyond the traditional bed-and-breakfast. Ours is a more contemporary feel for those who may want a weekend retreat without a country or vintage feel. Come this way please." The tour began, and true to her words, the rooms were not along the lines of the traditional bed-and-breakfast, but were uniquely and tastefully decorated in contemporary fashion. Although the rooms and colors were theme-centered, they were geared to the more young, urban taste. No heavy drapes, antiques or period pieces. There was a Florida room which included bright colors and seashell-themed towels along with matching accessories. There was a spa room that resembled a spa so much that April had to fight the overwhelming desire to book it immediately. It was inviting, with lush green plants, a weathered stone wall, white candles, white drapes and soft music. There was a New Orleans room, a few traditional honeymoon suites and several other themed rooms, all well decorated and inviting.

After the tour, Marcus concluded, "This is really impressive. You're right, it's not the traditional B and B. Be sure to give me some of your business cards, I'm certain some of my colleagues would love this place."

April looked out and commented, "Even the New Orleans-styled courtyard is beautiful. You've done a wonderful job. I know this will be a success because people embrace uniqueness and this is truly unique."

"It'll be a success if the community supports it." Cozette looked around and nodded. "I was a little intimidated by the neighborhood at first, but this area is so rich in history and tradition. Other B and Bs have thrived for years in this area, and I just thought, why not give it a shot."

April gave some reassurance. "This community needs businesses like this, they'll support it. I'll be sure to introduce you at our next meeting, too. Be sure to bring plenty of business cards, flyers or whatever, you'll have plenty of people interested. Now, we don't promote businesses during the meeting time, but afterwards, we have networking opportunities for businesses."

"Thank you both, I needed that." Cozette unexpectedly gave them each a friendly hug before continuing. "You two really are lovely people. Let me know when you're ready for a weekend, or perhaps a weekday stay."

The suggestion caused April and Marcus to exchange a quick furtive glance. Marcus responded by cupping his hand over Cozette's and saying, "We certainly will. Thanks again for the great tour." She gave a few of her business cards to each of them and said, "You guys enjoy the rest of your Sunday." She left them with a broad, knowing smile, as if she had guessed some secret the two of them had shared.

Hand in hand, they left the establishment. When they got to the car Marcus asked, "Feel like taking a little walk?"

April's head leaned slightly to the left as she said, "On a beautiful day like this, why not?"

The two started a casual stroll along the street, quietly admiring the architecture and after a few minutes April said, "So, tell me more of what you know about the area." She liked that he took so much pride in their neighborhood. He was not only knowledgeable about the architecture of the area, but had an extensive knowledge of the political and social aspects of the area as well. He pointed out different points of architectural interest on several of the buildings as they strolled along. The walk lasted nearly an hour, but the time went by quickly as they enjoyed the scenery, the people mulling about and the occasional music heard from eateries they passed.

Once they returned to the car April commented, "This was the most enjoyable Sunday I've ever had. Thanks, Marcus." She enjoyed talking with Marcus, she felt comfortable, and it was nice that they had so many things they could talk about. They once again shared ideas about writing a book.

Marcus opened the car door for her, but before she could step inside, he took her in his arms and said, "Then you agree we have to do it again soon?" He didn't wait for her answer before he brushed her hair from her face and lightly kissed her lips. He squelched his desire for more than a kiss as he took both hands and held her face, kissing her lips again with a more demanding, fiery kiss. They withdrew slowly, and April sat down in the car.

"I agree," she said afterwards, and Marcus closed the door. She had to ignore the desire to return for seconds, unlike what she'd done at breakfast. Despite the fact that he was far more tempting than the wonderful breakfast they had shared, she thought it best to take small bites. There was plenty of him and plenty of time, she thought. She watched as he walked around the front of the car and entered the driver's side.

"I like the fact that you're such a gentleman. Your parents taught you well." She noted how he pulled her chair out, stood up when she did, opened the car door for her and waited until she was seated and closed it. She liked this man…a lot.

The drive back to April's was full of lively chatter. When they reached her house, Marcus parked and turned to her. "What do you have for the rest of the day?"

"I've got some research to do. I'm trying to find my aunt and uncle in Cleveland." Marcus looked curiously, but April held up her hand. "Don't ask, it's another one of those family secrets. I'll tell you another time." She reached over and took his hand. "I really enjoyed being with you today."

Marcus leaned over and the two shared a kiss that sparked more passion than it should have. "Wow, that sure was a nice end to the date. Mind if I have one more?" Marcus leaned over and the two kissed again. "Think I'd better walk you to your door, otherwise we could be out here for a long time. You know you're hard to resist, right?" Which elicited a coy smile from her that only served to call attention to her lips. Marcus could only shake his head as he retreated from the car. This was going to be a challenge.

At the door, the two embraced and shared another passion-filled kiss. April pulled away, they were moving way too fast. She could easily get lost in him. "I would invite you in, but I have a lot to do," she said apologetically.

"Well, enjoy the rest of your day. I'll call you tomorrow." Marcus turned and left. April watched as he got into his car and drove off.

"Yep, that's one tasty morsel," she mused to herself. She turned and went inside just in time to see Midnight jump from the window, where he'd obviously been watching. "You are way too nosy for a cat."

Later that night, April continued to think about helping Summer fight her internal demons. Reluctantly, she picked up the phone. "Hey, Mom, how you doing?" Biting her lip to one side, she knew this conversation was probably going to end badly, but she had to give it a try.

April had accomplished her goal of being financially independent. Her practice, by all measures, was a success and she had invested wisely. She had set the goal early on, long before therapy helped her realize her mother had spent her life searching for financial dependence and happiness in men. April knew she had struggled for years to become the person she was today— educated, independent, confident and happy…most of the time.

"'Bout the same as always, why?" A voice dripping with bitterness that years of cigarettes and liquor had made raspy and low greeted April. If one had taken a good look at Mildred Nelson, she was a contrast; she was a petite frail woman who still had some of the natural beauty of earlier years. But upon looking closer, one could see the physical damage of too much alcohol, too many cigarettes and too much hard living and bitterness. Although no physical scars were on her face, if one looked closely enough they could see the scars of wars past.

"Uh, just checking on you. Do you need anything?"

"Why, what you got?" *Why couldn't she pretend to be civil for a brief minute?* April thought to herself. Her mother was indeed the most bitter woman she'd ever met. She'd been through a number of husbands and men and still was the most unhappy person April knew. She often wondered what had caused her mother to be so bitter.

"What did you do today?"

"What I do every day, sat around and looked at the television, not that there was anything worth looking at on this idiot box."

"Maybe you'd like to come out and spend some time with me."

"Not in that place of yours, it's more like a damn zoo, with all those animals. I swear I don't know where you got that mess from." Mildred began coughing and April could hear her struggling to catch her breath.

"Mom, you all right?"

"I'm fine, just allergies."

April thought about something that hadn't crossed her mind in years. "You think I forgot how much you loved Susie?"

"Susie, now that's a name I haven't heard in a long time." For the first time in years, April could hear a softness in her mother's voice.

"Yeah, you loved Susie, didn't you, Mom?"

"That dumb dog up and left me just like everybody else did."

"Susie died, Mom, she was old, she got sick and died. She didn't leave you. Who else do you think left you?"

"Don't try that damn psycho mumbo jumbo on me, I look at enough Oprah. Ain't nobody left me that I didn't want to leave."

April realized for the first time that it was her mother who unintentionally introduced her to what would become a lifelong pursuit. Her mother had refused to allow animals in the house, but when Mildred's mother died, she took in Susie, her mother's dog and constant companion for many years. Mildred could have easily given the little mixed breed away, but kept the dog for years. She actually gave the dog more attention than she gave her daughters. Susie had become Mildred's constant companion, just like it had Mildred's mother for years.

All three of Mildred's daughters laughed at how she would talk to Susie and acted as though the dog understood what she said. It was the rare occasion they saw their mother's softer side, and it was always with Susie. But when Susie died, Mildred withdrew from her family. She left the burial of the dog to her husband and she stayed in the bed for four days. Mildred did not come out of her room or speak to anybody during that time.

"You can bring me a carton of cigarettes and something to drink if you wanna just do something."

"I would like to treat you to dinner, or maybe a movie, but you know how I feel about cigarettes and alcohol."

"Well, then, I don't know why you even called. If you wanna just see how I'm doing just say that, don't ask if I need anything and then get on your high horse about cigarettes."

"I wasn't... You know what, Mom, I love you and if you really need anything, like food, or feel like taking in a movie, call me. Otherwise, I'll check on you next week. Also, I ordered some food for you, please don't try to return it and get something you don't need. I've asked the store not to exchange or refund you anything."

"Check on me for what? All you do is ask the same damn questions, and if I want to take it back, I will. Otherwise, I can refuse the delivery. Don't forget who's the momma here."

"Sorry, Mom, I was trying to help." Her mother had worn her out in that little time. She didn't feel up to arguing, so she said, "Bye, Mom, and I'll call you next week and ask you the same questions again."

All April heard was the dial tone. "Lord, I know I am supposed to honor my mother, but she makes it so difficult." April returned the phone to its cradle and let out a chuckle. She could picture Mildred on the phone, a beer within reach if not in her hand and a cigarette dangling from her lips. She was barely five feet tall and less than one hundred pounds, but she was tougher than anybody April had ever come across. April knew she'd inherited some of that toughness, and prayed she could always keep it channeled to more positive results.

She let out a sigh, walked over to her desk, pulled out a slip of paper with the information she needed and sat down. She looked at the paper and the information, booted up her computer and began a search on the Internet. April was certain that her mother's only sister, to whom her mother hadn't spoken in over twenty-five years, knew the root of the callousness. She smiled at the thought of her aunt.

Her Aunt May and Uncle Henry had moved to Cleveland, Ohio, back in the early seventies, and for a brief time stayed in touch. April remembered the last time they were in St. Louis visiting. It was summer and the couple were enjoying themselves visiting friends and partying. They were a fun-loving couple.

Aunt May had always been told she was a dead ringer for Lena Horne, but April thought she was even prettier. Her medium brown skin was flawless and her smile could make the sourest person smile. She had eyes that, despite their darkness, seemed to radiate light. She was gaped at wherever she went. Aunt May never seemed affected by it, though. She always said, "Beauty fades, but smarts last forever. Don't let beauty derail you, follow the pursuit of intelligence, it'll get you where you want to go every time."

She remembered one time when her aunt had taken her downtown shopping and was stopped by a policeman for speeding. One look into those dark soulful eyes and the slightest smile of those seductress lips sent the policeman into male mode.

He was no longer a policeman but a man who saw a beautiful woman and responded by issuing her a warning. "Sorry to stop you, ma'am, but you were speeding a little. Why don't you slow down a bit? Wouldn't want anything to happen to you." All the while he was looking at her and smiling from ear to ear. He tipped his cap and let her go on her way. Aunt May smiled over at April and winked.

Aunt May and Uncle Henry had returned late from a party given for them by close friends. Mildred had locked and chained the door. She dared any of the children and her husband at the time to get up and let them in. "If they ain't in here by midnight, they can just go back to where they was." Her squinted eyes and hands on her hips defied challenge from anybody.

At two-thirty in the morning, April was awakened by loud knocks. "Come on, Mildred, open the door." Followed by loud laughter and giggles. "I told you she was going to be mad if we stayed out too late. You don't know my sister, she's as evil as they come."

More laughter. If April wasn't afraid of her mother hearing, she would have laughed, too. But instead she just sat in bed whispering for Summer until she heard her mother.

"You silly cow, I told you this ain't no damn train station, we ain't open all night. You can't bring your ass back here at a decent hour, just go on back where you came from. I'm sick of you thinking you can do what the hell you please 'cause everybody think you so pretty and so nice. Well, that ain't working tonight. I suggest you and that worthless piece of nothing you call a husband go back to the party."

April froze in fear. Even at a young age she wondered, how could her mother say such hurtful, mean things to anybody, especially her own sister? She looked over at Summer and

Autumn, who were sleeping soundly, completely unaware of the disturbance going on in their home.

"Come on, Mildred, I'm sorry, we were just having such a good time. I told you to come with us, everybody asked where you were." Silence, and then an eruption of such bitterness it made April shrink deep under her covers.

"Well, now, I know you're just lying. I can't stand you or any the people you were with tonight, and they can't stand me. You think I'm too stupid to know what they say about me behind my back? Don't think for a minute I'm 'bout to believe somebody in that crowd asked about me.

"All y'all care about is you. You the damn star everybody wants to see." A silence so deafening that April swore she had to check her ears because it was as quiet as she'd ever heard. It was an eerie, deadly quiet that makes one look around for movement or something to let them know that they are still in the world. After a few minutes all she heard was the start of a car engine.

The next day Aunt May and Uncle Henry's suitcases were on the front porch. Her mother didn't say a word about what happened and had made it clear she didn't want anyone mentioning "that heifer's name."

She never got a chance to see her aunt and uncle again. April would occasionally intercept a call from her aunt when their mother was out, but since Mildred never returned the phone calls, Aunt May stopped calling. Shortly afterwards, Mildred insisted the family move and they never heard from Aunt May again.

Her mother's only living relative, and she'd been cast out because she'd come home too late from a party. The next day, when April told Summer and Autumn the story, each found it hard to believe, but knew it was true. Mildred had always been tough. The three sisters swore they'd never abandon each other no matter what. As young as they were, it would impact them in ways they never realized until they were older. The trio clung to each other even more.

Their father's family had been banished from their home years before. Mildred's alcoholic rages had alienated them before any of her children were born. None of the sisters knew why, they just didn't see or spend time with family members from their father's side. It was another of their family secrets that someday they hoped would come to light. It frightened April that her mother could be so cold and distant, almost heartless.

April, Summer and Autumn all agreed that their mother had always been jealous of her sister. Mildred Nelson had been a beautiful woman in her day, but she was one of those women who knew she was beautiful and let you know she knew. Her disposition made her ugly, people didn't want to be around her. She wore a perpetual frown that over the years had etched hard, cold lines into her face. Her eyes were devoid of the warmth of Aunt May's. She rarely laughed, so people never saw her beautiful smile. Later in life, years of drinking and bitterness had turned her into a woman nobody recognized or knew. Her gray hair hung down in an undefined style, this woman who at one time nearly lived at the beauty shop. The alcohol had clearly ravaged her once smooth café-au-lait skin, the skin under her eyes was dark and her eyes looked too big for her face. Her cheeks had sunken in and she had become so haggard looking that on the rare occasion that April visited she could barely look at her. Mildred had rejected April's invitations to join her for a visit to the beauty shop. Instead she told April, "What you going to the beauty shop for? All you do is shampoo that mop of yours. Just give me the money and I'll do what I want." While April sometimes found her mother's caustic comments mildly entertaining, others found them to be rude.

April reached for the phone and dialed information for the city of Cleveland. Since Mildred had cursed her like she was a stranger begging for money the last time she mentioned Aunt May's name, she was on the hunt for her aunt's phone number through the only way she knew how. If that didn't work, she decided she'd try the Internet or if need be a private investigator.

She and Summer needed the attachment of another family member to help them understand their past. Maybe there was an answer to their mother's coldness that Aunt May could explain. It would help Summer understand that too many un-answered questions had driven all three girls to some form of dependence to compensate for what they missed at home growing up. April had to fill in the holes and gaps from her youth not so much for herself, but for her sister. She and Kenneth had agreed that the way to help Summer was to answer some of the questions about their past.

She decided then it was imperative for Summer to talk with Carmen as soon as possible. They were in fact their mother's daughters, but they were not their mother. That mantra kept repeating in her head, it was a necessary thought for her to remember. She had hung on to it for years, even during her discussions with Carmen.

April took extra care preparing for work on Monday. She wore a colorful sundress which she rarely did and just a hint of makeup. Since she wore a white coat most of the day she rarely dressed up for work. Bridget was surprised that morning when April walked in.

"Dr. Nelson, you look great!" Bridget smiled broadly at her boss before continuing, "Is there something going on I should know about?"

April looked at her and laughed as she headed toward her office. "Nothing gets past you, Bridget, but I will say I enjoyed that B and B you recommended."

Bridget was overjoyed. She was quite dedicated to April and

wanted her to find someone special. Her boss was all business on the job and rarely talked about her personal affairs, but Bridget knew that April didn't receive many personal calls from men at work. She was delighted to hear that she had gone out, and judging from the uncharacteristic sundress and makeup, it was obviously a date with someone special…a male.

"So, when can Samantha start?" April asked as she was putting her lab coat on.

"Not until next week, but she's coming in a few times this week, so I can train her on the computer and show her the set-up. She's going to do great." Bridget had already turned on April's computer, with her schedule for the day displayed.

"I hope she's half as good as you. I talked to Nia, and she's stopping by next week with the baby. I can't wait to see her." April giggled before continuing, "I thought she was going to have that baby in this office."

Bridget joined in with a giggle. "You and me both. I couldn't believe her water broke and she kept on working. She didn't tell anybody, talking about how we were almost done for the day."

"We ran out of here and left everything on!"

"I was afraid the ambulance in this neighborhood would take too long, so I figured the best thing to do was take her." April was still thinking about that day. It was Nia's first baby and she had been having contractions. April had insisted that she not come to work, but Nia showed up, saying she would be bored just waiting at home.

At three o'clock April was just walking into her office when she heard someone in the bathroom moaning. She knocked on the door. "I think I'm ready to have this baby!" was the response she got. When Nia opened the door, she was flushed.

"How far apart are the contractions?"

"About a minute!" Nia could barely stand. April helped her from the bathroom and called out to Bridget, "Get my purse, I'm taking her to the hospital now! You come, too."

Bridget came running with April's purse. "Just lock the door and turn on the burglar alarm."

"I'll get her to the car. Please make up a sign, 'Closed for family emergency. Sorry for the inconvenience.' We'll call and reschedule this afternoon's appointments."

Once at the hospital, April called Nia's husband, who arrived and was a nervous wreck. It all worked out, and Nia gave birth to the most precious little baby girl April had ever seen. She was looking forward to seeing beautiful little Kerry Lloyd again. She and Bridget were to share the title of Godmother.

As soon as Marcus got to work he was in demand. He worked nonstop for hours. He made it his business to spend time with each patient, explaining any required test, or X-rays, and spoke in layman's terms. Patients loved him for his bedside manner.

He stood and studied the chest X-rays and chart of a patient he had suspected had primary pulmonary hypertension. The patient was only thirty-nine and was experiencing respiratory difficulties of the pulmonary system. He wrote his notes in the chart and took another look at the X-rays. He put it all to the side, and glanced at his watch. He was always busy, but he was determined to make time to call April and check on how her day was going.

His one fault as far as he was concerned was never taking the time to foster a relationship. He'd had plenty of dates and relationships, but never took the time required to develop a meaningful relationship. His schedule was full and that meant little time for anything else.

His other flaw was his jealous nature when it came to someone he cared about. As an only child he grew up always protecting what was his and himself, he didn't have any brothers or sisters to protect. He sometimes found it difficult to control his temper regarding matters of the heart. He would work on it, he told himself.

Nurses had pursued him relentlessly and he'd gotten a reputation of being an elusive devoted bachelor, almost to the
point of being a womanizer. It wasn't a reputation of which
he was proud, and it had caused him to take a more critical
look at himself. He decided no more dating coworkers and
no more casual dating. If he was going to spend time with
someone it would be with someone special. April was that
someone special, he was certain of it. Marcus would take
time to get to know her. He called April a little after one in
the afternoon.

When she answered, he reared back in his chair. "Hello, I
called to see how your day was going."

Her feet ached and her stomach growled, but none of it
mattered, she felt good hearing his voice. It had been too long
since someone had called to ask about her day. "Hello, Marcus,
it's a little busy, but otherwise it's a good day. What about yours?"

"About the same. Hopefully you've managed to at least
squeeze in lunch. I'm about to break for lunch."

"No, I haven't eaten yet."

Marcus knew he didn't have much time, and there was a
possibility that he could get paged during the middle of lunch,
but he could not resist seeing her again, no matter how briefly.
"Think you could join me for a quick lunch? Nothing fancy,
just something from Hodge's. It's less than five minutes from
your office. And I've written down a few book ideas I'd like
to share with you."

April looked quickly at her planner. "Sure, I can make
that." She was taking off her lab coat as she spoke.

"You look beautiful." Marcus tried to sound casual, but the
appearance of April in a sundress that bared her soft, slim
shoulders was too much for him. The bright colors highlighted her flawless skin and auburn hair. He fought the desire
to take her in his arms as he pulled out her chair. He liked the

naturalness of her hair and he bent over slightly to smell it when she was seated and he stood over her.

"Thanks. It was luck that we arrived at the same time." April looked into his eyes as he sat down and decided that his eyes were gray. He wore a cream-colored silk shirt with light brown slacks and a smile that caused her heart to thump loudly in her chest. They ordered lunch and engaged in small talk.

Marcus took out a notepad from his briefcase and said, "I wrote down a few ideas and thought we'd brainstorm on an initial outline. I don't have much time for lunch and I'm sure you don't, either, so let's get started." He tried hard not to notice the slight shimmer of light that played on her shoulders. He suppressed the desire to touch them.

"Sounds good to me," April agreed, but not before deciding she wanted to feel his hand on the small of her back again, and wanted his lips to caress hers with fire and a hint of seduction, the way they had yesterday.

His knowledge of the neighborhood surprised and delighted her as they discussed the preliminaries of the book. He knew many of the older residents that could be interviewed for the book, and that perhaps could give them some foresight on the social climate of the neighborhood's earlier years. April enjoyed his company immensely and silently hoped that this wasn't just a business venture. She wanted very much to know more about Marcus.

After lunch he walked her to her car. "Thanks for meeting me on such short notice. I'll call you later. Think you'll have time for a visit to the library soon? We can do some research together." Marcus didn't want to appear too eager, but couldn't help himself as he noted how the beautiful, warm afternoon paled in comparison to April's beauty. He'd just met her, but could tell she was beautiful inside and out. He hadn't seen that in a woman in a long time. It made him yearn for her more.

April stirred under his warm gaze. "It has been very nice.

I've got a few meetings in the next few days and I must visit my sister, but yes, we could do that." Her eyes reflected hints of brown light that made Marcus smile.

"Promise?" he asked, with such wanting.

April started the car and tried not to look into his eyes, fearing hers would show the craving for him she felt. She actually craved him…craved the feel of his arms around her again…his lips pressed against hers, delivering the satisfaction she found each time their lips met.

She wondered briefly what it was about this man that drove her to such distraction and made her eager to spend more time with him.

"Promise," she said tenderly, and watched helplessly as he leaned over and kissed her gently. Her eyes remained closed seconds after the kiss and she was glad that she was already seated. She felt her knees go weak, and could feel a slight hum and warmth generate in the pit of her stomach.

Chapter 5

"What do you mean, I've had enough? I'm a paying customer. I'll tell you when I've had enough."

The bartender shook his head. "Ma'am, do you want me to call you a cab?"

Summer looked up. "I'm sorry, are you talking to me?" If not for her advanced stage of drunkenness one would have thought she was insulted by the question. "Are you implying I'm intoxicated?" The words had barely left her mouth when she burped. Laughing, she covered it and reeled back so far she lost control, falling off the bar stool.

Two young men rushed to help her to her feet. "You awright, lady?" the first young man asked. He didn't even look old enough to be in a bar drinking. He was short and stocky, with a weightlifter's powerful build. The other man appeared somewhat older, but not much, and not nearly as heavy or strong. Something in his eyes made her retreat. They were

hooded and slightly slanted, she couldn't look into them, and
something about his quick movements made her not trust
him. Even though she was drunker than she could ever
imagine possible, the fall sobered her up somewhat and she
knew a shady character when she saw one, drunk or sober.

She knew she'd have some bruises to explain. "Thanks, I'm
fine, just lost my footing."

She staggered when reaching for her purse and the younger
man said, "Ma'am, is there someone I can call for you?" The
stocky young man asked and appeared to be genuine.

She shook her head as if trying to clear it and slurred, "What?"

"You're in no condition to drive, can I call someone to
pick you up?"

The tall skinny man with the shifty eyes intervened. "I'll
drive you home for twenty dollars."

"Man, this lady doesn't know you from a can of paint, so
just back up."

Summer's head went back and forth as if watching a tennis
match. It made her dizzy and sick to her stomach.

"Fool, she don't know you either, so you shut the…" His
voice was forceful and too loud.

Summer interrupted the show of male bravado when she
hiccupped. "No, please don't argue." Her head was pounding
now and her stomach was turning.

"You need to go to the bathroom, you look like…" Before
he could complete the sentence Summer hurled all over the
bar stool and floor.

"Mercy be!" The bartender shouted with disgust. He then
called to one of the waitresses in the back. "Melanie, come
out here and escort this woman to the can, please. I've gotta
clean up this mess." He turned and left hurriedly, obviously
in search of cleaning supplies.

Melanie, a young woman of about twenty-two, appeared

with more attitude than clothes. "I ain't no escort, she can find the bathroom by herself."

"Melanie, please just do as I ask," the bartender shouted from a back room.

"Come on, lady, you can clean up back here." She took Summer, who had started to feel ashamed, gently by the arm.

Releasing her arm from Melanie, Summer countered, "You're right, I can find the bathroom by myself. I don't want to inconvenience you."

The girl folded her arms across her chest and rolled her neck and eyes. "I know you not trying to get uppity, with puke all around your mouth and down your blouse." Melanie worked her neck from side to side. She then unfolded her arms and placed them steadfastly on her hips, ready for a challenge.

Her streaked blonde hair was plastered to one side of her head with a curl at the end, the back was piled high with a French roll that resembled the Eiffel Tower. She had some kind of colorful glitter in her hair and enough makeup to be an honorary member of the Tammy Faye Baker Hall of Fame. Her clawlike acrylic nails were long enough to be downright frightening.

Summer looked at her, standing with her hands on her hips and more attitude than any overly made up barmaid should have. "Well, excuse me Miss Manners, I was just saying I can manage by myself." Summer let out a small sigh and added, "Girlfriend, you could really use some makeup tips. Your hair-do is definitely a don't." She let out a light giggle.

Melanie's jaws flexed tightly and Summer knew she was about to go off, but the well-built guy intervened.

"Hey, Melanie, why don't you get me a club soda." Flashing a twenty dollar bill, he got her attention.

"Sure, Sonny, it stinks over here anyway." She looked Summer up and down shaking her head, and murmured, "Silly cow," loud enough for it to be heard.

Summer was about to go after her when she felt the grasp of two strong hands. "Miss, the bathroom's that way." The young man was turning her toward the direction of the bathroom. "Go on, I'll wait for you and if you want I'll call a cab for you." He smiled and she saw a row of white teeth that were so straight they looked false. He was clean cut with just enough wisdom in his eyes to make her think maybe he wasn't as young as she thought at first sight.

"Thanks, young man, you're awfully nice. And I'm a Mrs." She patted his hand as she threw her purse over her shoulder. Staggering to the bathroom, Summer felt like her insides were being forced up, and she made it to the toilet just in time.

After emptying her stomach, she splashed cold water on her face, cupped her hands and cried softly. After a few minutes there was a knock on the door. "Miss, you awright in there? Here, take this, it'll settle your stomach."

When Summer opened the door, the young man was there with club soda, pretzels and a smile that made her blush. "Thanks." Taking the glass and pretzels, she said, "I really am fine." She couldn't help but notice how the muscles in his arms flexed as he handed her the club soda.

"Well, yeah, I can see that as the old players would say, but are you feeling okay?" He was flirting with her, this boy who obviously was closer to her son's age than to hers.

"Yeah, I'm okay. Did I hear them call you Sonny?"

His cockiness unnerved her somewhat as he smiled and said, "Sonny Johnston, and yours?" She noticed how chiseled his facial features were. His eyes were dark and slightly slanted, reminding her of the handsome actor on the soap opera she had been watching the last few weeks when she'd returned home early from work, or had taken the day off. His hair was cut close on the sides with just a little height on top. His bronze-brown skin contrasted nicely with the sheer blue silk shirt he wore. This young man was obviously no stranger to the gym, his muscles seemed to scream for attention. He had full lips that curled up at the corners, giving him a slight but sexy smile, even when he wasn't smiling. Lips that could only be described as tempting to someone else. She, after all, was an occasionally happily married woman. She hoped that he wouldn't mistake her polite conversation for something more meaningful.

"Uh, thanks again, Sonny, but I'll be okay. I'll call my husband to pick me up." Thinking that if he heard she had a husband, maybe the attention would stop.

"I can call him for you if you like." Searching his eyes for sincerity, she almost laughed at the thought of him calling Kenneth.

"No thanks, I don't think my husband would appreciate hearing something like this from a stranger." He smiled that boyish-man smile again and she felt herself start to return the smile, but stopped herself.

"Sure, I can understand that. I'll be at the bar if you need any help. But you still haven't told me your name."

"Oh, I'm sorry, Summer…Summer is my name."

"Summer Summer, that's an odd name. Or is that you trying to give me one name when I gave you two?" Grinning devilishly, he made her smile broadly. She noticed for the first time how well shaped his mustache was. This was a man who took a lot of time to groom himself. She recognized the slight scent of Polo.

"Summer Hughes." She waited for the usual response her name evoked.

His head turned to one side, and almost in a whisper he said, "You know, somehow it fits you, beautiful and unique."

He smiled again and laughingly said, "Almost lyrical. But you know what sounds even better? Summer and Sonny, or better yet Sonny and Summer. Sounds like a singing duo, huh?" His eyes looked directly into hers, searching for a hint of response. He seemed to be setting the stage for an enticement. *The eyes always give you away,* she thought.

Summer began to wonder again if he were as young as she thought initially. He handled himself too confidently to be a young man. He wasn't quite as overt as most young men. His flirting was subtle and easy, almost natural. She had been away from the dating scene a long time, but not so long that she couldn't tell a seduction when she saw one. She thought they were making these younger models a lot bolder, and a lot more tempting since the last time she'd played the field. He handed her a business card. "I'm a handyman by trade, I can repair, fix anything. Take my card, pretty lady, in case you need some work done around the house."

Her mind wasn't as clear as it should have been, but why he was so interested in doing "work" for her? She knew then that he wasn't talking about repairs to her house, he was talking about repairs to her. Maybe she'd only imagined his flirting with her, maybe it was his way of securing additional work, flirting with older women to get them to hire him. Surely he could see she was old enough to be his...aunt.

They stood looking at each other for a few more minutes of uncomfortable silence before she said, "Well, I should finish cleaning up. Thanks again for the club soda and pretzels." She closed the door and stood with her back against it. She felt like her skin was starting to crawl away from her. How could she have gotten to this state? Allowing a mere child to flirt with her, and as if that weren't bad enough, enjoying it. She glanced at her image in the mirror and shook her head. That belligerent Melanie was right, she was acting simple-minded.

After several minutes of cold compresses, club soda and pretzels she was starting to feel human again. How was she going to explain her getting too drunk to drive home to her husband? How was she going to explain to him that she suddenly felt worthless and unimportant? How was she going to explain that she'd defined herself the past years by her success at work rather than her accomplishments as a wife, mother and good-hearted woman? She decided then she'd clean herself up, get something to eat and be in good enough shape to drive herself home. She couldn't face the sadness that would surely envelop Kenneth's face when he saw her.

She felt lower than she ever had, but at least she'd admitted the truth to herself. When people asked her what she did, she said with great pride, "I'm with LaFlair," and she could see how impressed people were by the way their eyes lit up, usually followed by plenty of "ooo's" and "ahhh's."

It was by all standards an impressive company to work for, and at one time she'd felt proud to be a part of it, but that time had become a distant memory. Now all she felt for LaFlair was contempt. She'd lost herself in the company, and that was her fault, but they had lost themselves in themselves and that was their fault. Just like she had to pay, they also would pay.

She reached in her bag and took out her small bottle for emergencies. She knew better, but she felt compelled to become numb again. That's what it did for her, made her numb so she could cope. Finding the bottle, she opened it and was interrupted by a call from April on her cell phone. She tried to act as though everything was fine but she answered with a vacuous, "Hello."

"Hey, sis, it's me." April could tell from the hello that something was wrong. "Are you okay?"

Summer burst into tears and said, "No, I'm a mess! Please come help me. I've been drinking, I'm sick and I can't drive."

When April arrived with Marcus, she felt sick at the sight of her sister. Summer's usually impeccable clothes were wrinkled and disheveled. She'd obviously attempted to wash her face, which still contained telltale signs of makeup, giving her a blotchy appearance. Her shoulders were slumped and she looked totally defeated.

April hugged her sister. "Come on, you're coming home with me for the night. I'll call Kenneth and tell him something." April saw the disappointment in her sister's eyes.

All Summer could manage was to mumble, "All right." She went obediently with her sister like a young child. She still had the small bottle in her hand. April took it and set it down on the table.

"This is a friend of mine, Marcus. He'll drive my car and I'll drive your car." She smoothed Summer's hair and kissed her forehead. "You'll be okay. Can you stand?" Summer smiled weakly at her sister and tried to stand. Marcus grabbed her gently as she started to stumble, and he lifted her up and carried her to the car.

Marcus was touched by the patience April showed. He placed Summer in the car. "Thanks," Summer muttered. With a blank expression she said, "It's nice my sister has someone to help her. She's so strong, but even a strong woman needs help once in a while. You strong, too, picking me up like that..." She was going to say something else, but she just patted his hand as he buckled her seat belt. Summer fell asleep before April even started the car.

Marcus followed them to April's house. April had called Marcus, asking for his help with her sister. She hadn't gone into detail, just that she needed his help with her sister. They had planned a trip to the library that evening to do some research. After April had put Summer to bed, she came and joined Marcus on the living room sofa.

"Summer asleep?" Genuine concern was etched on his face and April knew she didn't have to explain, but felt compelled to at least apologize. Although they'd only dated a short time, she'd gotten the impression that Marcus was a very compassionate man. He could read and understand people quickly.

"Yes, she is, and I'm sorry our evening has to be postponed."

"There's nothing to be sorry for, family always comes first." He put his arm around her shoulder and drew her closer. They sat quietly for a few minutes and April drifted off into a restful sleep. He watched her for a few minutes. She was clearly exhausted.

Marcus whispered, "Always taking care of others, you need someone to take care of you," and settled back on the sofa where he dozed off after a few minutes with her nestled in his arms. The feel of her head on his chest was natural, one that he enjoyed enormously.

Kenneth returned April's call. The ringing phone woke her and Marcus, and he unwrapped his arm from around her to allow her to answer the phone. The two had only been asleep for a few minutes, but they had gotten into a comfortable position. He enjoyed holding her while she slept, and the strength of his arms around her made her relax and feel quite protected.

Neither said anything as she walked toward the phone. "Hello, Kenneth, can you hold on for a minute?"

Marcus stood. Realizing she needed privacy, he said, "I'll talk to you later." He kissed her and let himself out. He double-checked to make sure the door was closed, and got into his car. Initially, their plan was to visit the library together that evening. He smiled at the thought of even spending time with her at the library. "I've got it bad, looking forward to an evening at the library." He laughed to himself and decided he at least would pick up a few books from the library.

Their intention was to research local neighborhood history for their book. They both agreed the neighborhood held a lot of history, but for some reason people only noted the history of the nationally known Anheuser Busch Brewery that called their neighborhood home. The area was also known for its great many restaurants of various cuisines which spoke of its diversity. The political history of the area was something of interest to them both. It was known to be the area that could elect a mayor. It was rich with cultural history as well but that was never explored in depth. The previous books explored the earlier cultural history of the neighborhoods, but did not explore the changing demographics of the area. They had decided their book would entail the rich political and cultural history of the neighborhood, past and present.

Marcus pulled into a parking space at the library, looked at his watch and thought he'd call April later when he returned home. He wanted to check on her and Summer. There was a lot he didn't know about April, secrets that he did not want to stand between them. He may not have come from a home with secrets like hers, but he understood adversity and what it meant to rise above it. He shook his head as he entered the library, he was thinking how much it took for April and her sisters to overcome whatever secrets they held. He didn't have to worry about money in college and medical school. He could only imagine what a hardship school had been for April, but she had managed to champion over it and succeed. She was the kind of woman that took control of her destiny. He liked that about her…liked it a lot. She wasn't looking to marry a doctor, she was a doctor, a title he knew didn't come easy. He held a great amount of respect and admiration for her. She was worth waiting for, he would take his time with her. He thought about their last kiss, and the way she felt nestled in his arms and knew that taking his time with her wouldn't be without its challenges. His heart and body ached for her, and that would be difficult to ignore or control.

* * *

April dreaded talking to Kenneth to tell him what happened. She and Kenneth talked about what they could do to save Summer from her continued descent into depression. They agreed counseling would be best but both knew that Summer would resist it. April decided then that Summer and Carmen would meet at a social gathering. Kenneth agreed with the plan, and the two began making plans for the meeting.

Later that evening Marcus called April. "I'm so sorry I fell asleep on you. I could have at least fed you before you left." She was in bed reading, but closed the journal and put it on the nightstand.

"No, I was fine. I was more concerned about you and Summer. How is she?"

"It's hard to say. Summer keeps things to herself, an unfortunately inherited family trait."

Marcus immediately wondered if April also shared that trait, but before he could ask, she volunteered, "Carmen has helped me work through that, though. I grew up in a house where it was best to keep things to yourself. My mother didn't encourage expression from her children. We all pretty much kept quiet."

"What about your father?" His voice was soft and soothed her. He had retired for the evening and had been lying in bed thinking about her.

"Don't remember much about him, except him being a quiet man."

"What about you, April? How are you?"

"I'm fine most days, but then there are those times when it's just hard watching my sister become detached, and thinking that the resolution to her problems are in a bottle."

"I understand that, and I want you to know I have very broad and strong shoulders anytime you need one to lean on.

I know we've only just met, and maybe you don't feel very comfortable being so open with me just yet, but I do under- stand about family and what it means to have so many people depending on you." His words touched April's heart, and for the first time in a long time, she allowed her defenses to come down. She knew he was sincere, and that touched her.

"Thank you, Marcus, you have no idea what that means to me."

"Well, you're welcome. It's getting pretty late, and I've kept you on the phone long enough. I'll talk to you tomorrow, you get some sleep."

All April could do was mutter, "Good night."

When April left for work the following morning Summer was still asleep. Summer called her later that day.

"I can't believe these lawyers are always advertising on the radio and television about how they can help you, and when you seek one out, they claim you don't have a case. I'm sick of it all. I've gone through two and all they did was take my money, claiming later that as an employee at will, most com- panies have the right to let you go at any time. That's common knowledge, so what kind of legal advice was that?" Summer felt helpless for the first time since she was a child.

She sipped on the rum and Coke, her fourth in the past two hours. It was taking more and more for her to get that high that liquor seemed to give her in the past. She knew it was a sign that her body was getting used to the new drug, and it took more and more of it to make her feel the numbness she longed for. She was forgetting things and barely remembered April bringing her home... Was there a man with April? She tried to remember, but her head ached.

She hoped that April wouldn't notice the bottle she'd emptied and hid in the bottom of April's trash can. She still hadn't worked up enough nerve to talk to Kenneth or to return home and it was nearing two o'clock in the afternoon.

"I told you a friend of mine is dating a lawyer that could help you. Why are you so set on trying to do this on your own? Use all the help offered by anyone willing." April was writing notes for her next neighborhood meeting while eating a small fruit salad for lunch.

"Why are you so set on worrying about me? I told you I'll be fine. I know where to look for help when I need it." Summer's voice was void of the usual interest it held when talking to her sister.

"What worries me is that you don't think you need help. We all need some help every once in a while. Isn't that what you said yesterday? We all need help sometimes. I worry about you because I love you." April set the pen down she was writing with and sat back in her chair. She then asked Summer, "When did you get so selfish and self-centered? You haven't given a thought to your husband or son. Don't you think that sounds at least a little bit familiar?" April knew she was being hard, but felt it was necessary.

The silence on the phone was deafening. "Listen, Summer, I've gotta get back to work. Will you be there when I get home?" She was putting her lab coat on.

"No."

"Have you spoken to Kenneth today?"

"No."

"Well, don't you think you should at least call him and let him know you're okay?"

"You've spoken to him," Summer answered dryly.

Frustrated, April sighed and said, "That's not the same as you talking to him. Listen, I've got to go. I left a business card on the kitchen counter for you. Someone I know could help you, and you need help, whether you're willing to admit it or not." April's voice hovered between aggravation and sadness.

April turned to leave, but not before saying, "Please take the card and call her."

"You really do need to get you some personal business. I don't need any help, I'm just tired."

Summer could never remember having this kind of conversation with her sister before. Unlike most sisters, they never fought each other, even as children. Their home was traumatic enough, they needed all their strength for fighting those who had made their lives difficult enough as young girls. A huge lump formed in her throat thinking about how she'd insulted her sister.

She walked over to the cabinet and pulled out a glass, and then searched the cabinet below for the bottle of liquor. She put a few ice cubes in the glass and then poured a small amount of the contents of the bottle into the glass. She stared at the amber liquid in the glass on the table. It seemed to be dancing a wicked dance of consumption. She knew all too well how it consumed all who dared to abuse it; took away everything, body and soul. After talking with April she was even more depressed.

When Summer returned home her head began swimming. She poured herself another drink and sat staring blindly out the kitchen window. Her mind wandered to the conversation she and April had had the night before. April pleaded with Summer to seek professional help before she destroyed herself and her family, before she turned into their mother.

Summer's eyes flooded with tears when April made the comment about her turning into their mother. April told her that there was no doubt that Kenneth loved her, but how much was he willing to put up with, and for how long? April was persuasive and her concerns were valid, but somehow Summer had convinced herself that she was doing the best she could, and felt the drinking helped her cope. She thought she could make herself stop anytime she wanted. Right now she wasn't sure if she wanted to stop the numbness.

Chapter 6

April had barely called the meeting to order when Marcus walked into the room. He wore a white shirt tucked neatly into his jeans and loafers. April marveled at how luscious he looked. His long athletic legs gave the jeans appeal that made her start to get warm. His appearance caused quite a stir as some of the women began whispering and sizing him up. He seemed unaffected by it all as he took a seat near the back of the room.

He acknowledged April's eye contact with a wink. *You are one sexy thing,* she thought to herself, and returned the wink. The meeting was heated with discussions about the rise in car thefts and home burglaries in the neighborhood. They agreed to beef up the neighborhood watch and would seek out more volunteers in the neighborhood to join the organization.

Mr. and Mrs. Anderson, her next-door neighbors, agreed to gather the other neighborhood retirees to make plans so they could sit in and observe one of the judges in action.

They had all agreed to target the one judge who was too soft on criminals. Even repeat serious offenders were released or given light sentences so they could prey on the neighborhood again. They had discussed the best use of video recorders that had been donated to the organization by a local retailer to help them record suspected criminal activity.

The meeting lasted longer than usual because of a guest speaker and the heavy agenda. April smiled when she saw Cozette walk in. She would be a welcome addition to the group. When the meeting finally ended, Marcus stood and began walking to meet April, but before he could get to her several women approached him. "I've never seen you at the meetings before, are you new to the neighborhood?" Liz Graham extended her hand to Marcus.

"No, I'm not, I've lived in the area for a few years and only recently decided to come to the meetings. I saw an article about the group and thought maybe I should check it out." His broad shoulders and smile almost brought Liz to her knees as she continued to hold his hand.

"Goodness, Liz, you act like you've never seen a man before," Patricia Ramirez intervened. "Excuse her, what did you say your name is?" Patricia flashed her prettiest smile and flung her hair over her shoulder in an obvious attempt at flirting. When that didn't get the desired response she moistened her lips and batted her eyes. It was an old-fashioned attempt at flirting but she was willing to try anything to get the attention of the tall, handsome stranger.

Marcus returned the smile and said, "Excuse me, ladies, but I need to see Dr. Nelson."

Cozette had joined April and thanked her again for inviting her to the meeting. April introduced her to the Andersons, knowing they'd take good care of her. She was introduced to several people and began passing out business cards and an-swering questions about her B and B.

Marcus quickly strolled over to April. "I'm surprised they allowed you to escape," she said good-naturedly. She'd had plenty of conversations with the women about the lack of available, working, drug-free, not-living-with-their-mothers, straight men in the area.

Marcus bent down and kissed her cheek, which elicited a col-lective gasp from the group of women who were now looking at the two like they were already on neighborhood watch.

April laughed and waved at the women. "Don't worry, I know him."

They all laughed and Patricia responded playfully, "Ask him if he has a brother, friend, cousin or even an uncle." Patricia raised both brows and gestured with her hands as if expecting April to ask Marcus the question. When April shook her head no, the women all chuckled and went about their business.

"Good of you to come, I wasn't expecting you." She tried not to show her pleasure but was fooling no one.

"I am a resident of the neighborhood, thought it was time to come see you in action. I was impressed. I read the article about you and the group in the South side Journal. I like your fire and passion." The way he said it made April wonder if he was talking about the meeting or something else. She con-cluded it must have been the meeting since they'd only had a few dates and too many late-night phone calls.

She'd purposely stayed away from him. His lips and arms were too demanding and her body was too willing to comply. They'd talked several times on the phone and just the way he said her name made her feel like getting closer to him.

"I'd like a decaf now, what about you?" he asked with a smile that made her lose her train of thought. She was gath-ering her papers and putting them in the briefcase.

April looked at him. "What?" She had tried her best to ignore his scented cologne, but his obvious male presence made her realize how much she'd missed him in the past few days.

"I said…"

"I'm sorry, I heard you, there's a coffee shop near here if you want to follow me." She closed the briefcase and asked the secretary if she could have the minutes done in the next week or so, she would mail them to members who had missed the meeting. They would be updated in plenty of time for the next meeting. The secretary assured her it wouldn't be a problem. Since all of the members were volunteers, April made it her business to never demand anything from them. She thanked them for their contributions. She understood they had other obligations. After a few minutes more of neighborhood talk with various volunteers, she gathered up her belongings and said, "Boy, am I beat. That decaf is going to have to be brief."

She then looked over at Marcus and could tell he was disappointed, but there was no way he was getting her all heated up tonight, she didn't trust herself enough to know if she'd let him leave. He was a tall, handsome distraction that she didn't have time for right now. Her plate was already too full. And besides, she wanted to take it slow…didn't she?

He followed her out of the building toward her car and tried diligently to ignore the tempting swing of her hips. He smiled internally and thought, *I'd follow you anywhere.* He was not going to let her businesslike manner deter him.

The coffee shop was a favorite of policemen and night workers who would gather there before or after their shift at the nearby brewery. It was clean and the coffee was good and hot, so it met all their needs. They sat in a booth and ordered two cups of decaf and shared a piece of apple pie.

"I really liked a lot of the things you said in the meeting.

I'm afraid I've been one of those neighbors that have taken for granted that the police will do their jobs. I have a burglar alarm on my home and car and just hadn't given much thought to how bad the neighborhood had gotten or what I could do to improve it." Marcus took a forkful of pie and offered it to April. She slowly wrapped her lips around the fork and took in the pie.

Marcus tried to ignore her sensuous lips, "Hmmm, this is really good pie." April didn't notice him staring at her as she licked the remainder of the pie crumbs from her lips.

Marcus was determined to stay focused on his thoughts, and tried to keep the conversation on track. "I do some mentoring for at-risk young men in the area. Thanks to you I plan to join the organization and become more active when I can. Attending a meeting once a month isn't nearly enough." Marcus sounded natural and sincere, but his eyes returned to her lips.

"I want to see as many good neighbors like yourself involved as much as possible. We want to take our neighborhoods back, one block at a time. We have elderly people who are afraid to walk the streets in the daytime or the evening. That should never be. My neighbors have lived in their house for over forty years and now are afraid to leave it, and are afraid to live in it." April shook her head as the sadness of it took hold. Marcus admired her passion and determination.

"They look to me for help, we watch out for each other." She thought back to the comment Donald had made and added, "Some people don't understand why or how I continue to live in the area. They seem to think I should sell my house and move away to a nice quiet neighborhood. Preferably in the suburbs." She picked up her cup of decaf and took a drink.

"I guess that would be the easy thing to do, but you don't strike me as the kind of person who makes it a habit of taking the easy way out," Marcus retorted as he peered at her over his cup. When he set the cup down she looked at his moist lips and resisted the urge to lean forward to kiss them.

"No, I don't, but there are times when I wish I could. It gets challenging at times." She continued to hold her cup in her hand, sat back in her chair and smiled.

"Are we still talking about the neighborhood group?" he asked with a sly smile on his face.

April looked at him and brought her own coffee cup to her lips in an attempt to hide her desire and the tiny smile the comment brought. She loved looking at his lips, they seemed to always be inviting hers to join them. She barely whispered, "Yes, we are, but just barely." Her attention was focused on his eyes.

Marcus decided to continue. "My friends ask me why I continue to live in the area, too. But I'm five minutes from the hospital, many of my patients I see in the grocery store, at the bank and so forth. I think it makes me more personable to them. I live in their neighborhood. They see me without the white coat. The community almost has a small-city, personal feeling to be so close to the patients whose lives you touch. I have a daughter, mother and grandmother who have all come for visits to my office and they all live in the neighborhood, so why should I give that up? I love the area, its rich history, diversity. I love that it's being revitalized."

April simply nodded her head in agreement. They both sat comfortably in silence for several more minutes before Marcus said, "Tell me more about your family."

April had never had a man inquire about her family after knowing her such a short period of time and she wasn't sure how much she'd share with him. Her family wasn't something she spoke freely about, especially her mother. "Well, I told you I come from a family of three, all girls. My youngest sister died a few years ago, and Summer lives in St. Charles with her husband and son."

"What about your parents?"

"I don't spend much time with my mother, and like I said, my father left years ago…" April hesitated, thinking of the best way to describe her mother before continuing, "…and my mother managed to raise us in spite of herself."

Marcus found the last comment odd, but wasn't sure if he should pry. He did ask, "How's Summer doing?"

"She's okay, needs some help, but refuses. She's had a setback at work and I think it has her feeling insecure and unvalued." April looked away and felt sad. She didn't want to discuss the situation with him and shifted the conversation.

Marcus looked curiously at her and instantly knew it wasn't a subject she was ready to share openly. He would take the time to find out why the thought of her family made her look so sad. It pained him that she didn't feel that she could talk to him about whatever problems her family was facing.

"Tell me about your family," April reciprocated.

"I'm an only child, my parents are still married. They retired to Florida a few years ago." Marcus took another drink of decaf and added, "I try to visit them several times a year, but it becomes difficult with my schedule."

"An only child, huh? What's that like?" She couldn't imagine growing up in the tumultuous home she lived in as an only child. She relied on her sisters for support.

"It was great, but I don't have anything to compare it to. I do have cousins that I'm close to." Marcus motioned for the waitress to refill his coffee. "You want more?" he asked April.

"No, thank you." She pushed her cup to the side and asked, "You don't have any children?"

"No." He looked at her curiously. He didn't remember seeing any visible signs of children when he was at her home but knew that didn't always mean anything, so he asked, "You've never mentioned children, I just assumed you didn't have any, do you?" He could picture a cute little girl looking just like her, wild curly hair and all.

"Not a one, but I do have a nephew who's a junior in high school. I feel like he's mine. We are very close." She tried to read his thoughts and the smile he wore was curious, she thought.

"That's nice, I've often wondered what that must be like. I've regretted not having children. Sometimes I think us first-generation college graduates put too much into our careers and not enough into our personal lives. Actually, I know that to be true in my case. I hope it's not too late, I definitely want children."

His eyes questioned hers, but she refused to answer back, she could almost read his mind. He was asking the question, "Do you want children?" with his eyes, but she diverted the question by saying, "It's not too late, you're still a young man. And rather virile looking, I might add." April smiled wickedly and Marcus saw the hint of mischief in her eyes. He liked her playfulness. If she wanted to talk about her desire to have children, she would have, so he left the subject alone. It would be a question he would ask her later, after they'd spent more time together.

"Why thank you, I think. And you are mighty appealing yourself." His eyes held her gaze.

"You think?" She refused to look away and the two continued their gaze.

Marcus leaned forward and with undeniable conviction said, "I know." April studied his face. He was truly a handsome man, but more importantly, his eyes revealed an honesty that she could trust. Getting to know him since their first eye dance from across the room at the fund-raiser had intensified. The once subtle allure she felt had somehow turned into a burning desire to have him eagerly buried deep inside of her. She refused to let that overwhelming desire overtake her, she wanted certainty that he was all that she thought he was.

"I don't wear much makeup or dress fashionably. In high school kids teased me about my hair." She self-consciously tugged at her headband to make sure it continued to hold her hair in place. "I never liked putting chemicals or anything on it so it's just natural."

"Don't apologize, I like it, very wholesome. You're a naturally beautiful woman, you don't need any makeup. I think your style of dress fits your personality, very earthy, warm." Marcus took another sip of his decaf and his eyes returned to hers.

"That's about the nicest thing I've heard from a man in a long time." April smiled modestly and with both hands brought her cup to her lips and took a drink.

"I find that hard to believe. What kind of men have you been going out with?" Marcus added a pack of sugar to his decaf and stirred.

"Evidently the wrong kind," she replied.

"Well, I hope that's about to change." Looking at her intently again, his eyes spoke volumes while his mouth remained closed. He took another drink of his decaf and asked, "What made you want to become a veterinarian?"

"I really didn't think much about what I wanted to be when I grew up until I was almost out of high school. When I thought about it, the only thing that had remained constant throughout my life was my love of animals. I've loved animals since I could remember. You know how small kids draw pictures of their family—dad, mom, siblings, etcetera? I drew pictures of animals and their families. A daddy lion, momma lion, cubs. My favorite trip was going to the zoo once a year at school. I didn't have a lot of friends growing up because we moved so much, but I loved visiting the friends who had pets. I think I played more with their pets than I did with them.

"I watched any program about animals on television growing up. I snuck frogs, grasshoppers, turtles, anything into the house. I'd keep them for a while and prayed my mother wouldn't find them. I eventually had to let them go because I knew what would happen to them if I didn't. I read every book in the library on animals, and the subject in school that I enjoyed most was science. Dissecting the frog in biology class was the real deal maker." April had to laugh before continuing, "The only pet we ever had was a little mixed breed that we got when my grandmother died." April stopped and looked inquiringly at him. "I'm sorry, I was getting carried away, wasn't I?"

Marcus let out a sound of unmistakable male laughter, punctuated with a smile that melted April.

"Did I answer your question?"

"You most certainly did."

"Do you like animals?" she queried.

"Yes."

"Are you teasing me?"

"Nope."

"Huh…something tells me you are. Why did you choose to be a pulmonologist? I know it's quite an extensive area and requires extra schooling and residency."

"Actually, I think the field chose me. I was extremely close to my paternal grandmother who took care of me while my mother finished college and my father was away in the military. I believed the sun rose and set around my grandmother. She was the closest thing to an angel I've ever seen— warm, loving, patient. She always found time for me, spoiled me, doted on me. When my dad went overseas, he insisted that my mother and I live with her. My grandfather had remarried years earlier, but I would occasionally see him. I didn't like him because he'd left my grandmother. You know how kids think."

Marcus stopped and sat quietly for a minute before continuing, "We were out shopping for school clothes when I was in first grade, and my grandmother had an asthma attack."

April had just lifted her cup, preparing to take another drink of her decaf, but stopped in midair. "It was serious, but she survived, and I made up my mind that I would always take care of her, and believe it or not I decided then I wanted to be a doctor 'who helps people breathe.'" Marcus made quotes with his fingers, indicating the quote from his youth.

"I didn't know then what it was called, but I've had the desire to help people with pulmonary disease ever since."

"Is your grandmother still alive?"

"No, she died of natural causes at the age of ninety-two."

"Did you ever forgive your grandfather?"

"I did when I was much older, and wiser. We made our amends and I did work up the courage to ask him why he'd left my grandmother."

"Are you serious? How old were you?"

"I think I was around eight."

April laughed, "You were that brazen at eight?"

"Most kids don't know they're being brazen, they just want their questions answered."

"What did he say?"

"He basically said that she was too bossy, but what I learned later was that he really meant she wasn't a pushover. She didn't take a lot of stuff from him or anybody else, she knew what she wanted and pursued it. Some men are too weak-minded to understand and find that desirable in a woman."

"Oh," April said. Finally she brought her cup to her lips

and took a drink. Marcus did the same, not allowing his eyes to leave hers. They sat quietly for a few minutes and April thought they had a natural chemistry. She liked the fact that he had no problem looking directly into her eyes when he spoke. He never looked away. She'd seen enough men who could spend the evening out with her and at the end of the night couldn't tell you a thing about her eyes. Marcus was the first man to make her feel comfortable enough to share personal details about herself and her family. And he shared information as well, which brought them closer.

"May I ask you a personal question?" Marcus asked after a few minutes of silence.

"Oh, that depends on the question, you certainly may ask it, but I may chose not to answer. You seem to know the right questions to ask," she answered playfully.

"Do you feel some kind of spark that's more than a physical attraction between us? A hint of something much bigger than either of us are willing to admit?" He looked at her curiously and waited for her to answer.

April's response was reluctant, but she couldn't help being honest. "Undeniably, I do." She thought to herself, *Not much gets past this man. I like that…like it a lot.*

"Okay, good. I didn't want it to be just me." He relaxed and picked up his cup again.

April started laughing. "No, it's just not you, but I do like to take things slow if you don't mind. I've grown to appreciate what it really takes to get to know someone well before you become intimate."

"I don't mind at all. I understand taking it slow. I've made it a habit of rushing into relationships, and they've always ended before they started. I'd like to see us last. And besides, you can become intimate without sharing each other's bodies." His intensity had returned, as had the urge to hold her in his arms again. When he looked at her lips again, his mouth became suddenly dry and he took another drink of decaf.

"You know, Doctor, I really like your bedside manner." Her voice was enticing and he responded.

"You haven't seen it yet, but I do believe you'll like it." April took the menu from the metal holder on the table and began fanning herself with it. He was saying all the right things, and the challenge was raised another bar. It was definitely going to be difficult not jumping him.

Teasingly she joked, "It certainly has gotten warm in here."

Marcus flashed a smile that was laden with seductive charm, causing April to return it with her own sensual smile. A smile that incited him to pick up the other menu and fan himself. "Yes, it has," he muttered while looking at her inviting lips that had beckoned him since the first time he saw her.

April had barely gotten inside the house when her doorbell rang. Peeking out to see who it was she opened the door for Donald.

"Hey, you, I wasn't expecting to see you." He leaned over and tried to kiss her lips but she offered her cheek instead.

"Oh, it's like that now, huh?" He seemed offended. She looked at him and wondered, what was he doing at her home so late and uninvited?

"Like what?" she couldn't help asking with more attitude than she normally used with him.

"I usually greet you with a kiss on the lips."

"I thought we decided the other night we'd be friends." April walked into the living room with Donald behind her.

"You decided," he pointed out, and took his usual position on the sofa without being asked.

"What brings you over?" She looked at him getting comfortable and wondered, was he always so assuming with her, and why hadn't she noticed it before?

"You." He looked at her and smiled. He sat back on the sofa and stretched out both arms.

April walked over to the recliner and sat down. She yawned, hoping he would get the hint. After a few minutes of silence she said, "It's late, Don, and I had a meeting after work, can we make this quick?" Her tone was impatient.

"I got some good news today and I wanted to share it with you." He smiled and his voice became lighthearted. "I've been given a city contract in Seattle and plan to move there in three or four months to get the ball rolling, even though the project won't start until the first of next year."

April felt happy for him. "That's wonderful news, you've worked so hard to get it. Congratulations."

He walked over and sat on the arm of the chair and leaned over, trying to kiss her lips.

"Don!" They'd agreed friendship was best for them.

"I know we're just friends, but actually, April, I was hoping you'd considering moving with me." He reached into his pocket and pulled out a ring box. April was exasperated as she slowly took in a deep breath.

Donald stood and then kneeled beside her and said, "April, I love you and I know you can come to love me." He opened the ring box and exposed a beautiful diamond engagement ring. "Please marry me."

April was dumbfounded. She truly enjoyed his company and loved him as a friend. She didn't have the kinds of feelings for him a woman should have for a husband. Her mind was flooded with thoughts before Donald interrupted, "I know it's a lot to ask now, and maybe you want to think about it." He searched her eyes for a "yes," but his heart heard "no" when she remained silent. He stood up and straightened his pants, returning the ring box back to his pocket. "I see." He was disappointed and hurt.

"I'm sorry, Don, but I just really don't love you in that way. All we could ever be is friends, and I do value that. I'm sorry…"

Donald held his hand up to stop her. "No need to be sorry, April. I think you are making a mistake." He took her by her arms and pulled her gently to her feet. "You know I've loved you for years, and I'm asking that you consider the possibility of us spending the rest of our lives together. I'm willing to make the sacrifice and decline the Seattle request, that way you can remain here with your family. Just think about it, no commitment for now, just think about it." He pulled her close and kissed her forehead and held her close again.

She gently pulled away. "I can't, Don. I'm sorry, but friends is all I can see for us."

"I understand, but that doesn't change how I feel about you, and you know I would do anything to change how you feel about me." He smiled the captivating smile that he used the first time he lured her into his bed.

Ignoring the smile, she said, "I must tell you, I've met someone."

His response was immediate. He pulled further away. "What do you mean, 'met someone'?" She took that opportunity to step further away from him before continuing.

"Just that, I've met someone I'm interested in, someone I think is special." The thought of Marcus made her smile, and she walked over to the chair by the window and sat down.

"Why didn't you tell me that before I came in here and made a fool of myself." His eyes followed her but he didn't move. He then walked away and sat on the sofa.

"I hardly consider you proposing to me as making a fool of

yourself, and if I remember correctly we had this conversation about us remaining friends, and only friends. You agreed."

"I was there, remember, and you said nothing then about meeting someone, and…" He looked at her and a flash of darkness crossed his face. "Have you slept with him?"

"Of course not! You know better. Besides that, it would be none of your business, anyway." She looked up at him as he stood and paced.

"I don't know. You haven't said a *word* about him before now." His voice was dangerously close to a sneer.

"We just recently started dating and he came to my meeting tonight. We had coffee afterwards."

"So you haven't gotten serious?" He was now wringing his hands and pacing.

"We are certainly headed in that direction. There's a strong attraction between us. We have a lot in common."

"I see." Disappointment was clear on his face as he lowered himself onto the sofa.

"Please don't act like that. You should be happy for me." April walked over and joined him on the sofa, covering his hand with hers.

"Like what? Like you've just stepped on my heart? Damn you, April, you could've told me about this sooner. Why should I be happy for you?" He truly didn't get it, she thought.

"I'm sorry, I thought you were my best friend. I thought we came to an understanding. I want what's best for you, I thought you wanted the same for me. You're the one who came in here tonight out of the blue with a proposal."

Donald scratched his head and she watched as his eyebrows flexed in a worried expression. "Yeah, you're right, I do want you to be happy." His eyebrows relaxed, but his tone did not convince her.

"And I want the same for you. There's someone out there looking for you, someone who will know how special you are."

Chapter 7

When April got to work she went about her tasks with speed. She had a full day and was trying not to think of Summer. She had to concentrate on her work, her attention was required. Every once in a while the situation with Summer would drift into her thoughts, or she would think about the hint of longing in Marcus's eyes when he looked at her.

"Dr. Nelson, you're not going to believe this! You've got to get out here."

April was completing the neutering of a poodle and looked up at Samantha. "We're just about done here, will it wait about five minutes?" She looked over at Bridget, who was assisting her, and all she got was a curious look.

"Oh, yes, it'll wait, it's not an emergency, but you just need to see this!" She backed out of the room and closed the door, but not before she squealed with laughter.

April moaned to herself, "Oh, oh, that doesn't sound good."

She patted the sleeping poodle on the head and placed it in the recovery room. Bridget laughed as she removed her gloves and walked over to the wash area.

"My cousin doesn't get excited about nothing, so I'm very curious. I wonder if it's like a two-headed snake or something?" Bridget and April laughed. "I hope not," Bridget added and shook her head, making April laugh even more.

April removed her gloves and gown, then walked to the sink and scrubbed. By the time she was done her curiosity had peaked as she headed toward the waiting room.

The fragrance hit her before she got there. When she arrived the entire room was filled with all kinds of roses. There was a large assortment of American Beauty roses with a huge banner that read, "Life with me could be a bed of roses!" She found the card and read the message from Don.

April stood in shock as some of her customers stood smiling and apparently quite amused with the scene. Samantha had joined the staff and replied, "Dr. Nelson, this is the most romantic thing I've ever seen." Bridget was bubbling with happiness, but it was short-lived when she noted her boss's expression.

April began scattering the vases of roses throughout the office so they weren't quite so overwhelming and went about the rest of her tasks. Samantha looked at Bridget, who just hunched her shoulders, indicating she didn't know what was going on.

April looked at her watch and was surprised by the time. It was nearly 1:30 and she hadn't had anything to eat since an early morning breakfast of toast and juice. Her stomach began to rumble and she felt famished. She decided to call Marcus and invite him to lunch since her afternoon schedule was a little lighter. She paged him and within five minutes he returned her call.

"Good afternoon, beautiful. How's your day going?" He had

just returned to his office from making rounds. He was looking at the stack of patient files and welcomed the distraction.

"It's going well, what about yours?" April took off her white coat and placed it on the back of her chair. She didn't want anything to constrict her while she was on the phone with Marcus. She liked feeling soft when talking with him, no clinical white coat while on the phone with him. She laughed at her giddiness. This was indeed something new and foreign to her.

"Busy as usual." He put the file down and massaged his forehead.

"I called to see if you had time for lunch?" April pictured his lips and she smiled to herself.

"No, but I'll make time. You and food that's not prepared in a hospital are the best offer I've had all day." The tension was suddenly gone and he looked at his schedule for the day to make sure he could spend as much time as possible with her.

"Let's meet at Hodge's over on Chouteau in thirty minutes."

"I'll be there." They said their goodbyes and April immediately began thinking more about where her relationship with Marcus was going. She liked the fact that he understood her commitment to others, understood she didn't have the best family history, and so far none of it had run him away. She felt such a strong attraction to him that it scared, yet delighted her. She wanted to explore the feeling.

As soon as April walked into the restaurant her eyes met Marcus's and he waved her over. He stood up, leaned down and greeted her with a kiss on the cheek. "I was afraid you wouldn't make it."

"Why would you think that?" April asked curiously, her cheek still feeling warm from the kiss.

"No reason, I was just excited about seeing you. Anxious,

I guess, I want to make sure you're doing okay. You seem to want to look out for everybody but yourself." His tone was serious as he sat down and leaned forward with his elbows resting on the table.

"I know, but I haven't forgotten about your offer. I may have to lean on your shoulders."

"They're here anytime you need them. No excuses or reasons. Anything you'd like to share, or I could help you with?"

April thought about it and decided to give him the abridged version of what Summer was experiencing. "Yes, but let's order first, I'm starving."

Marcus agreed and the two began studying the menu. After they'd settled into lunch April began telling him about Summer's situation. She told him about her concern and for the first time she admitted her mother was an alcoholic.

"My father left when we were very young. I don't really know why." She looked pensive for a minute and added, "I barely remember anything about him." April's tone was sad as Marcus listened intently to her.

Her family lived next door to a woman whose husband had left her with four children. She worked at the hospital with April's father and had become fast friends with April's mother as well.

April found out later from her mother that the woman was even friendlier with her father, and was the reason that her parents ended up always arguing and fighting. Although in the recesses of her mind she could never remember her father arguing or fighting with her mother, she could only remember him being soft-spoken and looking beaten all the time. Not physically beaten, but mentally—shoulders slumped and a slow walk like he was tired from carrying a very heavy load. She told him about her mother's many

failed marriages and subsequent abuse of alcohol and neg-
ligence of her children.

Her mother moved them to a nearby housing project
shortly after her father left. It was an experience that always
hovered somewhere in April's mind. To this very day, she
could visualize the small, cramped apartment with the
concrete walls and floors. The sounds and smells would last
a lifetime. She attributed it to her father's leaving and blamed
him for all that had gone wrong during her childhood.

Hers was indeed a painful childhood, filled with disappointment, confusion and sadness. Her mother was neglect-
ful in many ways. She didn't encourage them to pursue any
interest outside of the home. They never participated in
mother and daughter activities that their friends experienced
with their mothers. The only happy times that she could recol-
lect were always with her sisters as they grew older and were
able to spend time away from home.

Marcus could see the pain on April's face and it pained
him. He reached out to gently stroke her face. Although he
had wonderful, doting parents, who filled his childhood with
wonderful memories, there were many parents who were in-
capable of such love and attention.

"Are you okay talking about all of this?" His voice and face
echoed his concern and when April looked at him it warmed
her heart. Marcus never wanted anything to ever hurt her
again and his face and gentle gesture showed it.

April loved the way his soft hands felt on her face. "Yes,
I am okay, but actually I haven't talked to many people about
it. It's too painful sometimes."

"I'm glad you feel comfortable enough to talk to me. I
think you're a very special lady to have gone through all
that you have and managed to become the woman I see
before me." His admiration for her had grown exponentially

and he couldn't help but tell her so. "You are nothing short of amazing."

His reaction surprised her, April thought. She didn't expect him to be so direct and complimentary. She thought somehow he'd lose interest in her after telling him so much about her family. He seemed to meet each hurdle and leap above it. Marcus was getting more and more entrenched in her heart and it was a feeling she enjoyed.

"Have you referred Summer to Carmen?" Marcus had completely ignored his lunch, as had April. They were deep in conversation and neither had touched their food or beverage since early on in the meal. Their eyes and attention were focused only on each other and the conversation. He wanted to help her and she reached effortlessly out for his help.

"Oh, I have, but she's resistive to any kind of outside help. She feels like she'd betray some family secret. Actually, I think some residual guilt from my younger sister's murder may be the cause." She hadn't meant to say it but she definitely had Marcus's attention and he queried her.

"You said your sister died, I didn't know she was murdered." He gently took her hand and said, "I'm sorry to hear that. You are carrying a lot on those beautiful shoulders. Tell me what happened." He stroked her hand and leaned forward attentively.

"It's still difficult for me to talk about." April lowered her head as sadness enveloped her.

"I'm sure." Marcus tilted her head slightly up with his finger. "But understand, you're not alone, you can talk to me anytime you want. I'm here for you." His eyes looked at her pleadingly and she knew his offer was genuine. He had become a bigger distraction than she was willing to admit.

"Thanks, that means a lot. If I hadn't gone to see Carmen I'm not sure if I could have gotten through it." April took a drink of water and continued telling him about how Autumn was killed by her jealous boyfriend. Despite her and Summer's continuous efforts to keep Autumn away from the man, she continued to run off to be with him. She met him in Houston, Texas, while attending college there. April was certain she sought the elusive love and attention from the man that she never got at home. She squandered a full scholarship because she spent more time with the man than she did attending classes. April tried to tell her that a man who was interested in her and her future would not have allowed such a thing. She and Summer tried every logical and illogical argument to keep Autumn away from him.

During the early stages of the courtship he worshipped her and showered her with attention. Autumn was overwhelmed by the attention and when she met his family, who embraced her, she was seduced into a relationship that grew violent over the years. She admittedly felt like something that had been missing was now found. Autumn never said what it was, but April had always assumed it was a sense of family, of loving parents.

Autumn made excuses for the man's increased physical abuse and was determined to make the relationship flourish. April and Summer tried desperately to convince her that the failure of the relationship was not her fault. It wasn't until after her death, when April was telling the story to Carmen, that she realized Autumn was trying not to become her mother, who'd never had a successful relationship with a man.

Autumn didn't understand that staying in an abusive relationship wouldn't make it a good one. Whenever any of them looked at their mother, they tried their hardest not to be like her. It had harmed them all to varying degrees.

April explained to Marcus that it was why she took the situation with her sister Summer so seriously because even though the scenario was different, she saw the same kind of self-destructive behavior. Kenneth loved his wife, but their marriage was in trouble.

"Maybe you can arrange for Summer to meet Carmen in a social setting and let her get comfortable with her first. Sometimes that helps people to relax. And I know Carmen would be amenable to that, she did it for me with a friend of mine who was having difficulty dealing with some issues."

"That's really a good idea, Marcus, thanks." April began to ponder how she could pull the meeting off because she knew Summer would not knowingly agree to meet with a therapist. She felt relaxed with Marcus in a way that she'd never felt before. He was understanding and compassionate. They continued to talk about work and what the rest of the workday was like for them. They talked briefly about the book and shared information both had learned while talking with others about their ideas for the book.

"I'd like to get tickets to see *The Lion King* in late September. I know it's kind of early, but they're expecting a sellout. I'm thinking of a Saturday evening performance. Would you like to join me?"

"That's a ways off, think we'll last that long?" She smiled at him sensuously.

"I know we will." His confidence amused and delighted April as she enjoyed teasing him. Marcus examined her closely. He thought she exhibited that kind of allure that had nothing to do with wearing a low-cut blouse or revealing too much skin. Hers was the deeply rooted, quiet kind of appeal that made men look twice and make all kinds of promises to keep that smile on her beautiful face. He couldn't imagine why she was still single. His only thought was that she was smart, and very selective about what she wanted. She wouldn't settle for less, of that he was certain. He liked that a lot, he wanted to be the one she selected.

His continuous gaze didn't escape her keen eye and she wondered about it, but went on to answer him. "Sure, that sounds great, I've heard nothing but wonderful things about it. The reviews have been complimentary." April thought back to the last time she'd spent an evening attending a play, and couldn't remember. She admittedly had spent too many late nights in her office, attending meetings, a fund-raiser or doing some other activity. Marcus had made her realize that.

Almost as if on cue, both began to eat their neglected lunches. "This is really good," Marcus said, after taking a bite of his burger, then asked, "How's yours?"

April had barely stopped chewing before her pager went off. She looked at it and saw her office number.

"This is a good burger. Excuse me, I've got to place a call." April went into the bathroom to return the call to Bridget. "Dr. Nelson, I hate to bother you during lunch, but there's a gentleman here insisting that he talk to you. He claims your cell phone is turned off. I tried to explain to him that means you don't want to be disturbed."

"That's okay, Bridget, put him on the phone." April's free hand automatically rested on her hip as she was known to do whenever she got ready for an argument. She knew Donald was being aggressive because he cared for her but she found it annoying.

"Hello."

"Hello, Don. What are you doing at my office?" she asked with directness.

"What, is it off-limits to me?" He was being sarcastic, she thought. She didn't like it when he'd try to bait her with questions like that.

"No, it's just that you've not been there since the first time we met." April's hand was now planted firmly on her hip and she was facing the mirror. She glanced quickly at her posture and removed her hand from her hip.

"Well, I wanted to surprise you and I wanted to know if you liked the flowers. Kinda my last plea…" Looking over at Bridget, Donald turned away before saying, "…about Seattle." He knew Bridget was listening, and clearly was interested in the conversation.

"The flowers are lovely, Don. I have said all I'm going to say about Seattle."

"I just wanted to be sure, I want you to be sure." Donald could hear the distance in April's voice and asked, "Are you with someone now?"

"Yes," was all she said. She tried to be understanding and hoped that he would, too.

"I'll call you later." She couldn't discern what his tone meant. He didn't sound angry, just disappointed and perhaps curious. He'd never had any real competition for her friendship or attention with another man before. April was concerned about him. He was a dear friend and she didn't want to lose that.

"Are you okay?"

"Oh, yeah, couldn't be better. I'm sorry about interrupting you. Go and enjoy your lunch." April immediately wished she hadn't asked Bridget to put him on the phone because now she was getting an earful. She didn't want to bring her personal affairs into her office.

"Donald, can we talk later?"

"No need, I was out of line. I thought maybe there was a chance we could… Never mind, I'm sorry. I'll talk to you later." The silence that followed caused her to doubt if they would talk later.

April flipped her phone closed and took a deep breath. She looked in the mirror and sighed at her image. She splashed cool water on her face, reapplied her lipstick and fingered her hair into place.

"Something important?" Marcus immediately asked.

"No, just a misunderstanding."

Marcus noted the short, curt answer, and knew that the phone call had annoyed her. "When can I see you again?" Marcus leaned over and peered at her as he took her hand.

"I thought you just asked me to go with you to see *The Lion King.*"

"April, that's over a month away. As a matter of fact, I'm thinking of going to Antique Row this weekend. One of the stores has been on the lookout for lamps for me. They called and said they may have something for me. I'd like to get your opinion. You got any plans?" She liked the feel of her hands in his, it felt natural.

"I do now. I work until noon on Saturday, but I'm free after that."

"Good, then, it's a date."

"Do people our age date?" she asked playfully.

"It's been a while, but yes, I do believe we still date."

"I find it rather difficult to believe that you haven't been going out or dating." She knew women who would drop to his feet and do whatever he wanted them to do. He was more man than she'd seen in a long time. Afraid of giving away her thoughts, she reached for her glass of water.

He smiled and refused to look away from her—even when she reached for her glass of water, he continued to hold her free hand. Despite her strong persona, he knew how delicate she was. She was a rock for others, but he knew there had to be times when she wanted someone to be her rock.

"It's been mostly self-imposed. I usually work almost sixteen hours a day. I don't have a lot of time for dating. And

I really didn't have a lot of luck dating, so frankly I'm looking for something more."

"More what?" April asked and then put a forkful of salad in her mouth.

"You." His intense stare had returned and it made her want to melt into his arms. He hoped he wasn't being too direct, but it was necessary, he thought.

"I think that's a nice compliment, but why me? Why now?" April tried to ignore the feeling of warmth as it spread throughout her body. He drove her to distraction, she thought as she watched the corners of his mouth turn up into a smile with just a hint of a secret.

"You know how you're always told to follow that first thought? The first time I laid eyes on you, I knew it was something different, something drew me to you. There's something between us, something more than dating. You feel it and so do I." Marcus picked up his hamburger and took a bite of it. It had gotten cold, but he chewed and swallowed it. He pushed the plate away. He wanted to focus his attention on April.

"It may be that you haven't dated in a while. I think they call it being horny." They both laughed good-naturedly. She tried to make light of his interest, but deep down she knew better. She could judge character and she knew his interest in her was beyond the physical. She felt the unstated.

"No, sweetness, I'm not driven by lust. It's much deeper than that." Marcus took another swallow of water. "Although I must admit, I do like the possibility of us in each other's arms on a warm summer night with the window open and a soft breeze blowing across our naked bodies."

"I'd say that was pretty lust-driven." Her mind conceded to the thought, and a small smile hinted at her lips.

"Well, maybe just a little," he admitted with false modesty and they both laughed again.

"I find you to be a very special woman, someone that I look forward to spending more time with, getting to know even better."

He thought back to the times when he had dated. It seemed the rule was after three dates, it was sex followed by the woman making references to having always wanted to marry a doctor. He didn't totally blame the women, he blamed himself for not taking the time to get to know them, just like they hadn't gotten to know him.

April was different. She was independent, vibrant, beautiful, grounded and everything he'd ever wanted in a woman. His body seem to go on alert every time he thought of her. He wanted desperately to get to know her. He would take the time to pursue her.

"I guess what I'm saying is that I hope you will seriously give me the time needed to explore this feeling we seem to share." No more games, he wanted to add, just explore the possibilities.

"I've got a lot going on now."

Marcus stared at her with such longing, it caused a slow blush to cover her face and throat.

"I know you have a lot going on, I told you I've used that excuse in the past myself. But now is just as good a time as any to explore what we could have. I'll give you space and time, but we do need to spend some time together. Let's hold off on the book idea for a few months and just focus on us." His voice became low, almost demanding. He cleared his throat before adding, "There is something special between us, April. I know you feel it, too."

April looked cautiously at Marcus and became perplexed. Was he truly asking to get to know the real her? If what she'd already told him about her family didn't send him running, she couldn't imagine what would. She lifted her eyes to heaven and thought, *I owe You big-time*. She felt her prayers had indeed been answered.

April liked the idea, but was still somewhat skeptical, after all, she didn't have a barometer with which to measure this new type of burgeoning feelings for a man. The one female family member that she knew had a trusting and lasting relationship with a man was falling apart. Summer and Kenneth's marriage had been filled with passion and romance. They were her paragon for a relationship. From the first time Summer called and told her sister about meeting Kenneth, theirs had been a meeting of two that had become one.

That secret fear of turning into a bitter woman like her mother crept into her thoughts again. Although she didn't want to grow old alone, she didn't want to grow to depend on a man for happiness, either. Her mother's dependence on men had wounded her. She was ready to move forward in closing the wound. This was the time, and Marcus was definitely the man.

She smiled at Marcus and said, "Yes…yes, I think you're right. We should focus on us, but there are some things I need to help my sister with that will require time."

Marcus returned the smile and took her hand into his. It felt natural for both of them. The tender way in which he held her hand made April believe he'd always be tender with her.

"I don't know about you, but I've got to get back to work. Are you ready to leave?"

"No, but I've got to go. This was very nice, thanks for lunching with me."

That evening after work, April took her dogs to the park for a walk. It was a walk for them, but more of a jog for her. They kept a fast pace, even the smallest one, Champ. Afterwards, she tossed balls to them in her backyard. The dogs loved playing a game of catch, while Midnight sat watching nonchalantly on the patio.

She was exhausted when she picked up the phone to call her sister for the first time in a few days. "What are you doing?" she asked Summer.

"I just finished reading a book I bought several months ago, and just got around to reading. I just came out to sit on the patio and was just thinking about you, actually."

"I hope it was good thoughts about me."

"I could never think bad thoughts about you."

April exhaled a sigh of relief. She then thought about when was the last time she'd done reading for leisure. Most of her reading was limited to medical journals, but she knew how much her sister loved to read. "I'm glad you're taking the time to do something you enjoy. Where's Kenneth and Drew?"

"Girl, where else? Out playing basketball. I swear that child has an obsession with basketball and so does his father."

For the first time ever their relationship had been strained and it pained them both.

The two sisters hadn't spoken in days which was highly unusual. Even when traveling away on business or vacations, the two had adopted the habit of talking each day. Although the conversation was light in nature, an undercurrent could be felt. April hadn't told Summer about Marcus yet. Summer was so intoxicated the day April picked her up at the bar, she never asked who he was.

"You remember the time you told me Kenneth asked you if you wanted to go out one Friday night after work and you told him you were too tired?"

"Yep, what's that got to do with anything?"

"Do you remember what he'd done when you came home from work?"

Summer thought for a few minutes and a smile lit up her face as the thought developed in her mind. "Oh, yeah, he had Luther playing, candles lit and a hot bubble bath waiting for me. He had ordered dinner, sent Drew to spend the night with friends, and as the kids say, 'it was on.'"

Their laughter echoed through the phone. April continued, "And what did he do the next day?"

"Girl, you know the man was too cute. I came home from shopping and he had moved all the furniture in the living room up against the walls. Had created us a mini dance floor, complete with strobe lights and disco music. We had a ball, I have to admit the man is creative. But what's that got to do with anything?"

"So when you meet a man like the one you have, it's good to hang on 'cause they can be hard to find. I think I've found a good man who makes me happy like that."

April waited for her sister's response and thought about Marcus. He was creeping into her thoughts more and more.

"I knew there was something going on with you. Who is he? How long have you known him? What's going on?"

"Don't get too nosy, we are still getting to know each other. He's very nice. We met through a mutual acquaintance. And that's all I'm going to tell you for now. I'm more concerned about how you're doing."

The silence came, and they allowed it. Both of them were sorry for the way they'd spoken to each other on the phone.

After a few more minutes of silence, April spoke softly. "So, what's up with you? How've you been?"

Summer thought about the question and entertained the thought. She wanted to respond truthfully, but that would have been painful. She wasn't fine, and she hadn't been fine in a long time. If she couldn't be truthful with her sister, who could she be truthful with? A year ago she would have responded differently. She knew at that instant, even though it was just considered polite conversation, that her answer to the question wasn't to be taken lightly. Deep trouble was carrying her down a fast river current of winding turns with lots of rocks and branches to battle and bruise her. For the first time, she confessed she needed help.

"I'm a mess, April. I'm in a big mess and I am a mess. It's all out of control and I don't know how to get things back to where they were." She broke down crying, sobbing and shaking.

"I'm on my way over." Grabbing her purse, she was out the door and on the highway within minutes. That was the way sisters were as far as April was concerned. They'd grown to depend on each other from the time they were very young. She'd lost one sister and she wasn't going to let anything happen to Summer.

April had managed to trade vet services for therapy sessions with Carmen because she still felt the need to occasionally openly discuss some of their childhood trauma with someone who wouldn't judge her or her family. Only her sisters knew the emptiness and lack of motherly love they felt growing up. It had impacted all three women in ways that seemed irrelevant, but she knew their past still had a grip on her and her surviving sister. It was time for Summer to understand that grip and to release it.

She'd tried to encourage Summer to go with her to therapy, but her sister had refused and accused her of betraying family secrets to a stranger. April reminded Summer that they only had each other to talk to and they needed to release some of their inner secrets and frustrations. But Summer still refused.

April tried to tell her that was why she did it, so she would have a nonpartisan view, someone who wouldn't be judging, someone who could help her get the answers, someone who'd just listen. April hadn't been much of a crier as a child, but after about the third session with Carmen, she was crying like a baby. It was an incredible cleansing of sorts for her, indeed a breakthrough toward helping her understand where she'd come from and how it impacted who she was now. How all that had happened along the way molded her into what she was today, and that she was not responsible for the doings or actions of others. She couldn't save her parents' marriage. She was not responsible for her father leaving the family. Only he could answer the question of why he left. April couldn't stop her mother from drinking, and she couldn't stop her sister from being with an abusive man. Initially it made her feel helpless and out of control, but in time she grew to understand that she was not able to control the actions of others. Most importantly she learned that she and her sisters missed out on a nurturing relationship with her parents. Like so many others, they sought that missing nurturing in other ways.

She was convinced that Summer would benefit from sessions with a therapist. Summer was the strong one, she'd always been the one who'd taken care of April and Autumn. April thought back to the time she got drunk as a teenager. One of her friends called Summer to come and get her because she couldn't remember where she lived. It was Summer who came and rescued her sister, and had the forethought to sit her in the cold shower while fully dressed so she could sober up quickly.

Her mother would be home shortly, and Summer knew that April would get the beating of a lifetime if her mother found she'd gone out and gotten drunk. Summer was the one who'd cleaned up the telltale signs of vomit and the stench of stale liquor and cigarettes. They laughed about it years later, but at the time, even though she was just a teenager herself, Summer was the one with a clear head and the maturity to act quickly. Her instincts always allowed her to take over and think clearly.

By the time April reached Summer's home, she wasted no time asking her sister, "So, what do you plan to do about getting yourself out of this hole and getting your life back on track?" April had a concerned look on her questioning face, and her eyes mirrored the concern etched on her face.

Looking around, she continued, "I know you're not willing to give all this up and your family to alcohol, because you and I know how quickly *that* can take everything away from you, leaving you with nothing, not even yourself."

April stood up and walked over to the large picture window in the living room and took a deep sigh. "You know, Summer, growing up, I always thought I'd be the one to mess up and lose everything, not you. Why do you think I've been seeking help? I had to fight the urge to pick up the bottle, just like you and everybody else who has an alcoholic parent, whenever things in life start to get rough."

April turned to look at her sister, seated on the sofa, before continuing, "It's not easy, but nothing we choose to fight for ever is. Even at sixteen I was fighting the urge to drink. I wanted to know why Mother sought it so much. What was in that bottle that seemed to cause the pain to go away? That's why we all chose to try and figure out what was so magical in a bottle that it could make every pain go away. Make you not give a damn about anything or anyone. Make you numb."

Summer looked at April achingly and knew what she was talking about. Their mother and her dependence on alcohol had been a mystery to all of them.

April turned again to look out the window. "I can remember kids laughing at me because I wanted to be a veterinarian in high school. Just because I wasn't studious didn't mean I didn't have dreams or plans beyond high school. With all that we went through as children, somehow that seemed unfair, too. It made me more determined to be a success. I think in some ways it continues to drive me today. No one can ever tell me what I can't accomplish."

Turning to look at her sister again, she continued, "But you, nobody ever laughed at you. You always commanded respect, just by the way you walked into a room. Nobody ever said you couldn't do something. Even Mother always thought you could walk on water."

Summer, who had been staring blankly at the wall, turned her attention to April, who had come and sat next to her on the sofa. "Mother never thought I'd amount to anything and you know that. She never respected anything I did."

Holding her hand up, April stopped her. "Don't start that with me, you know better—well, maybe you don't. So let me break it down for you, sister. Of the three of us, whose school plays did Mother attend? Out of the three of us, whose high school graduation did she attend? Huh, Summer? Who did she call into the living room late at night to recite some poem for one of our many uncles? Who was the one that she always said was pretty? Maybe not so much after the liquor had gotten to her, but earlier on. Surely you remember."

Tears had begun to form in April's eyes and her mouth had become rigid. She was way past due for a good cry. The thought of losing another sister was more than she could bear. Summer went over to hug her sister as she patted her back. "I guess that was her way of showing what emotions she was capable of, but I swear it never felt like love to me, and Lord knows I never remember her saying any of those things." Her voice was low and soothing.

The sisters stood and hugged for a few minutes before April cleared her throat. "I'm supposed to be comforting you and look at you, as usual you're being the grown-up and helping me. God, I don't know where you get the strength from."

"Please, April, you've pulled me out of more fires than even I am willing to admit. I just wonder sometimes what our perceptions have to do with reality. Seems to me we remember things differently according to our perspective at the time. I swear you were Mom's favorite. I remember the time she and husband number three, I think it was, aka Snookie, got into that fight and she pulled that gun on him. You were the one who jumped into the middle of them, begging Mom not to shoot him and to give you the gun. I swear it was like watching something on TV, you were just a mere thirteen years old and were asking your mother not to shoot someone so she wouldn't go to jail. I thought for a minute she was going to shoot you. Poor little Autumn was just in the corner, crying her little eyes out."

"Yeah, I remember you yelling, 'Get out the way, April, let them kill each other!' Which sure got both of their attention." The sisters laughed nervously at the memory.

"You were brave even at thirteen. I thought Mama was going to beat you half to death, but she stopped to catch her breath, looking at you without saying a word. It was beyond tense in that room for about five minutes. We kept looking at each other curiously, wondering what Mama was going to do. You remember how she slowly walked to the sofa and sat down? Like it was the most natural thing in the world. I think even Snookie was holding his breath. She casually lit a cigarette, blew out the smoke like she didn't have a care in the world. When she finally spoke, she said, 'What's wrong with y'all, looking at me like I'm crazy?'"

The two sisters laughed nervously again. Summer said, "Yeah, it's funny now, but at the time, I thought, 'My God, my mother was ready to shoot somebody,' and if I remember correctly, it was over something like him keeping ten dollars of his paycheck and giving the rest to her. She thought he'd kept twenty and was so angry." April looked over at Summer, who folded her arms around herself and rocked back and forth as her mind drifted to the awful night.

April tried to ease the pain for her sister as she said, "After they calmed down, and Snookie showed her the only money he had in his wallet, they went to the bedroom and all I could hear was them making those sounds." Summer shook her head at the thought. She and her sister had been through a lot.

Summer looked at April and said, "Yes, you remember it correctly, after fighting, they went into her bedroom and made the springs squeal till dawn, and I wonder why I'm drinking, and poor Autumn went looking for love in the wrong man."

"No, I don't wonder why you're drinking, I wonder why you're drinking now. I think it's your way of trying to deal with what's happening at work. You've certainly dealt with more pressure than this before, but you didn't resort to the bottle for answers. This time you need to figure out what it is about this situation that makes you feel so helpless. You've never been one to play the victim role before, so what's different this time?"

"I don't know, it's like all the things from the past came and slapped me upside the head all at once. I've been thinking a lot about all the stuff we went through as children, and for some reason, it's been bothering me."

"Why?"

"I wish I knew. Suddenly I feel very tired, helpless and out of control, like I just want to lie down and do nothing. Like all the fight's gone out of me. I've never told Kenneth any of this stuff, and somehow the longer I'm with him the harder it is for me to even think about telling him. And I've never talked to him at all about Autumn, about what really happened." That was the one taboo subject the sisters never discussed, their baby sister's death. It was the most painful memory of all, too painful for even them to discuss, so they rarely brought it up.

"I just want you to go and talk to this lady one time, I'll even go with you. I promise you if you don't feel better, I'll never bug you about going again."

"And who is this lady, some faith healer or herbalist that you've gone to for spiritual healing?"

"Laugh if you want to, sister, but I feel good taking my natural herbs and meditating. It's good for your body and spirit. But no, this isn't that kind of specialist, this one's a head specialist."

"Oh, no, I'm not going to no shrink."

"I didn't say she was a shrink. I swear, you need to come out of the Dark Ages. But listen to me before you close your mind to what I'm saying. She has really helped me deal with some of the things we went through as children. Helped me to understand that really, maybe things were different from our perceptions."

April paused to formulate her thoughts. She fingered the fabric on the sofa before continuing, "You were the one who said perceptions can change the way we view things. Just give yourself a chance to be open and honest with someone besides me about what we've held on to, things that we can let go of. How can you get over something if you keep it a secret and never understand what it truly means to you? If you can't discuss it without breaking into a million pieces? Please, Summer, I promise you'll feel better."

Before she could object further, her sister pleaded again. "Please, Summer, do this for me. If not for me, then for Kenneth and Drew." April thought Summer was smarter than anyone she knew. She knew her sister would do just about anything for her, and she the same, but her husband and son were a sure deal maker. There was no way Summer could turn her down. "Please, with sugar on top."

That childhood plea brought a tear and a hug from Summer. "All right, I'll think about it. You make me sick. You aren't slick, hitting me where I live." She held her hand to her heart.

"And I have something I want to tell you." April sounded serious as she slowly backed away from her sister.

Summer sat down in the chair at the kitchen island. April was quiet, and took a deep breath. "Are you intentionally trying to drive me crazy. What is it?" Summer's look of curiosity made April smile.

"Like I started to tell you on the phone, I've met someone. Someone really nice. I like him a lot." April almost giggled as the words sprang from her lips.

"Oh my goodness. Look at you, you're blushing!" Summer immediately became giddy. "And you look so happy. You must really like him."

April's smile couldn't hide the truth. "I do, and he's, he's…I don't know, different." She couldn't think about Marcus without smiling and thinking about his deadly lips.

"He must be special, I've never seen you at a loss for words when it comes to men. What about Donald?"

"Donald is just a friend, nothing more, just a friend. I've been comfortable for years allowing him to be the one constant man in my life. I was safe with him because I don't love him, so I don't have to make decisions about where our relationship is going. I was too blind to see that he was feeling something different, though. I've backed off from our friendship so that he can accept it for what it is." April suppressed a quick guilty look.

"It suddenly dawned on me the other day that I've not had a good role model for a happy couple except you and Kenneth. I see so much of Mother in me and sometimes it frightens me." She looked to Summer for understanding, and she nodded in agreement.

"I know, sometimes I find myself behaving like her, lately, more than even I am willing to admit. I know a lot of what's happening now is because I've never dealt with some of the scars she left on me. Not the physical ones, the emotional ones."

"No doubt we're our mother's daughters, but so was Autumn and look how it destroyed her." April flashed back to how Autumn refused to stay away from the man who abused her. Kenneth loved Summer, but even he had his limits and men had left for less, she thought. Living with someone who holds secrets and tries to drink to keep the pain away could be trying for anybody, April told her sister. For the first time, they wondered if that was the cause of their parents' breakup.

"I know, April, and sometimes I think about that, too. I try so hard not to allow Mother's influence keep me from being a good wife and mother. Even now, sometimes I just don't know how we managed to grow into such good women." April walked over to the cabinet and took out a glass, then she went to the refrigerator in search of something to drink. She settled for a glass of orange juice and walked to the kitchen island where Summer sat, and sat beside her.

After several minutes of silence, Summer asked April to tell her more about Marcus. The two laughed like schoolgirls as April described her attraction to the man and how his touch made her giddy. April explained that the two were taking their time getting to know one another. "I'm actually dating! And enjoying it. It's been too long. Marcus is patient, very understanding. Sometimes he looks at me and doesn't say a word, and the funny part is, he doesn't have to. I feel the connection without the words."

"That sounds nice. You sound very sure of him." Summer was happy. It was the first time her sister ever admitted to being close to a man. Love was right around the corner, Summer thought.

"I am, most of the time, but we are still at the getting-to-know-you stage." April stood up and walked to look out the window into the backyard, and admired the beauty of it.

"You always said you wanted a man who makes your toes curl. Does Marcus make your toes curl?" Summer giggled and was happy with the thought of her sister finding someone she found so enthralling.

"He makes my toes curl, but we haven't gotten to the physical toe-curling stage yet, if you know what I mean. But given the way he makes me feel, I see plenty of toe-curling in our future."

April couldn't help but laugh when Summer looked at her. Summer joined in and laughed, "Oh, I get you, sister. Now, that is always something to look forward to. I still remember the first time Kenny and I made love, mercy!" Summer closed her eyes and thought about how good a man her husband was. "And you know what, it was after we had really gotten to know each other—we took our time, too. I think that's a good thing."

April walked over to her sister and embraced her. "Kenneth still loves you so much, you guys have something so very good."

"I know, I'm working on it, April, honestly I am." She smiled tenderly at her sister.

They continued to smile while embracing one another. Just as they walked into the family room, Kenneth was coming through the door.

"You two look like *Thelma and Louise*. I swear I can almost see mischief in your eyes when you two get together." Kenneth smiled to himself as it seemed Summer looked slightly different, like maybe some of the burden had been lifted. He knew his sister-in-law hadn't planned a visit. Summer must have called her for help and they'd evidently had one of their girl talks. The two definitely had been entrenched in some deep conversation, he was certain of it.

These sisters were as close as any two could ever be, and if needed, he could call on his sister-in-law for help in getting his wife back to herself.

He kissed his wife on the lips, and for the first time in weeks, didn't smell the pungent smell of alcohol. His heart became lighter at the thought of his wife winning the fight against whatever demons she battled. He bent down to kiss his sister-in-law on the cheek. "How have you been, April?" he asked.

"I'm fine, Kenneth, and getting better." The lack of passion in Kenneth and Summer's kiss didn't go unnoticed by April.

"Okay, what personal-growth book are you reading this week?" He sat his briefcase down on the kitchen island.

"Man, you two are such doubting Thomases. I don't need a book to tell me how I feel, and I resent the insinuation." She was smiling and teasing her brother-in-law, who she felt was more like a brother.

"Now, I do have something I'd like for you both to read. A friend of mine wrote and published this book, it's called *The Missing Passion.* It's for people who've been married a long time and maybe need a little help to rekindle the home fire, if you know what I mean." She mockingly raised and lowered her eyebrows in comic fashion.

Kenneth and Summer looked at each other, blushing, as both were taken a bit by surprise by April's casual, but on-target observation. "No, we don't know what you mean, we haven't lost our passion." Summer's sentence was declarative, but it fooled no one as an uncomfortable silence engulfed the room. In the past few weeks, each had withdrawn into a shell, only coming out for occasional polite conversation and putting on a front for their son. Each wondering if their marriage would survive this sudden drifting they were doing, and if the marriage did survive, would the passion?

They understood people stayed together for all kinds of reasons. April told Summer about one of her friends who was trapped in a loveless marriage in which both spouses had numerous affairs. They stayed together for financial reasons, and because their only child was a freshman in an expensive private college. Neither wanted to give up the lifestyle they'd created, nor the status of being married that each thought was beneficial in their careers as partners in an advertising agency.

The family business had thrived, but not their marriage, as the friend had occasionally pointed out. Their own mother had been married six times, and always bragged that she didn't see what the big deal was about staying married, since most men weren't worth more than a few years of your life, anyway. After a few months they were boring, obnoxious, remote-controlling slobs, who left nothing in your life but a sofa with a lump in it that contoured to his body, and a mountain of bills.

With each husband, their mother drank more and more and by the time husband number six came along, she was more often drunk than sober, and therefore bragged in later years that marriage number six was a blur, with her barely remembering his name. It was strange, but after her first marriage, she never took any of the last names of her husbands. That fact always puzzled April and she often wanted to ask her mother the reason, but never dared to.

April stood and said, "Well, judging from that really pitiful kiss you just gave your wife, I'd say you two are in denial. Especially considering that you two have always greeted each other with a kiss and hug that would make even me blush and wish I had that kind of love for somebody. But I'm going to leave it at that. I'll call you later, Summer. Take care, brother. I'll drop the book off next week—if nothing else, it will make for some entertaining reading." She smiled wickedly, knowing they got the point.

April kissed her sister on the cheek and gave her a hug. She tiptoed up to kiss Kenneth, and whispered in his ear as she began to withdraw from kissing his cheek, "You're a good man, Kenneth, please take care of my sister." He could almost touch the concern in her voice.

"Now, I'm getting out of the 'burbs, 'cause you know all

these streets and houses look alike at night. Tell my baby Drew I love him and I've got something for him. Don't forget my party Saturday after next." She blew them both a kiss and left.

The ambiguous silence after her departure left each of them feeling uncomfortable and uncertain. Neither was sure where to take the conversation or what to do. This was truly foreign to them, as their lives together had always been laden with lively banter and demonstrative shows of affection. This was indeed new territory for the seasoned couple.

Chapter 8

April was running late on Saturday due to a few emergency walk-ins, but she'd called Marcus and told him to pick her up around three o'clock. She was at home putting on her finishing touch by adding a touch of mocha lipstick, when he rang the doorbell. She had put the dogs in the basement after spending a few minutes with them and was now ready to go.

Marcus was dressed casually, but April felt her feelings intensify each time she saw him. She was more and more imagining him without the clothes that he wore so well. She ached at the thought of him naked and the protective feel of his arms around her. Her smile reflected some personal thought as she greeted him. "Hey, handsome, you look nice."

Marcus liked her directness, but found it difficult to always control himself around her. His initial thought was to sweep her up in his arms and carry her off to the bedroom. "Thank you, but I swear you are more beautiful each time I see you. I don't care what you're wearing."

The compliment made April blush. "The way you talk, Dr. Davis." She added a bit of a laugh and the two completed the greeting with a brief kiss. A kiss that although brief and meant only as a greeting, sparked heat between the two of them. April fought back the desire to wrap her arms around his neck and give him the kiss she wanted. Despite the fact that she was the one that insisted they take it slow, her desire for him was growing quicker than she wanted.

Marcus watched in agony as April walked ahead of him to the car. Her long, shapely legs seemed to go on forever. She was shapely in all the areas that were important as he watched the swing of her hips. She wore khaki shorts and a white tank top, and her hair hung casually around her shoulders.

During the drive, April said, "I must tell you, I don't know anything about antiques, so I don't know how much help I'm going to be."

"That's more than I know about antiques. I just want your opinion on the lamps I may purchase. I like looking at antiques and collectibles, and know what I like, but I don't spend a lot of time learning about them. I rarely buy antiques."

"I do like looking at them, too."

"See, something else we have in common," Marcus joked.

They spent the afternoon browsing and walking along Cherokee Antique Row. The area consisted of retail shops packed with antiques and collectibles. The six-block area was known for not only its fine antique shops, but also historic homes, so there was plenty for them to enjoy.

April was looking at an African-American collectible doll while Marcus browsed another section of the store. He watched her for a few minutes and knew that she was interested in the doll. He watched as she delicately smoothed the doll's hair, and the tiny smile on April's face made him think she was remembering something from her past. He walked over to her. "She's a beauty."

April agreed, "Yes, she is, but she's too expensive."

"How can you put a dollar value on something that makes you smile like that?"

"Clearly these people have," April retorted, as she looked at the price tag and added, "and a really high one at that."

Marcus looked at the doll again and back at April. "Are you going to get it?"

"No, I think I'll pass on it this time. Maybe later." April reluctantly returned the doll to its decorative stand.

"Who, or what were you just thinking of when you held that doll?" His question surprised April. He was too good at asking the right questions, she thought again.

"I had a similar one when I was little, I think it was the last thing my mother gave me as a child." It was clear that April wanted the doll.

"Why are you always doing for others, and not for yourself? Buy the doll for yourself, April."

She walked away, casually waving her hand. "I'm ready to move on, let's get something to eat."

Marcus looked at the doll and then at April's retreating back.

They settled down for an early dinner at an intimate little bistro. "This is really quaint, don't you think?" April asked.

Marcus looked around. His thoughts had been on April and the doll. "Yes, it is. You like it?"

"I do, but ask me after I've eaten."

Marcus smiled. "What are you having?"

April was going to visit her mother that evening, so she reluctantly said goodbye to Marcus after their dinner. They had planned to meet Sunday morning at April's church for services.

April was sitting outside her mother's apartment building in her car, with the engine still running. She glanced in the rearview mirror and fluffed her hair. She turned off the ignition and pulled her lipstick from her purse, freshened up her lipstick and put a smile on her face. "She's still your mother," she moaned to herself as she got out of the car. She'd stopped and picked up her mother's favorite dinner; fried catfish, greens, macaroni and cheese, with a side of sliced tomatoes.

Mildred's apartment was on the first floor, so April was there in a few steps. But Mildred was standing there with the door open. "I saw you when you pulled up. What took you so long to get out of the car?"

"Hello to you too, Mother." April walked past her mother and saw her roll her eyes.

"What you got in the bag?" Mildred didn't pretend to be interested in greeting her daughter.

The apartment was a sad place. Mildred didn't clean it nearly as often as she should have. The stench of stale cigarettes and liquor was overwhelming. Despite the fact that April had recently bought new furniture for the place, it looked out of place. The walls were dingy, as were the windows, and Mildred refused to make the place a home by cleaning it thoroughly or adding small touches to it. She yelled at April for wasting money on bringing her fresh flowers, and any cleaning help that was offered was vehemently refused. April tried just picking up things, and doing general cleaning, but her mother would ask her to stop, and not in a nice way.

April finally had given up and allowed her mother to live the way she wanted. She just tried to make sure her mother had food and shelter. She paid her mother's rent every month. Mildred never even so much as said "Thank you."

"I brought your favorite, catfish." She set the bag on the kitchen table and pulled out a chair.

"Uh, you can't stay, I have company coming over." Mildred was walking over to the front door. Without so much as a bat of an eye, she opened the door and stood there quietly.

"What?" April wanted clarification. Her mother was asking her to leave without any explanation other than she had a visitor coming.

"You heard me, I got company coming over, you gotta leave."

April stared blankly as her mother stood at the door. She finally stood up to leave. "I'll call you. But I find it hard to believe you're asking me to leave because you have 'company' coming. I'm your daughter. You really know how to hurt, Mother."

When she got home that night, April wondered how any mother could be so cold toward her children. It was the reason she doubted if she'd ever have children. She lay in bed that night and thought about how she'd felt the first time she'd held her nephew in her arms, and more recently, Nia's baby. It felt wonderful, and she'd gotten a rush like no other. They truly were bundles of joy, and her heart almost burst the first time her nephew hugged her and told her he loved her. But she questioned if she had the instincts to be a good mother—what if she had inherited her mother's cold heart? At some point in time her mother could have possibly been warmed by the hug of a child, but not in April's memory. Her mother had always been distant. She couldn't risk it. After all, she was her mother's daughter.

Marcus joined April on Sunday for church services, and later they enjoyed a long bike ride, followed by a movie at her home.

They were sitting playing a game of chess when April asked, "Do you think men and women can be just good friends if they've—" she studied him closely before continuing "—been intimate with each other?"

He wondered where the question came from and thought about it for a minute. "I don't know. You mean, sexually intimate?"

She nodded her head. "Yes, meaning they've slept together."

Marcus looked at her as she quietly looked at the board. "I've not been friends with any of the women I've slept with. I think most of the time you break up, and that just ends it. Why do you ask?"

"Just curious."

He looked at her as she pondered her next move on the board. "Oh, no, it's more than curiosity." She immediately looked up. He read her too well, she thought.

"Maybe, but I have to defer the conversation. I want to beat you. You've already won one game. I'm concentrating, be quiet." She turned her attention to the chessboard again.

Marcus laughed and picked up his glass of wine. "Woman, there isn't that much concentration in the world. I was the champion chess player in high school. And you're the one who asked the question."

"On, no, you were a nerd in high school?"

"Quite the contrary, but I secretly joined the chess club. I got a set for my birthday and fell in love with it." Marcus took a drink of the wine and set it down.

"When's your birthday?" she asked while continuing to study the board.

Marcus smiled in anticipation. "April 27."

April turned her attention from the board. He had to have been teasing her. "Are you kidding me?"

"No, why would I kid about something like that?"

"Because my birthday is April 28. Thus, the name April, plus my mother was unique about naming us."

Marcus picked up his glass again. He thought it was a coincidence that his birthday was in April, and now to find that her birthday was a day after his was something he attributed to Providence. "What are the chances of that? That is really extraordinary, don't you think?"

"You bet it is, almost overwhelming." April brought her hand to her chest. She couldn't hide the excitement. "Wow, that's something!" She looked at him in amazement.

"We have a lot in common, I think it's just something to add to the list. Better yet, let's start planning our birthday celebration." Marcus was smiling broadly now.

"It's a bit early for that, don't you think?" she laughed. "It's like, what, nine months away?"

"That's not long, it'll be here before you know it. The sooner the better, but we can wait until I beat you at this game." He sat back and laughed, "Go on, make your next move so we can start planning."

April studied the board one final time and knew he was going to beat her again. "Okay, maybe this time you win, but don't forget I rode the socks off of you earlier on that bike trail. You were huffing and puffing, I thought you were going to have to doctor yourself," she kidded.

"Now, that was just cold," Marcus laughed. "True, but cold."

"Yeah, whatever, but I tell you what, next time I'm going to beat you at chess." The two ended the game and snuggled together on the couch, enjoying music and conversation the rest of the evening. When it was time to leave, Marcus stood reluctantly at the door with his hands on her waist. "Have a good night," he whispered. He could barely talk, he wanted her so badly.

"I already have, thanks to you." April put her hands around his neck and drew him closer. She kissed him goodbye, and the two grudgingly separated.

Chapter 9

The party was at full blast when Summer and Kenneth pulled up. As soon as they got out of the car they heard the soulful wail of Chaka Khan asking you to stop on by. They both laughed as they reminisced. The front door had a sign that read, "Party in progress, enter at your own risk." The door was unlocked and the two stepped inside.

They smiled at the ensembles. It was a 1970s theme and everybody was in full regalia. Afros, bell bottoms, large hoop earrings, peace signs and lots of gold chains were everywhere. Some of the men had on the long wigs replicating Super Fly, and several had canes. The record changed and the Isley Brothers began singing, "Fight the Power." Everybody started to gather around. It was a hilarious sight, Summer thought, but she really lost it when she saw her sister.

April wore a huge blond afro wig, a multi-colored halter with hot pants, platform boots and about fifty bracelets on one arm. Her face was fully made up with thick black eyeliner and lots of black mascara. Only April could carry off such an ensemble and still look beautiful, Summer thought.

The partygoers had formed two lines; one side had the females and the other side the males, and they would meet at the beginning of the line and dance down the middle toward the end of their respective lines. One man shouted, "Soul Train!" which made the other people shout slogans of the seventies and raise their fist in the air.

Kenneth looked at Summer and asked, "You want some of this?" He began doing a seventies dance, hunching his shoulders and doing the penguin dance.

She laughed and said, "If you can swing it, bring it!" and they joined the line. April was coming down the line when she saw Summer and Kenneth. She flashed them the peace sign, threw her head back and did a spin. The crowd went crazy with laughter and shouts.

The party was bustling with many of April's friends from college, colleagues and some people from the neighborhood watch group. Summer knew most of the people but there were a few she had never met. "Looks like everybody's having a good time," Summer said without missing a dance step. Looking around, she asked, "Is Donald coming?"

"No, he's in Seattle for a week."

"Where's Marcus?"

"He's working late, he'll be here in about an hour," April responded as she continued to dance.

"I can't wait to meet him." Summer snickered. "Where did you find the hot pants?"

April turned around and shook her bottom. "You don't recognize them?"

Summer laughed, "*Nooooo!* Are those the ones you bought

when we went to that retro store over on Delmar?" The two stopped dancing and moved off toward the kitchen area.

"One and the same. Found the wig there, too. And you said I'd never have any reason to wear them."

"Girl, only you could pull off a party with this much flavor. This is way cool! Or should I say, this is truly righteous." Summer caused them both to laugh. She looked around at the beads that hung strategically around the house, the incense burning and the lava lamps. April had found a velvet picture of a woman with a huge afro riding a black panther. There were posters of movies from the seventies on the walls and the strobe lights made Summer giggle. "Drew told me to take pictures. He's going to have a good time making fun of us." Summer removed her camera from her suede beaded bag.

"Oh, I got that covered, too. I hired a professional to video-tape the party." April pointed toward a gentleman who was standing in the living room with his camcorder aimed at the partygoers dancing.

"The best part is that he's doing it for free, he's one of my patients. Well, I guess his Siamese cat is actually my patient. I never thought I'd meet a cat more finicky than Midnight, but his cat, she's something else. And he pampers that cat like she's a queen." The two laughed at they watched the guy videotaping the party.

"Looks like you thought of everything," Summer commented as she looked at the disc jockey, who was also dressed in seventies garb.

"Kenneth looks like Huey Newton with that tam and black leather jacket on. And brother-in-law still got some moves. You better get on in there, looks like that sister is smiling a little too much at your husband."

Summer looked and for the first time in years felt a tinge of jealousy. "She sure is. Excuse me, I got to cut in."

"Okay, but don't hurt her." They both cracked up again. Summer was dancing toward Kenneth when she saw a tall, handsome man enter the party. He had on a wig with pork-chop sideburns, a knit shirt with a large collar, knit bell bottoms and a black jacket. She swore to herself the man looked totally seventies and had one of those walks like Denzel, way too cool and very confident.

She walked up to the stranger and took his hand. "Hey, superfine dude, come on and dance with me." She didn't know the man, but liked the relaxed feel of his hands. He was obviously comfortable, she thought. There was a hint of familiarity about him that she couldn't place.

He smiled easily at her and said, "Sure, foxy mama," and broke out into some dance from the seventies. Summer was laughing so hard she could barely dance.

"What's your name, brother?"

Marcus waited briefly for some sign of recognition, but thought about the state Summer was in last time he'd seen her. He smiled and pointed toward April. "Ask your sister, Summer." Summer looked over to see April approaching with a smile on her face wide enough to drive a Mack truck through it.

"Hey, I thought you were going over there to get your husband. What are you doing with my man? You better check yourself, before you wreck yourself." April tried to sound threatening as she put her hands on her hips for emphasis.

Summer played along. She turned and continued to swing her hips to the music. "You didn't tell me he was such a super-fine dude, and so…so…humph. Right on, sister." They all laughed heartily and finally Summer turned toward Marcus and asked, "How'd you know who I was?"

"Strong family resemblance." He had to shake his head. They were truly sisters, very similar not just in looks, but full of fire and passion in a take-no-prisoners kind of way.

"Even with this big wig and makeup?" It suddenly dawned on Summer where she'd seen Marcus and she felt embarrassed. She didn't let it stop her, though, but it gave her cause to think.

"Even with the wig and makeup." They all danced and made their way toward Kenneth. The music stopped momentarily and a slow song started. The party mood quickly changed and Summer took the opportunity to introduce Kenneth and Marcus. The woman that was dancing with Kenneth thanked him for the dance and left without an introduction. After a few slow dances the party became lively again as James Brown's demanding voiced filled the house.

Summer went to the kitchen for a bottle of water and saw the lady that had danced with Kenneth. The two exchanged smiles and hellos. April walked in and asked the lady was she having a good time.

"I haven't had this much fun since…actually, I can't remember having this much fun. Girl, this party is really boss!"

The three burst into laughter. April looked at the two women and asked, "Have you met my sister, Summer?"

"Not formally, she was gracious enough to let me borrow her husband for a few minutes on the dance floor." She extended her hand and the two shook hands.

"Carmen, this is Summer. Summer, this is Carmen, a friend of mine from my college days."

"Hi, it's nice to finally meet you. Your sister brags about you constantly. It's nice to meet the legend." Summer blushed slightly and looked at April. "You work for the cosmetic company, right?" Carmen asked.

"Yes, I do." Summer felt comfortable with Carmen and watched as she casually took a few hors d'oeuvres from a platter and began putting them on a plate.

"I love their mascara. I've used it since I was a teenager,

but I've noticed it doesn't wear like it used to." Carmen popped a shrimp into her mouth.

"They've changed the formula slightly. You may want to consider switching because they plan to discontinue it next year."

"Really? Thanks for the heads-up. I love that eyeliner and mascara you're wearing. Are those false eyelashes?"

"No, they're mine. Do they look false?"

"No, they look natural, they're just so long and lush, you could make mascara commercials. You've got beautiful eyes."

"Thanks. I thought my makeup was fading. I've been sweating so much. I know my hair is tore up under this wig."

Carmen popped another shrimp into her mouth and asked, "Have you tried these? They're delicious!"

Summer smiled and reached for a shrimp and popped it into her mouth. She closed her eyes and savored it. "Hmmm. They are good." She grabbed a plate and began filling it with food.

Sensing her plan was working, April excused herself. "I'm going to dance with my man. I'll see you later, Summer." She then looked at Carmen and joked, "Don't eat all the shrimp, Carmen, I know how you are once you get started." She looked at Summer. "She could always out-eat all of us in college and never put on an ounce."

April left the two women chatting, hoping that Summer would take the bait and make an appointment with Dr. Carmen Dubois.

Marcus was looking more scrumptious than the shrimp, April thought. He put his arm around her waist and said, "You look great. Your sister is some kind of charmer, just like you said. But I'm sure she says the same thing about you."

"Did I tell you how great you look in the Shaft getup?" April's eyes danced with mischief.

"Nope." Marcus put his hand to his ear so that he could hear the compliment.

"I take it back if you're going to tease me."

"I wasn't going to tease you, I just wanted to hear you say something nice to me. You looking so fine and foxy."

His eyes looked appreciatively at her from head to foot and traveled back up before he kissed her lips.

"Thanks. And you look so good you're making me want to be a bad girl tonight."

The smile that spread across his face made April grab his hand. "Come dance with me before I really get bad." Another slow jam was playing and Marcus pulled April close to him. The two danced without conversation. Each seemed to enjoy the movement and feel of the other's body.

Their coordinated movement was natural and one would have believed they'd danced several times before. The lights dimmed and the disc jockey began playing "Misty Blue" by Dorothy Moore. The room did a collective sigh as couples began to sway in unison with the music.

"Anyone can see they're really in love." Marcus nodded his head toward Summer and Kenneth, who were looking lovingly into each other's eyes while they danced. "I talked briefly with Kenneth and he's a great guy. He spoke highly of you, which was no surprise."

"He's a wonderful man, husband and father. I love him like a brother." April smiled at them but then turned her eyes on Marcus. His hands on the small of her back felt as natural and refreshing as sunshine. Just as she nestled closer to him she saw Donald standing in the foyer, watching her.

She pulled away from Marcus. "Excuse me, I have an unexpected guest." Marcus didn't like the way she suddenly pulled away from him and the stiffness of her body. He glanced in the direction of her eyes and watched as the man standing there looked as though he were throwing daggers with his eyes and assumed it was Donald. She had told him about her friendship with Donald. The look in Donald's eyes didn't render that description. He looked like a jealous lover.

April walked over and asked, "What are you doing here? I thought you weren't coming back till next week."

Donald's eyes never left Marcus's as the two stood in a silent duel, each daring the other to look away. "I decided to leave this afternoon so I could check out the party, have a little fun and leave early Monday morning. I don't have to be back until Tuesday." He finally broke his stare at Marcus and looked at April.

"Is that the man you were telling me about?" His tone was hard and cold.

"Come on, I'll introduce you two."

"No, that's okay, maybe later. I'm starved. What do you have to eat? I came directly here from the airport." He seemed strangely distant, April thought.

"There's plenty in the kitchen." He took her by the hand and began walking toward the kitchen.

April removed her hand. "Since when do you need a hand-held escort to the kitchen, Don?" April was not about to become a pawn in her own home. She wasn't sure what kind of game he was playing, but she didn't like it.

"I was just going to bring you up to date on my Seattle trip." His eyes darted toward Marcus, who had begun a rapid, purposeful stride in their direction.

"Is there a problem, April?" Marcus asked in a deep voice that demanded attention.

"Not at all, Marcus. This is Donald Perrault. Don, this is Marcus Davis."

The two men unenthusiastically shook hands. "The song is almost over, April, I'm sure Donald wouldn't mind you finishing our dance." He extended his hand to her and she took it. Donald went into the kitchen, mumbling to himself.

"You are devilish," April murmured once they were dancing again.

Marcus held her closer than before and replied, "I'm not being devilish, he interrupted our flow. You feel good in my arms. I *thought* for a minute there was going to be a problem."

"Why?"

"He looked mad as hell to see you dancing with me." Marcus was toying with her and she knew it. His words came out casually but something in the way he held her told April that he was being serious.

She looked up at him and tapped his chin with the tip of her finger. "Stop being so devilish."

"You saw him. If looks could kill I'd be sprawled out on the floor right now."

"Well, you were looking pretty serious yourself."

"Any man looking at my woman like that, yeah, it's serious."

"I didn't know I was your woman."

"Well, you are." He pulled her closer and she nestled her head to his chest again. When the song was over April took a deep breath, kissed him lightly on the lips and thanked him for the dance. She excused herself and went into the kitchen for a cold drink because the hot dance had really gotten to her. Marcus was looking just a little too good, and the way he made her feel in his arms was sinful. When she got there she found Donald sitting at the island alone. He'd fixed himself a sandwich and gotten a beer.

"You look awfully comfortable," April joked.

"So did you."

"What does that mean?"

"I saw how you were all hugged up with whatever his name is."

"His name is Marcus, and honestly, Don, playing the jealous lover doesn't suit you."

"How can I play the jealous lover when you won't admit that you love me?"

"I never said I didn't love you. I do love you." April watched as Donald's eyes traveled to the entrance to the kitchen. She turned and saw Marcus, who had just turned to leave. He'd obviously heard April admit her love for Donald.

"I love you like a friend, Don. Did you see Marcus standing there and try to bait me?"

"All's fair in love and war." He held his plastic cup as if toasting. April huffed and left. She called out to a retreating Marcus.

When they were standing face-to-face she took his hand. "You didn't hear all that I had to say. I love Don like a best friend. Not like a lover."

"But you two have been lovers." He sounded expectant.

April looked sheepishly before replying, "Yes, but it didn't last and we're friends now. Only friends, I promise you."

Marcus stared at her briefly and said, "Then you need to make sure he understands that. Seems to me he's holding out for something else." His voice was demanding and pleading at the same time.

"I have told him, it's just that for the longest time there hasn't been any other man in my life. He's never had to share me."

Marcus knew that she was the kind of person who was upfront and wouldn't intentionally hurt a friend. "Well, you have a man now, and he has to understand that. A man that is more than a little crazy about you." His eyes bored into hers and she was grateful when Summer and Kenneth interrupted.

"April, you're running low on ice. Do you have any more downstairs?"

April looked at Summer and Kenneth and mouthed, "Thank you."

"Yes, I do. Come help me." She pulled Summer by the arm

and hurried to the kitchen, where Donald still sat. They both looked at him and opened the door that led to the basement.

Summer couldn't contain her laughter. "Girl, you got men in there almost ready to fight over you. Did you see the way they were looking at each other?"

April wasn't amused. "Yes, and it's not funny, Summer."

"Yes it is. I wish you could have seen your face while you stood between the two of them. Kenneth was about ready to intervene." Summer couldn't stop giggling.

April had to laugh, "I wasn't expecting Don and he wasn't very happy with me being in Marcus's arms."

"I could tell that, but you two looked awfully cozy and comfortable to me. So what happened?"

"Nothing, they're trying to be civil, but it's not working. I'm not going to let it stress me out." April walked over to the freezer and pulled out two bags of ice. "Here, take this."

She handed one to Summer and asked, "What about you? Is not drinking at the party bothering you?"

Summer thought about it and said, "I guess not, I'm having such a good time I haven't wanted one. I've been drinking lots of water because I've been dancing so much. I remembered vaguely where I'd seen Marcus, and I felt like such a fool. How could I get into such a state? But I swear I'm working on it."

The two started back upstairs. "I'm really trying, April, and honestly, you don't have to worry about me." Summer's tone was sincere, as were her eyes as she looked directly into her sister's eyes. For the first time, she realized what a burden she had placed on her sister.

"I'll worry about you until you stop drinking, and you won't stop drinking until you figure out why you started drinking."

Summer turned around. "I swear, April, I haven't had a drink in weeks." She didn't tell her sister that she'd gotten a business card from Carmen and had already scheduled an appointment.

"Besides, you need to put one of those men upstairs out of their misery. Go on and choose one and send the other one packing!" Summer giggled again.

April was forced to laugh again. "I made my choice, the other one is just suffering from an overdose of testosterone. I don't know if Don's being jealous or just being protective, but it's starting to wear thin. I think it's time for a talk with Don."

"Every woman should be so lucky," Summer joked. "Girl, I'm not mad at you, I never thought of you as a player." They both laughed again.

"You know that's not what I'm doing."

"Yeah, I know, but you must admit it is nice to have two wonderful, desirable men ready to fight over you. Have mercy, you got it going on, huh, sis?"

When the two sisters returned to the kitchen Kenneth, Marcus and Donald were standing around, talking.

April shook her head. "This could mean nothing but trouble," she murmured to her sister. Kenneth and Marcus rushed over to assist the women with the bags of ice.

Donald made a too late move and was edged out. "Oh, I was going to get that."

Marcus smiled as he took the ice from April. "Don't sweat it, man, I got this." April could almost see the mischief and innuendo in Marcus's eyes as he smiled slyly at her.

"Yeah, well, you may now, but I've had it," Donald grumbled.

April cut him a look that could have melted the ice she was carrying. "There's no need for you two to flex your male bravado in here. Nobody's impressed."

Summer and Kenneth excused themselves and quickly returned to the living room, laughing in conspiratorial whispers. April folded her arms across her chest as the two men glared at each other. "You're both acting like adolescent boys. There is no competition here. I'm disappointed in both of you."

The two finally stopped glaring at each other and turned their eyes toward her, and each started to approach her, but she held her hands to stop them. "Look, I'm having a good time, and I won't let you two ruin it for me. Don, can I speak with you for a minute?" April clicked her tongue and walked to the living room where the music was pumping and the bodies were jumping. Donald followed closely behind her, with Marcus following him.

Just as Marcus got to the living room a tall, slim man approached and stopped him. "Aren't you Dr. Marcus Davis?"

Marcus turned his attention from April long enough to respond to the question. "Yes, I am." Then he turned his attention to Donald, who was now following directly behind April alone. He wasn't liking the attention Donald was getting.

The man continued, "You don't remember me, but we met at a conference in Atlanta last year on…" Marcus turned his attention back to the man, who wore a peace sign headband over a shoulder-length wig, a rainbow-colored shirt, which looked like it was covered with a million love beads, and striped bell bottoms.

Looking closely at the man, he recollected the meeting and said, "Oh yes, Dr. Joshua Silverstein, I remember. How are you?" Marcus extended his hand and the two men shook hands.

"Great memory. I'm fine. I'm here with my wife, Rachel." He nodded in the direction of a group of people in the living room.

"Where do you know April from?" Joshua inquired.

"We were introduced by a mutual friend and we're dating." He smiled and scratched his head. "At least, we were up until a few minutes ago. I think she's a little upset with me right now." The two looked at April as she stood talking rather animatedly to Donald. Suddenly he didn't mind the attention she was giving him.

"She doesn't look very happy talking to that guy, either. She's a mysterious one. Very bright and independent." Marcus looked at Joshua and realized he hadn't asked how he knew April. Judging from the personal observation Joshua had made he wasn't sure if he wanted to know how he knew April. Marcus could tell from her posture the conversation with Donald wasn't pleasant. She was animated while he stood with his hands in his pockets, his eyes downcast.

"April can put you in your place faster than anybody I know. Very unpretentious. She's the only woman I've ever met who's completely impious toward social class. Don't care where you come from, she talks to the company president and the janitor in the same manner." The two men just shook their heads up and down in agreement.

Marcus finally asked, "How are you two acquainted?"

Joshua looked at Marcus and whispered, "We dated a few times in med school." Looking over to his wife he continued, "But I told my wife we were just friends. Which I guess we were. I wanted more, but she didn't. Said she didn't have time for a relationship."

Marcus looked at the man and a momentary flash of jealousy consumed him. He gathered his thoughts and realized that the two had dated years before he even knew April so he had no reason to be jealous. He nonchalantly inquired, "Which one is your wife?"

"The short brunette over there with the pink bell bottoms and white blouse with all the love beads. She's talking to Summer and Kenneth."

His eyes seem to radiate as he spoke of her. Marcus felt a softening as he thought that there were times that he had to force himself not to look at April like that. He longed for her so much it frightened him and he knew it would frighten her. He knew the attraction was mutual, but he was not sure how she felt about it. Joshua was right about one thing, she was a mysterious one, which to Marcus was a part of her attractiveness.

Out of perfunctory courtesy, Marcus said, "She's pretty." But his eyes quickly returned to April and Donald. April was quietly listening to Donald but had her arms folded across her chest. Whatever Donald was trying to sell her, she wasn't buying it.

Finally she looked over at Marcus and when their eyes met he felt compelled to hold her in his arms again. Marcus excused himself from Joshua and made it over to the disc jockey where he requested a special song. Just as the disc jockey started to put the song on Marcus walked over to April and Donald.

He apologized for interrupting and asked April to dance. "I've waited all night for this song, please come dance with me." He extended his hand.

April looked at Donald and said, "I'll talk to you later." She excused herself, and walked onto the dance floor with him. She and Donald had just ended the conversation and neither were pleased with what was said. The DJ made the announcement for the special request and invited all those with someone special to get on the floor.

Donald had already turned to leave, but stopped briefly at the front door.

The first three bars of Barry White's "I've Got So Much To Give" came on and April melted into Marcus's arms. Donald turned in a huff and left unnoticed. The two danced quietly until the song was almost over when Marcus said, "I apologize for the scene in the kitchen. I understand he's your friend, but it's obvious he wants more."

April's heart softened and she looked up at him and replied, "Apology accepted, and you have to trust that I can handle Donald. He's been the only man in my life for a while, so he feels a little threatened. He'll work it out."

"I can't help but feel protective where you are concerned."

She laid her head back on his chest and they continued to dance in silence.

Later that evening April approached Carmen again and asked, "So, did you talk to her?"

"Yes." Carmen answered rather noncommittally while eating more shrimp.

"Well, what happened?" April was bursting with curiosity.

"I can't disclose that, since she's agreed to see me." Carmen winked and let April know when her sister was coming in to see her. April spent the rest of the evening playing a good hostess and enjoying time with Marcus. She shared that Summer had finally gotten to meet Carmen, and the party was an official success.

"That was a wonderful suggestion, Marcus," April whispered.

"I just suggested that you get the two of them to meet socially, you did all the rest. Have I told you lately how amazing I think you are?"

"No, but it's nice to hear, thank you." He picked up a shrimp and fed it to her. She did the same, and the rest of the evening was spent with them teasing each other with food, slow dances and lots of passionate kisses. To say the evening was hot would have been an understatement. Try as they might, the two could not keep their hands off of each other.

Everyone at the party noticed, and Summer was happy to see it. She and Kenneth smiled at the couple a few times and joked about how long Marcus would last. "He'll do fine as long as he doesn't say or do something really, really stupid," Summer whispered to her husband. They also enjoyed being close that night. It was as though they were on a date. They laughed and talked. It had been a long time since they had enjoyed an evening together.

April went to the kitchen to check on the food. When she returned she saw Marcus seated on the sofa, talking to Joshua. She turned her head to one side and wondered what the two of them were talking about.

Marcus looked over at her and said something to Joshua, who smiled, and the two rose from the sofa and shook hands. Joshua headed toward the kitchen where his wife was, and Marcus walked over to April.

"Were you two over there talking about me?" she purred, trying her best to look kittenish.

"Yes, we were."

When it was obvious he was not giving up any details, April lightly punched his arm. "You don't have to be so honest about it. What did he say?" She was curious and felt oddly curious that the two had spent some time talking about her.

"A gentleman doesn't gossip." Marcus was teasing her and she enjoyed it.

She countered, "No, a gentleman doesn't, but I'm asking you, not Joshua."

"Oh, it's like that now." Marcus took another drink of the beverage he held in his hands, all the while his eyes never leaving hers. Even his eyes seemed to be teasing her.

"Yeah, so tell me."

"Nope, ask the gentleman." Marcus smiled and pulled her closer to him with one arm. "When can we do this again?"

"What?"

"Get sweaty and close?" His voice was demanding and April saw the desire in his eyes.

"Soon." His hand was on the small of her back again and she felt comfortable—way too comfortable, she decided.

"Promise?" he asked.

"I promise," she said and tipped up to meet his lips with a kiss that caused them both to blush. April could hear some of the partygoers giggle and knew they were being watched. She laughed and thought, *I have gone way too long without this man.*

When she saw Summer whisper something to Kenneth, she guessed her sister probably thought the same thing.

Chapter 10

Later that night Marcus called April. "Hey, beautiful, are you alone?"

April let the question hang in the air a minute before answering, "Of course, I'm alone."

"I thought maybe Donald would try to backtrack over to your place."

"Are you jealous?"

"No, but I still say he wants more." Marcus's tone was not casual or teasing this time. April had to smile at the thought of him being a little jealous.

"I explained that we are friends and you seem to understand. Why are you all of a sudden jealous?" She lay in bed and looked at the other side of the empty bed, wondering what it would be like to look over and see Marcus lying there.

Marcus thought about the question and tried to explain.

"I'm not really jealous, I just know men, and I know that he wants more."

"What he wants and what he gets can be two different things. After all, he can only accept what I'm willing to give." She stretched her arm to the other side of the bed and it felt cold. She quickly withdrew and placed it across her flat stomach.

"Yes, you're right, but I still don't like the way he looks at you." The amusement in his voice had returned.

"Are you in bed?" she asked suddenly.

Marcus wished she hadn't asked because he'd wanted desperately to have her lie in his arms in his bed. Talking to her on the phone while in bed seemed about as close as he was going to get to his fantasy. "Yes," he murmured. He tried to clear the image from his thoughts as he asked, "How's Summer doing? She didn't take a drink all night."

"I think she's doing better, but it's slow progress. Her agreeing to see Carmen is wonderful."

"What about you?"

"What about me?" April's interest was piqued by the question as she pondered it.

"How are you feeling about things? I know this is a stressful time for you with all that's going on with your sister. We talked briefly about your mother, but I get the impression that there are some things going on there, too."

April shifted in bed and for the first time in a long time she felt like talking about her mother. "You are very perceptive. There are still some issues I have with my mother."

"I'm not trying to play psychiatrist, but is it anything you want to talk about with me?"

April shifted again in bed, but finally got up and walked to the kitchen for a drink of water. "Yes."

"I'm listening."

"I sometimes wonder if me or my sister have inherited my

mother's bad blood. I mean, I know it sounds crazy, I realize that it's probably more of my imagination than anything else, but sometimes I wonder if we're destined to be unhappy and bitter like her. If maybe we somehow, unknowingly or unconsciously, sabotage our relationships." April had finally admitted something she'd been thinking about for years. Something she'd found impossible to even share with Carmen or Summer. She walked to the kitchen and stood at the sink with her eyes closed as she felt her energy draining. The thought of such a thing made her weak and sick to her stomach.

She walked over to the chair and pulled it from the table and slowly sat down. She laid her head down on the table.

"April, first of all you have a lot of love and compassion for others, there's no way you could become bitter. You're a vibrant woman who enjoys life. From what I have seen there are people who love and adore you. I think the thing that your mother has passed on to you and Summer is the will to survive, despite the odds. There's nothing wrong with being strong." Marcus allowed time for April to digest what he said. He could hear the doubt and sadness in her voice. He'd gotten up, and sat on the edge of the bed.

Almost as if they detected her sadness, April's dogs came into the kitchen quietly. Champ sat under the kitchen table and rested his head on her slipper. She smiled as each of the two bigger dogs lay on each side of her. She reached down and took time to pet each one.

Even finicky Midnight joined in and lay at her feet next to Champ.

"Are you there, April?"

"Yes." She suddenly had the urge to think about things. She said, "I really needed to hear that from someone."

"Someone who's crazy about you? Someone who thinks you're the best thing that's ever happened to him?"

"Yes."

"Someone who's taking it slow because you asked, but it's driving him crazy?" His voice almost pleaded and it made April smile.

"Yes," she repeated reflectively. They both let out a slight laugh.

"April." His voice was so low and hypnotic she closed her eyes in an effort to gather her thoughts.

"I'm still here," she finally said. After a few minutes she added, "Would you mind if I said I wanted to be alone right now?"

"You're going to be fine, and no, I don't mind."

"Promise?"

"Promise. Good night, beautiful."

"Good night, handsome." April hung up the phone reluctantly. She didn't necessarily want to talk, but she longed to feel his masculine assurance, which was what she always felt when he was around. Somehow she knew that he had her interest at heart and she had never had that from a man before. It warmed her heart and she decided that the tall, handsome distraction had somehow gotten into her heart and had become a tall, handsome, overwhelming attraction that made her feel like singing. April fell asleep that night with Marcus on her mind and in her dreams.

"I won't, now let me get out of here before somebody shows up with an animal. Goodbye, Samantha, it was very nice meeting you. Watch out for these two crazy women, though, they'll work you to death!" They all laughed again, partly because they knew Summer had absolutely no desire to come into contact with any animal. Samantha thanked her again for the lunch.

"Bye," they all called out in unison.

When she left, Bridget asked, "Doctor, is Summer okay? She looks very thin."

"No, she's not okay, but she will be." April watched as her sister got into her car and drove off. Her heart sank at the thought of losing her. She'd already lost one sister, her father and mother.

Even though her mother was alive, she had been lost to her family for years. She was lost to alcohol and bitterness. She prayed silently that Summer was being open with Carmen. One couldn't carry around that much of a burden by themselves. Summer needed to sort out her feelings and determine what she was responsible for and what things she had no control over.

It was Thursday, and April left work early to meet with other members of the volunteer group for their monthly meeting. She had convinced a local businessman to donate an unoccupied building to the group for two years, rent free. They were responsible for the cleaning, painting and general upkeep of the building. Through an impressive campaign of letter writing and asking for donations, the building had been given supplies to make it a place they could hold their meeting in. A local retailer had donated office supplies and furniture, another had donated a refrigerator.

The volunteers were dedicated to April's efforts in making South St. Louis City a place for families to live without fear. They'd tried to keep their children and families safe by continuing to patrol the areas of known drug activity, loud music or gang activity. They got city records to search for absentee landlords who'd let their property become rundown and become safe havens for drug activity. Once the landlord was found, the city would issue summonses or fines.

Their slogan was, "Making our neighborhoods safe, one block at a time." The group was dedicated to making sure citizens, police, judges and politicians did their part in making the area safe.

Once inside the building, April turned off the burglar alarm and started getting the room set up for the meeting that was to take place in an hour. The building was hot and stuffy since the air-conditioning wasn't turned on when the building wasn't being used for meetings. She'd left the door open to allow for air to circulate and remove some of the stuffiness before turning on the air conditioner. She sat her briefcase on the table and was removing the pamphlets one of the volunteers had dropped off at her office only moments before she left to prepare for the meeting. Her thoughts were interrupted when she heard a noise. April turned to see four young boys standing in the doorway. The one standing in the front turned to the boy behind him and said something in a low voice.

The very last boy then closed the door and stood there while the other three approached April. She recognized them from the neighborhood and knew they'd had problems with the law. She recognized one as being in a group of men she'd personally called the police on when she saw they were involved in drug activity standing across the street from her home. The young boys swaggered toward her with menacing looks on their faces. They looked young, but their eyes spoke of a hardness reserved for someone who'd seen things they shouldn't have.

She took in the backward caps, pants sagging and oversize shirts. "May I help you gentlemen?"

The three looked at each other and the leader sneered, "We ain't no gentlemen. But yeah, you can help us by staying out of our bizness." His tone was meant to be threatening and April had no doubt the trio plus one had in fact come there to threaten her.

"And what business would that be?"

"You ain't stupid, Doctor, you know what I'm talking about." The leader looked at the three young men standing behind him and replied, "We professional bizness men like you. We what you might call pharmaceutical salesmen." The other two boys chuckled but their faces didn't soften.

"What'd you say your name was?"

"I didn't say, but you can call me trouble." A few of the other boys snickered and April tried her best not to appear frightened.

"Well, look, Mr. Trouble, all I'm doing is trying to make sure the citizens who live in my community can do so peacefully. We don't want to get in your business. As a matter of fact we don't want your business in our community." The face of the young boy hardened even more and it did frighten her that someone so young could be so ruthless looking. It dawned on her that no one would be in the building for at least another thirty minutes. These young men could come to do whatever it was they wanted to do to her and be gone before anyone discovered her. Her stomach tightened, and she decided whatever was going to happen was not going to be pleasant. She was not going down without a good South-side fight. She had mace in her briefcase, but she knew she wouldn't be able to fend all four of them off for long. But still she stood her ground.

"I know it's not easy out there. I understand what it's like to not have any hope or feel that there's nothing out there for you but what you're doing."

"Lady, you don't know nothing about us so don't try to act like you do. You're a doctor, probably ain't never had to want for anything."

"You're wrong, young brother, I grew up in the projects on this South side. Nobody ever gave me a thing. I worked hard and went to school. In college I had three part-time jobs, and all of them were legal. There are other ways to make a dollar, there are options for you, for all of you."

"Yeah, we could all get jobs at Mickey D's making minimum wage." The other members let out obscenities at the suggestion. "But we making big money and we aint gon' let you or nobody else mess that up for us." He held his finger up close to her nose and said, "I'd hate to see something bad happen to such a pretty lady...."

"And trust me, you don't want anything bad to happen to that lady, either." A voice boomed from the back of the building as Marcus began making strides toward the front of the room where the group and April stood.

April looked past the trio and saw the boy who'd been standing at the door struggle to get to his feet. Marcus had quietly knocked him to the floor. Within seconds he was standing facing the three menacing youngsters who'd turned their attention from April. Marcus towered over the three and looked just as menacing.

"Hey, Dr. Davis, ah...ah, whacha doing here?" The leader asked. All the while he continued to make distance between he and April.

"I'm here for the meeting and to see if I can help my woman."

The three turned simultaneously and looked at April. "Man, we didn't know she was..."

"Look, Quentin, it doesn't matter who she knows. The point is you can't go around threatening people because they don't want you selling drugs in their neighborhood. What you young men fail to realize is that this woman is protecting your mothers, grandmothers, sisters, children and others who live in this neighborhood. She's doing the job you should be doing, instead of out here selling drugs. And threatening law-abiding citizens."

The young men's pretense and hardness seemed to slide off their faces and April saw for the first time just how young they were. The fourth member, who had evidently tried to block Marcus's entrance into the building, shouted, "Come on, Quentin, let's roll."

Quentin looked at April and Marcus and said, "This ain't over."

"For your sake, I hope it is." Marcus looked each of them in the eye before they turned to leave. He walked behind them and closed the door after they left. He then went over to April, who had collapsed in a chair.

"You okay?"

"I guess so, but I swear I don't know what may have happened if you hadn't come when you did." She looked closely at him and wondered how he could shift his look from such a stern, no-nonsense, ready-for-action man to someone gentle and caring so quickly. Her pseudo bravery had left and she felt her knees begin to buckle.

"Do you have anything to drink here?" Marcus looked around the room.

April weakly pointed to another opening. "Through that door, we have a small kitchen. The refrigerator has soft drinks and bottled water."

"I'm thirsty, you want one?" He sounded remarkably calm, which was in contrast to his insides, which were boiling. The thought of the young thugs trying to intimidate April incensed him. He'd been trying really hard to practice restraint when it came to his temper. He tried not to show her just how angry or upset he was. He had come very close to swinging on Quentin when he saw him put his finger toward April's face. He had practiced more self-control lately than he had in his entire life, and he knew it was because of her.

"Yes, please," she murmured softly. All she could think about was what the boys were planning to do to her as she watched

Marcus go to the kitchen for their drinks. She'd been confronted before by thugs trying to scare her, but it was usually in public places where she felt safer. She realized that they knew where she lived, where she worked, and if they'd planned to cause her any harm they could. The thought weakened her more and she took deep breaths to gather her composure.

Marcus returned with two bottles of water and handed one to her. "If it's any consolation, Quentin is more bark than bite. I've known his family for years. He's more of a wanna-be drug dealer that needs some intervention." He gently rubbed her back in an effort to comfort her.

April smiled weakly at Marcus's attempt to comfort her. "Maybe so, but his threats sounded real to me." Taking the bottle, she unscrewed the cap and took a long drink and then placed the cool bottle against her forehead. She began to feel stronger after a few minutes and said, "I know it comes with the territory. It just makes me sad to see such a group of lost young men."

"That's why so many are trying to help them. Some of them we can save, others we can't. That's what keeps me in the neighborhood. I was one of those that could be saved."

"So, you were a roughneck back in the day."

"Yes, I was. My parents and teachers kept telling me I was smart and should pursue other interests, but the streets were more appealing than books. I'm just fortunate to have someone that cared enough to ride me until I turned around. That's why I live in the neighborhood, to give some of that back. Make sure some of these young men know they can make it without illegal activity." The firmness of his conviction left no doubt that he was indeed committed to making the neighborhood safe.

April's heart softened and she knew she'd found her soul mate. His words touched her and she stood up and wrapped her arms around him. He appeared surprised by the gesture but responded by wrapping his arms around her in response. April tiptoed and brought his face to hers and kissed him passionately. The passion she'd been holding back was all put into a single kiss that made Marcus obviously excited. She felt his excitement grow on her leg, which caused her to become more passionate. When the two finally parted there was no attempt to hide the passion that sparked between the two.

"Good evening, Dr. Davis." Marcus and April turned their intense gaze from each other and saw a group of young people who were smiling as they stood at the front door. They couldn't help but snicker as they caught the couple kissing.

"Good evening, Bobby, I'm glad you could make it." Marcus looked at April and smiled. He took her hand in his. "This is the lovely lady I was telling you about." Marcus introduced April to the group of young people.

After the introduction of the group, Marcus explained, "Bobby and the rest are here to volunteer their services. They understand it's their community too and they should be a part of keeping is safe."

"Yes, ma'am, so put us to work doing whatever you need for us to do." Bobby beamed as he looked at the others in the group, who all nodded in agreement. April was so pleased she hugged the group one by one and thanked them for coming.

"It's such a pleasure to see young people being positive influences in their community. There is so much to do here. Thank you all again." Her voice nearly cracked from the overwhelming pleasure her heart felt. She was truly overcome by emotions. She looked at Marcus and thanked him for his bringing the group. He had the nerve to blush, and she was tickled to see it.

The meeting was off to a rousing start with the reports of the arrests of several neighborhood drug dealers and the unexpected arrival of the police captain. He promised to make more officers available to the area and dedicate his force to aiding the group in their combined efforts to eradicate drug and illegal activities in the neighborhood. He commended the young people for getting involved and the rest of the group applauded their involvement as well.

Cozette was there again, offering her support. The Andersons gave their report on the observations they'd made of the judge. It was determined that he was too lenient on repeat and serious offenders. The group decided to protest at the downtown courthouse to let the general public know of their concerns with the judge. Cozette volunteered to be one of the protestors at the courthouse.

April couldn't keep her eyes off of Marcus and each time she looked at him he was staring intently at her, as well. She wondered if he was thinking what she was thinking. She certainly hoped so. April wanted to feel his arms around her again and wanted desperately to feel the warmth of his kiss and the passion he seemed to ignite in her.

Her throat became dry thinking about the kiss they'd shared earlier and she became eager to share more than a kiss. She laughed to herself as she thought about the old Betty Wright song, "Tonight Is the Night." She thought back to her seventies party and how they'd danced to the song. She could feel his growing excitement as they literally did a bump and grind during the song. It seemed the song had the same effect on everyone else at the party, so nobody noticed they were drenched with sweat afterwards.

It took all the control she had to send him home that night. She wanted to tackle him and make love on the living room floor. Her desire had been magnified to the tenth power since then but she'd managed to keep it in check. They needed to take their time and get to know each other before their passion claimed them. Passion had a way of clouding judgment; she wanted her mind clear when it came to Marcus.

After the meeting, Marcus followed April home and met her

dogs for the first time. They barked and growled at him initially but after less than ten minutes, they all played with Marcus. April shook her head in amazement. "They don't usually take to strangers. Those crazy dogs don't even like my sister."

Marcus laughed, "She's probably afraid of them and they can sense it." He continued to play with the dogs while April made tea in the kitchen. After setting the tray of brewed tea, sugar, cream and cups down on the table, she summoned the dogs and they obediently came to her. April put the dogs in the basement and closed the door. Marcus was in the bathroom washing his hands when they heard a knock on the door.

April looked at her watch and said, "Who could be coming over so late?" An initial fear washed over her as she thought of the threat earlier that evening, but she rationalized that the thug wanna-bes certainly wouldn't knock. Their style was more like a rock through the window, she thought. Hesitantly she walked to the front door, followed closely by Marcus, and looked out the frosted glass on the front door and saw her nephew, Andrew. "What in the world?" she murmured.

"Who is it?" Marcus asked.

April opened the door without answering and excitedly asked Andrew, "What's wrong?"

Andrew looked sadly at his aunt and quickly hugged her. He closed his eyes tightly and when he opened them he saw a stranger watching them. "Who's that?" he asked, and withdrew from his aunt.

"Oh, Drew, this is my friend, Dr. Marcus Davis. We just got back from a meeting. What's wrong, why are you here so late?"

Marcus extended his hand to Andrew and said, "Nice to meet you, I've heard a lot of nice things about you."

Andrew shook his hand and muttered, "Thanks, nice to meet you, too." He clearly had something on his mind. April's heart raced with fear as she did her best to sound calm.

"Can we talk privately?" His question sounded more like an invitation for Marcus to leave. He then walked toward the kitchen, not waiting for an answer.

April looked at Marcus with sympathy and he immediately replied, "Sure, you two need to talk privately." He walked over with a look of disappointment on his face that was only matched by the one that hid behind April's slight smile. He leaned over and kissed April lightly on the cheek. "I'll call you later."

"Promise?" she asked seductively.

"Promise," he answered, his voice dripping with entice-ment. Their night had been charged with fiery attraction. As April walked him to the door she wondered if the two of them would ever satisfy the elusive need to spend the night wrapped in each other's arms. As though reading her thoughts, Marcus put his arms around her waist and brought her to him.

"I think we need to plan some 'us' time." His eyes bored passionately into hers and he added, "Real soon."

"We will." April's voice was becoming slightly hoarse.

"Promise?" Marcus asked.

"Promise," she quickly replied. The two laughed and kissed good-night. April watched him walk to his car and mumbled, "Have mercy." His long, muscular legs were hidden by the warm-up pants he wore, but she could see the flex in them when he walked. She swore his derriere called to her hands, causing her palms to sweat.

When she walked into the kitchen Andrew was sitting looking out the patio door, deep in thought and looking so much like his mother her heart ached. She knew he was hurting and she knew her sister was hurting. "What's wrong, Andrew?" She pulled out a chair and sat down.

Andrew did the same thing, then explained his concern for his mother. She'd become distant and he overheard his parents arguing, which was something they rarely did. He felt his mother was having problems coping with events at work, but that her problems began long before the current work predicament.

April sat and listened to her nephew and marveled at his grasp of the situation. He was intuitive and smart, he'd figured out much of his mother's concerns. He didn't know much about her younger years and the fact that she blamed herself for her father's disappearance. Summer blamed herself for her sister's death and so many of the unhappy things that had happened during her youth. April knew an intervention was necessary. She silently prayed for guidance and strength as she talked candidly to her nephew about some of the events that she and his mother had experienced growing up.

Andrew listened intently and nodded as he understood what his aunt explained to him. He knew his mother had had a difficult youth but had no idea how bad it was. He felt sad for her but told his aunt his mother was such a wonderful mother that it amazed him, given all that she'd been through. April told Andrew he needed to tell his mother that. They agreed that he would spend the night with April since it had gotten so late.

April talked briefly to Summer and told her that Andrew was spending the night with her. He'd shown up and wanted to talk to his aunt in confidence. Summer didn't badger April because she knew why her son had gone there. The two spent part of the evening playing cards and talking. April talked to him about some of her high school antics and showed him the video of her seventies party. Andrew did some serious laughing and at one point simply just had to point to the television because he was doubled over. After the private viewing they sat down with glasses of grape juice at the kitchen table.

"So, Auntie, are you and Old Boy serious?"

April smiled as she tried to interpret what Andrew was asking. "Why would you ask that?"

"'Cause he was looking at you all funny, like he wanted to get with you."

"Well, Drew, I'm not sure if that means what I think it means, but yes, we are trying to get to know each other, and he's a nice man." Almost as an afterthought, she added, "And I like him a lot."

"He seems like a nice dude, I'm glad you got somebody nice. You deserve that, Auntie."

April smiled and so did Andrew.

As Marcus drove home that night, doubt began to creep into his mind. It was an old enemy of his and he wanted nothing to do with it. He wondered if he and April would ever get some intimate time together. He understood that she was busy with her family, her practice and her neighborhood group. He appreciated the fact that she could juggle so many activities, and he admired her dedication and passion. But he wanted time with her, time alone for just them, beyond the casual date. He'd committed himself to knowing her and believed that their time had come to move beyond dating. Now he wondered if she was running from him and if he would someday be a replacement friend for Donald. It was a troublesome thought that tore at his heart.

At least Donald at some point had been her lover; Marcus was jealous of that. He wondered if she would allow him in her heart so that she would understand and know how he felt about her. He'd not given any woman so much of his heart or himself and he hoped he wouldn't regret it. She had the potential to seriously hurt him like no one ever had, not even his ex-wife.

Marcus quietly entered his home and headed for his den. He did some of his best thinking there. He stopped momentarily in the foyer to check his answering machine. The light flashed one message which he knew wasn't urgent because anyone who wanted to reach him immediately had his pager

or cell phone number. He began to play the message and
smiled as Brianna's voice filled the foyer. Her voice was
sweet and kittenish as she reminded him that he was her
escort to some function and begged that he call her back. The
hour was late so he headed to his den to relax.

"At least she's persistent and has time for me," he mumbled
to himself. The doubt had crept in and was making him feel
insecure about his relationship with April. He knew she was the
real deal but his mind toyed with returning Brianna's call. He
sat down in the den and looked around. "I have everything I've
ever wanted right here except the woman I want to share it with."

He walked into the kitchen for a light snack. When he
opened the refrigerator to survey the contents, the phone rang.
He looked at the caller ID and saw Brianna's name. He
thought about avoiding her but went ahead and answered the
phone. It was late and he doubted if he wanted to hear
anything Brianna had to say, but that little doubt pushed him
forward. "Hello, Brianna." His voice lacked excitement or
warmth, but she was willing to overlook it. She immediately
launched into her dialogue about the function he had agreed
to escort her to months ago.

Chapter 12

Summer called her sister that evening as soon as she got home to share the news about the lawsuit.

"Well, actually, what I did was turn over the information to Paige's lawyers, and they seem to be certain they have a case. They seem to think LaFlair will settle out of court to avoid bad publicity. They may try to drag it on for a while just to try and wait us out, but all in all, it's very promising."

Summer was sitting in her office, gazing at old photos of happier times. She had reminisced about events and people she'd associated with at LaFlair over the years. She had taken the photos from her desk months ago with the intention of throwing them away. They had sat on her desk untouched until today. She glanced over at her wall. The wall was covered with awards and pictures of her accomplishments with the company. She no longer felt the urge to rip the awards and pictures from the wall as she had felt months earlier. Instead she looked at them as an old friend that she was about to say goodbye to. She slowly placed the photos back in her desk.

"And how do you feel about that?"

"I think word of mouth is the best kind of publicity. When word gets out to the general public that they are being sued by former employees for the way they were treated we won't have to worry about a public boycott. They certainly don't want the way they've shown preferential treatment to some of their distributors getting out, either. People won't buy their products. Distributors have known for years that their practices were somewhat shady."

"Sounds like you've got it all figured out." April was still updating her files on her computer. She stretched as she looked at the blinking cursor on her computer and decided she'd had enough for the evening. Bridget and Samantha had left hours ago.

"I wouldn't say all figured out, but I think I'm on the right path." Summer noted she no longer heard April's computer keys clicking. "What are you doing, wrapping up for the night?"

"Yeah, I'm tired. Why would Andrew feel like he needed to talk to me?" April closed out the file and shut down the computer.

"I've been busy lately, haven't been home much. He doesn't understand that I'm working things out quietly. I have a lot on my mind and I haven't been as attentive with him or Kenneth lately and…and it's just caused some distance between us all."

April knew that sometimes when being reflective she and her sister had a tendency to appear to become distant, but it was their way of thinking things through. "Well, that's good, but try to spend some time with your family, and let them know what's going on with you."

"Okay, Dr. Nelson, I will." Summer's voice sounded light and that pleased April.

April smiled to herself and said, "You know, I do the same thing."

"What's that?"

"Tend to want to be by myself when I have things to think about. It helps me to sort things out." April looked out the window at her car. She'd moved it closer to the entrance to her office to be on the safe side. It was dark outside and she had to be careful.

"You sorting out Marcus?" Summer asked.

"Yes."

"Do you want to be alone?" Summer's tone was soft.

"No, I want to talk to you about it. Maybe it's time we changed our pattern and talked about the things we're going through with our loved ones."

"Think you may be right about that."

"You're going to try and do that with Kenneth?" April surveyed the office to make sure everything was ready for the next day. She didn't like leaving a mess so she made sure her office was organized each night before she left. A cleaning service would be in to thoroughly clean it, but she still maintained that it was up to her to make sure everything was somewhat clean and orderly before she left.

"No, I'm not going to try." Summer paused and thought she could hear April intake a breath before she continued, "I'm going to do it. I love that man."

"Good, because I do, too."

"I don't want you there too late, why don't you call me when you get home? We can talk then."

April picked up her purse and car keys and headed toward the area of the burglar alarm.

"I'm on my way out the door now. I have my headset attached to my cell so we can talk for a few more minutes."

"Are we still on for Saturday?" Summer asked.

"You bet, I need new clothes in the worst way. Wearing smocks all day at work has made me lazy."

Summer laughed out loud. "That sounds like a dream job to me, not having to worry about what you're going to wear to work. April, I wish I had a tenth of the money I've spent on clothes just this year alone. And we won't even talk about shoes, handbags, pantyhose and all the accessories that go along with looking nice."

"I need something to wear out in the evenings. I go crazy trying to decide what to wear."

"Oh, I see, and are we buying something to wear on an upcoming date?"

"If you must know, Ms. Nosy, I'm going to a dedication dinner that I promised Donald I'd attend with him months ago. I want something new to wear." Summer remained quiet, waiting for the details, but after a few minutes she determined April wasn't going to volunteer the information she wanted.

"So, what's going on with you and Marcus?"

"I haven't gotten to spend as much time with Marcus as I'd like, but I'm working on it. We both have a couple of things going on that were planned months ago, so we're kinda attending the same function, but just not together."

"That doesn't sound good."

"We're both mature enough to know that we made commitments before we got together."

"Okay, if you say so, but don't allow those commitments to others come between the two of you. I know how you feel about him."

April laughed at the sage advise, and knew her sister was well on the road to recovery.

"So, what's keeping you from spending time with him?" Summer inquired.

"You know, stuff like work, family, work, my neighborhood association activities and more work. The usual stuff, but he's busy, too, and he seems to understand."

April pulled up to her house and sat quietly in her car while she enjoyed the sights and sounds of her neighborhood. Children playing, neighbors talking, dogs barking and the smell of home cooking. She walked into the house and was immediately greeted by her pets. Summer was excitedly talking about starting her own business.

After a few minutes, she kicked off her shoes and began pulling her hosiery off. Instantly she felt relieved. Summer continued talking while April took her hair and bunched it into a ponytail and fastened it with a holder. She removed her slacks and slipped on a pair of jeans. She reached into the closet and took out one of her favorite casual tops and slipped her arms through it. She buttoned it and tied it at the waist. She didn't work out but somehow had managed to stay slender, and she smiled at her small waist.

Summer was talking nonstop before finally saying, "Listen, I've got to order dinner, we all had a late day today. I'll talk to you tomorrow." Summer gently placed the phone in the cradle and looked for her takeout menus.

She quickly ordered Chinese food and then walked upstairs. She stared out the window as she closed the blinds. She thought about her last session with Carmen, which had only been an hour before she spoke to April. She stubbornly admitted the woman had listened tentatively and hadn't judged anything that she was told. At first, it was almost like she wasn't in the room, which made it easier for Summer to talk. Carmen got Summer talking and later she'd asked questions and made comments that caused Summer to think and form her own conclusions.

Somehow she'd begun to feel less vulnerable about the ugliness of her childhood. She somehow had felt responsible or at least at fault for her mother's drinking. She often thought she could have helped her mother, or maybe the reason her father left was because taking care of three children had gotten to be too much.

All the problems, all the secrets were being told, and slowly she was beginning to feel as though she could really learn to live with her past. For the first time, she understood how April felt a sense of catharsis when she revealed herself and all her secrets to Carmen. The burden was so much lighter, it was almost gone.

It was all as much a part of her past as her husband and son were a part of her present and future. She didn't have control over what happened to them, but she did have control over her ability to learn from her experiences and to turn those experiences into something that would prevent her from making the same mistakes. The mistakes her mother had made, and the mistakes she had made.

Up until a few months ago Summer had believed she'd been a wonderful wife and mother. What she was feeling now was that it had all been put in second place to accommodate her job. She had sacrificed time with her family, as all working women had, but somehow she'd allowed work to define who she was.

While she loved making a good living, who she was had nothing to do with what she did at work. She strolled downstairs and over to the bookcase and ran her fingers around the silver-and-gold frame of their last family picture. Drew was looking more and more like his father every day, she noted as a soft smile formed on her lips. Her eyes slowly zeroed in on her husband, his honest eyes, strong nose and lips that seemed always to say her name as if it were the only one he knew.

His deep dimples etched in both cheeks brought her knees to a weakened state, even while just viewing a picture. Her smile broadened and she thought back to the day they'd taken the picture. They'd spent the entire morning looking at college catalogs and discussing the merits of going away or staying at home. The debates had been lively as both the men voted for schools out of state, but she wanted her baby to stay at home.

He'd grown up too fast; one minute she was looking into his eyes as a newborn, and now they were selecting colleges. It had come too quickly and she hadn't been there to savor it all. She'd sacrificed too much time away trying to make a living. But Carmen had made her understand that independence was as much a part of parenting as anything else.

Young people needed to know what sacrifices it took to develop careers and jobs, that being a wife and mother is only a part of who you are, that you are other things, too.

Summer was taking April's advice that evening as she shared dinner with her husband. Andrew was working late and she decided she would talk to him later when he returned home. Kenneth loved Chinese food and was pleasantly surprised to see the table set for two with napkins, china and flowers. Summer was eagerly waiting for him and greeted him with a kiss and a passionate embrace.

They talked briefly about the events of the day and their planned vacation to Mexico. Summer talked with liveliness and was sharing the details of her interest in starting her own business. She was being more open than she'd been in months. Kenneth knew she had a lot on her mind and prayed that she would share it so they could somehow manage to get back to living the life they had before.

Halfway through dinner Summer looked at him prudently and said, "I haven't told you this, but I've been seeing a therapist to help me deal with this situation at work and some other things." The air between the two was suddenly charged as they both put down their forks almost in drilled perfect timing, while continuing to stare intently into each other's eyes.

"I know I should have told you." Gesturing with both hands

as if to calm her husband, she continued, "But for whatever reason, I just felt it was something I needed to initiate on my own. I haven't told anyone, including April." Kenneth sat back in his chair, waiting for more, trying his best not to feel the hurtful blow that his wife had just handed him. He somehow felt the chasm had just grown even wider.

"There are things about me that I wonder if you knew …if…if you'd still want me. I've wondered about them since the day we met, and sometimes when you say I'm being distant, I'm thinking about those things in my past that have eaten away at me for as long as I can remember."

Summer took a sip of her tea and continued, "There is no doubt in my mind that you love me, and trust me when I say this has nothing to do with that, but sometimes I just don't feel worthy of you, or the life I have now." She smiled weakly, hoping that somehow her husband would be understanding, just one more time. She loved him and didn't want to continue to drive a wedge between them with her insecurities.

Kenneth saw the beginning of a tear forming in the corner of her eye, which puddled and finally began a slow descent down her cheek. He took his napkin and tenderly wiped it away.

Taking his hand, she kissed it tenderly. "I've kept you at bay for so long about my past, Kenneth, and I know it has driven a distance between us. This situation at work has served as a catalyst for widening that distance, but I felt it before this situation came up. I want to save our marriage, I want it better than it was, I don't want any secrets between us. We are way past the time when I should tell you about me. Sometimes I feel like such a fraud. Like, I've created this superwoman for you to fall in love with, and she has nothing to do with the real me."

Kenneth took his wife's hands into his. "You could never be a fraud, we all have secrets we don't want to share. We all have reasons not to want to reveal everything about ourselves. But there are times when we need to shed those secrets for those we love and who love us. I won't let the past determine our future and neither should you. I know you have secrets, but there is nothing in the world that you or anyone else could tell me that would make me stop loving or wanting you. Nothing."

Kenneth watched as Summer took a deep breath and gained her composure. "Baby, don't you know by now that you and Drew are my world? You have any idea what our family means to me, what you mean to me?" Kenneth felt a large lump forming in his throat as we watched his wife's face slowly transform. He knew that on some level she was beginning to grasp that it didn't matter to him what her life was before they met.

Chapter 13

April had been keeping busy and the time was moving way too fast as far as she was concerned. Her extended summer hours kept her busy, and left little time for Marcus. He had explained that he was attending the hospital dedication with his mentor's daughter. They laughed because she explained that she had committed to going with Donald months earlier. Their laughter was short-lived because secretly, neither really felt comfortable with the arrangement. April wondered if the relationship was being tested, and if so, whether they would survive.

Donald arrived and picked April up at the scheduled time. "You look great!" He took her hand and playfully spun her around. "Let me look at you. I've never seen you look more beautiful. I hope the people will keep their eyes on my creation rather than looking at you."

"Oh, quit teasing me." She laughed as she spun around. "And stop, you're making me dizzy."

During the drive, Donald was excited about the dedication and talking rather animatedly about all the prestigious people he'd met during the project. He brought her up to speed on his last trip to Seattle.

Once they got to the hospital, the affair was in full swing as people were outside, admiring the building. The ceremony would start with a ribbon cutting, the usual speeches and then a dinner and dance would follow at a nearby hotel. April had avoided Marcus all week. She just didn't want to hear about him taking out another woman, even if they had agreed about the circumstances. When she did talk to him, and he brought the subject up, she changed the direction of the conversation. For this one time, she wanted to at least enjoy what they had shared. She was starting to feel a sense of loss, like perhaps this date meant more than Marcus was willing to admit. After all, it was his mentor's daughter. That meant his date would have all the right stuff—upbringing, culture, class—and, more important, she *would not* have the emotional baggage April had. She felt a sense of foreboding. She had secretly given Marcus her heart, and was afraid now that he'd lost interest.

The sun and weather were cooperating and the crowd couldn't have asked for a more beautiful day. The sun was warm and shone brightly on the building's glass. It was a perfect day to be outside, just a hint of a breeze, and not a cloud in sight.

The building was lovely. It didn't look like a hospital at all to April, it looked more like a library, she thought. It had quiet dignity and charm, just like Donald, she thought. She smiled at the thought as she glanced at him. He was to participate in the ribbon cutting and he looked very much the part of an important man. His confidence made her smile as he took his place with the other dignitaries posing for pictures. After almost an hour, the ribbon cutting and dedication were done and Donald took her on a personal tour inside the hospital wing.

The inside of the new wing was beautiful, bright and cheerful, which impressed April. The walls weren't gray or a sad blue. They were painted in vibrant colors of yellow and eggshell. After a brief tour of the new wing, the two proceeded to join the others at the nearby hotel where dinner and dancing were on the menu for the evening.

April stopped at the ladies' room to freshen up. When she came out, Donald escorted her to the main ballroom where the dance floor was packed with people dancing and having a good time. She hadn't expected such a large crowd and noted some of the people were more formally dressed. She looked down at her dress and said, "Maybe I should have worn something more formal."

Donald smiled at her and said, "You look fine. Come on, let's dance since *I* didn't get to dance with you at your party."

April rolled her eyes and let him lead her to the dance floor. They danced close, despite April's attempt to allow some distance between them. He held her closer to him each time she tried to put distance between them. It was a subtle but firm gesture.

"Let's find a table," she said when she tired of trying to keep a respectable distance between them.

With a smug grin he retorted, "We don't have to, we're seated up on the dais."

"Oh, I didn't know I was with a star." April batted her eyes in exaggeration.

"Well, you are, so just enjoy the dance." He pulled her closer and she didn't resist. She hoped that he didn't misinterpret her closeness for anything other than her unwillingness to create a scene by constantly pushing him away.

She felt him becoming slightly aroused and looked up at him

to say something but he kissed her temple and began caressing her back. He was trying to arouse her and she knew it was time to put an end to his attempt and once again pulled away from him. "Just give me this few minutes," he pleaded with her.

Just as she was about to say something, she caught a glimpse of Marcus standing at the entrance of the room. He was looking as though he were trying to find someone. His eyes scanned the room. Her heart began to beat erratically as she pulled away from Donald and turned to walk toward Marcus. She stopped suddenly when a tall, attractive woman extended her hand to Marcus and he enthusiastically greeted her with a hug and a kiss on the cheek. He was obviously looking for her and not April. Her heart sank and she suddenly had no desire to dance.

"What's wrong?" Donald asked.

"Nothing, I'm just tired of dancing. Do you mind if we take our seats?"

Donald's eyes searched hers for more meaning but found none. He nodded and the two headed toward the dais where they found their seats.

April scanned the crowd looking for Marcus and the woman but there were too many people in the room. She felt herself slowly coming apart and excused herself.

"I'm going to go to the little girls' room, I'll be right back." She smiled at Donald and left.

April was making her way through the crowd, hoping that maybe that wasn't Marcus she'd seen smile at the woman. She felt a slight panic as her desire to search the room for Marcus conflicted with the desire she had to be alone with her thoughts. She decided maybe a bit of fresh air would be better for her and she headed toward the front door.

Just as she got to the front door she heard her name. "April." She instantly knew it was Marcus. He thought he'd seen her earlier but when he tried to make it toward her his date grabbed him and put him in a grip that would have made a wrestler envious.

April turned to see Marcus looking so achingly handsome that it made her moan. She swallowed the large lump that had lodged in her throat. "Yes."

"I thought I saw you. I was looking for you earlier." He walked toward her as she stood fixed to her position.

April began to think maybe she'd imagined the happiness in his eyes as he greeted the woman, or maybe it wasn't what she thought. Just as Marcus stood in front of her April saw the woman approach them from the side.

"There you are, why'd you rush off?" The woman looked at April dismissively before turning her full attention to Marcus.

The woman was tall and beautiful, April thought. Her hair was cut fashionably short and tapered in the back. Diamond studs that were at least three flawless carats adorned her ears. The red formal dress she wore so well was definitely not off the rack. Her red nails matched her dress and her makeup was only rivaled by women in cosmetics ads. She had the air of influence. She definitely wore her money well. *A proper candidate for a doctor's wife,* April thought.

April had seen her kind before, when she was in medical school. Women like her flocked around the medical school students like ants at a picnic. She'd even heard them talking about what lengths they would go to in their efforts to marry a doctor. All April could do was shake her head. She had found medical school far too demanding and challenging to find time to date or chase men. She occasionally found time for a dinner date, but only viewed it as a diversion from the rigorous study schedule she had. There were those who made it almost a profession to seek out medical students exclusively to date.

The "candidates," as she'd grown to call them, all looked like this woman standing before her—tall, beautiful and well-maintained. Many of them had fathers who were doctors, so they knew all about being a doctor's wife.

April looked to Marcus, who began making the introductions. "Brianna, this is Dr. April Nelson. April, this is Brianna Langford. Her father was, and continues to be, a mentor and friend to me. Brianna and I grew up together." He looked from one to the other as he made the introduction. He was trying to read April's sudden coldness. Brianna inched closer to Marcus and she grabbed Marcus's arm in what appeared to April to be a death grip.

"*Oh!* You're a doctor. So you two are colleagues." Brianna seemed to find some comfort in that and began to relax her grip on Marcus's arm.

April tried to ignore the gesture, and said, "I thought you were just going to the dedication. You didn't mention you were coming to the after party."

"I let Brianna talk me into it."

Brianna smiled broadly. "That's what good friends do. Marcus has been so busy lately, so I thought a little party would be good for him. Wouldn't you agree?" She then turned her attention to April and looked her up and down, which did not bother April, but she held her nose just a little too high, and that did bother her. Still insecure about her humble beginnings, she didn't like people looking down their noses at her.

April was very close to becoming rude but decided that if Marcus wanted a "candidate," who was she to interfere? She looked at him and thought she'd recognized something in his eyes, but if it was there, it would be up to him to make the next move.

"Sure," April agreed.

"You look beautiful, as always," Marcus said to April.

There it was again, something in his eyes, this time she was sure she'd seen it. She would wait for his next move. She wasn't about to make a fool of herself.

Brianna noticed something, too. "Marcus, I'm sure Daddy is wondering where we are. Don't you think we should get going?" Marcus looked at her as if he had forgotten she was standing there.

"Sure," he responded. "But give me just a few minutes, I'd like to talk privately to April."

Brianna looked at April again dismissively and said, "You female doctors always look so…so casual." She lifted her head up and turned on her expensive designer shoes and left. Marcus and April stood together, watching her departure.

"If she wasn't so phony, I'd slap those expensive caps out of her mouth," April said once Brianna was out of sight. "I didn't think she was your type, Marcus."

"She isn't. You are." Marcus pulled her to him. "This isn't what you think it is, April. It's not a date. It's a favor. Besides, aren't you here with Donald?" He tilted his head, and she thought he looked a little too sexy to be out with another woman. Especially one as perfect as Brianna.

"Touché, Dr. Davis." April pouted even though she knew he was right.

"Are you jealous?" He smiled down at her as he pulled her close. She was close enough to inhale the scent she was becoming so familiar and comfortable with.

April pulled away from him. "Of what, who, her? Never." She couldn't help but smile at the lie herself. "Well, maybe just a little, she's quite beautiful and well put together." April smiled shyly.

"Yes, she is, but she's no April Nelson." Marcus smiled at her and pulled her to him again. This time he kissed her passionately.

After the kiss Marcus gathered his thoughts and asked, "So, where's Donald?"

April could barely compose herself, but she pointed and said, "In there waiting for me."

"Are you free after this shindig?"

"Why?"

"I'd like to come over."

"It'll be too late."

"What about tomorrow?"

"I have a meeting."

Marcus looked at her, trying to decide why she was intentionally avoiding him again.

"Besides, don't you have to take Queen Brianna home?" She smiled sarcastically.

Marcus chuckled and said, "Yes, I do, but I won't be spending any time with her."

"Call me later, then," April teased, and left Marcus as she went outside for some much-needed fresh air. That last kiss had almost made April strip his clothes from his body. She took a deep breath once she reached outside. The sky was just turning into night and was chock-full of stars. April closed her eyes and let the light cool her skin. She could still feel where Marcus had wrapped his arms around her. It felt wonderful. She wanted to go home and think, but knew she had cast away that part of her that made her wonder if perhaps she wasn't somehow worthy of love. Especially from a man like Marcus. She cast the thought out, squared her shoulders and made her way back into the main ballroom.

"I was about to come looking for you." Donald interrupted her thoughts.

"No need, I just wanted some fresh air. Do you think we can cut this short? I want to get home a little early." April looked around for Marcus but couldn't find him in the crowd.

"Sure, Is something wrong? You look a little flushed."

"No, I just have a lot on my mind."

He took her by the hand and kissed it. "Well, for now just enjoy this dinner, there's a lot of money in this room. You could easily solicit donations for your organization." He winked at her, knowing that the organization was something always on her mind.

Marcus watched the exchange from his chair and jealousy quickly filled him. Whatever Donald said made April toss her head back and laugh. Marcus wasn't sure what he was feeling. He knew that he wouldn't let April get away from him. He'd searched for a woman like her his entire life. He looked at Brianna and her overdone makeup, fake nails and overly expensive jewelry, and shook his head. He'd made one mistake with love but he'd never make another. April would be his, he was determined to pursue her at whatever cost. His eyes didn't stray far from April the entire night and he longed to be with her.

Once the ceremony began April watched as Donald became excited by the speeches made thanking him for his contribution to the new hospital wing. His company was cited as being innovative and committed to excellence in the field of architectural design. He proudly accepted the award, giving a brief speech. Immediately following the ceremony April was past ready to leave, but the two were constantly being stopped by well-wishers who gave their kudos to Donald.

Once in the car, Donald continued talking about the evening's activities and the award. He again mentioned Seattle and how much money the company would make from the design. It seemed every award meant more money to him and April tired quickly of the conversation, but remained silent and aloof. When Donald pulled up in front of her home he looked at her and said, "Can I come in for a nightcap?"

April had her hand on the door's handle and was more than

prepared to call it an evening. She looked over at him and noted how eager he looked. "No, I'm tired and I'd just like to be alone."

He took the key from the ignition and looked at her. "When are you going to let it go?" Donald's voice sounded impatient as he pulled the handle and stepped out of the car. April didn't wait for him to open her door.

She stood facing him as he got to her side of the car door. "Let go of what?"

"Your sister is a grown woman with a husband, child and life of her own. How will she ever work out things for herself if you're always there to help her?" Donald's tone continued to be impatient and for the first time April realized that he was hoping she'd changed her mind about the nature of their relationship. Marcus was right. Donald wanted more than she was willing to give.

"My sister is very capable of working things out for herself. My not wanting you to come in has nothing to do with my sister. I've had a long day, and I'm tired."

The two stood and watched each other for several minutes before Donald looked away. He started walking toward the house with April not far behind him. Once she put her key in the lock he turned her around. "I'm sorry, April. I understand that, I just feel like continuing the celebration."

"I'm sorry, but I can't, not tonight. I'm just too tired."

"You weren't too tired to be with the witch doctor tonight." Donald's voice dripped with venom as he continued, "I saw the two of you together earlier."

April was taken aback by the coldness in his eyes. "Well, we are dating, what would be so wrong about us saying hello if we were at the same gathering?" She looked at Donald. "What is wrong with you? I've never seen you act so, so…clingy."

"I didn't realize I was, but at least I'm not hiding."

April let out a derisive laugh that made him step back, "What makes you so intent on believing I'm hiding from you? I'm not hiding from you or anyone else."

"I think we'd better table this discussion before one of us says something that can't be taken back." Donald had started to back away.

"Too late. I don't appreciate you calling Marcus a 'witch doctor,' you don't know anything about him." April could hear the dogs barking and scratching at the inside of the door.

Donald stared at her with a look of disdain and laughed derisively. "I know that he had a classy, beautiful woman *clinging* to him all night and he didn't seem to mind." He didn't wait for her response. He turned and left in such a hurry, she wondered if she heard him correctly. She'd seen a side of him that she'd never seen before and didn't ever want to see again. She was losing her friend. She looked at his retreating back and realized he was jealous of Marcus. It was more than a friend being protective and looking out for her, he didn't want to see her with Marcus. They'd had arguments and disagreements before, but somehow this one was different.

Chapter 14

Later that night, true to his word, Marcus called April. "Are you alone?"

She laughed at the familiar question, remembering the last time he'd called and asked her the same question. "This sounds too much like a previous conversation."

"I know," he teased, but then added, "I'd like to be there with you." And there was no mistake about how serious he was.

April whispered, "I'd like for you to be here, too."

"So what's stopping us?"

"I want something beyond the physical, I want us to…" Marcus interrupted her, he didn't want her to think that was all they had to offer each other.

"We are beyond the physical." He wanted to tell her that he was in love with her, but didn't want to scare her off. She wanted to take things slow, and try as he might, he had fallen in love with her very quickly. He loved the way she walked, he liked seeing her head tilt to the left side when she was curious about something. He even thought about the faraway look she had on her face at the antique shop when she looked at the doll. He didn't tell her that she'd been the subject of nearly every dream he'd had since they met. He couldn't get enough of her, and making love to her was only a natural desire for him. A natural evolution of their relationship. He accepted that if she wanted to wait then he would wait for her, but there was no doubt in his mind that she was the one.

"It's been a while since I gave myself to a man in that way, and I promised myself that I would wait for someone special. I'm sure that's you. I want to be certain, I want to know more about you and I want you to know more about me. I promise you, I'm not playing games. It's been difficult for me to open up to you the way that I have, but I have. You are responsible for that. I've opened up to you about things I've never shared with anyone." April took a deep breath, which could be heard on the other end of the phone. Marcus knew it was difficult for her to put herself out in the open.

They allowed silence to hang between the two of them. "Have you had any luck locating your family in Cleveland?" April was thankful that he'd moved the conversation along.

"Not really, but I have a professional doing it now."

"A professional?"

"Yes, I've hired a professional investigator."

"Is there anything I can do?"

"Be patient with me."

"You don't have to ask, I know you're worth the wait." Marcus reluctantly told her about the conference he was attending in Chicago. He would be away for a week, and he already missed her. "I wish you could come," he told her.

"I wish I could, too. Maybe next time. This is short notice for me. I'd have to reschedule all of my appointments." April mentally thought about all the reasons she couldn't drop everything to make the trip with him. "I'll cook you a wonderful dinner when you get back."

"Now, that almost makes me think I can get through the week without seeing you."

April laughed. "You'll call me?"

"You know."

"Promise?"

"Promise."

She was enjoying the way they ended their conversations with a promise. It was an endearment that she found made her feel warm and fuzzy inside.

Chapter 15

"Damn, girl, I can't believe you haven't consummated this union. What you holding out for? He is the hero!" Summer pouted and tried to appear upset. She and April were enjoying a good Saturday afternoon of shopping at Frontenac Shopping Center. St. Louis natives simply called it "Frontenac," as if no further description was needed.

The upscale mall housed Neiman's, Saks, Lord & Taylor, Lillie Rubin and a host of other high-end retailers. Summer had insisted that April not be so cheap, and buy something extravagant for herself. There was no better place than Frontenac for self-indulgence. Even the parking lot declared the mall's reputation for opulence. The parking lot usually consisted of expensive cars like Porsches, Mercedes, Lexuses, Infinitis, a few Hummers and more than likely at least one limousine. It was as if a Chevy or Pontiac were not allowed. No public transportation to this mall, as management's apparent goal was to maintain the snobby reputation they'd held on to for years.

"Weren't you the one who told me a few months ago that it was a good idea? That you and Kenneth had taken time to get to know each other? We aren't rushing things, we are letting things flow naturally." April masked her excitement as she feigned boredom. She finally smiled and said, "But it's going to be soon, very soon. I'm probably too old for such nonsense, but I swear, looking at him makes me just heat up. His kisses are like nothing I've ever felt. And all I have to do is smell his cologne, and I nearly tackle him."

"Girl, don't even try and play me like that. You've had a dry spell for too long and now you've got a good man, you should be tackling him." As they walked around the cosmetics counter at Neiman's April was teasing her sister with silence, pretending to be interested in some cologne that was way too costly, that she would never in a million years purchase. She always claimed to be low maintenance and the exorbitant price of the cologne made her laugh.

After a few more minutes, Summer said, "Well, what's happening?"

"Besides having the time of my life?" She smiled as her sister began to get excited and pummeled her with questions.

"What does that mean? Are you finding more time for Marcus?" The cosmetic lady at the counter had a slight smile on her face as she intently listened for April's reply.

"Yes," was all she replied.

"Yes. Yes to what? Why are you trying to kill me with suspense? Come on, let's get some lunch, I'm starving."

"Yeah, starving to get all in my business. Let it suffice to say that Marcus is exactly what the doctor ordered." April arched her brow as Summer smiled knowingly at her sister.

The two were interrupted by a saleslady. "May I help you?"

"Oh, no, thank you," Summer replied, as she hadn't noticed the lady listening to their conversation, who was seemingly as curious to hear about the date. The saleslady leaned forward and smiled at the two.

She looked wistful as she said, "Well, have a good day. Sounds like you're having fun."

Both the sisters looked at the woman in wonderment, not realizing she'd been listening to their conversation. She leaned forward on the counter with her elbow, cupping her chin with her hand and, looking like someone in a stage of reminiscing she sighed, "I know I've had my share of nightmare dates, it gives me hope to hear someone having fun dating."

Summer and April stopped in their tracks and looked at the clerk, then at each other. April shrugged her shoulders and nodded her head. Snapping out of her reverie, the clerk handed the sisters samples of the latest fragrance. She looked at April and said, "Even if I don't know you, it gives me hope to know that there are still some good men out there." She put her elbows on the counter and told the sisters to have a good day.

Summer and April thanked the lady and left. "Girlfriend must really be in a serious drought season. She looked so pitiful when she said I gave her hope, I started to tell her maybe she ought to get on the Internet and find somebody."

"No you didn't, I can't believe you'd think of the Internet as a viable source to meet men with all the perverts and pedophiles on there. I don't even allow Drew to go into chat rooms." Summer did a shudder as she thought about it. "Don't tell me you think that's a viable way to meet men." April had to laugh at the frantic sound of her sister's voice. They continued to stroll along and window-shop.

"No, Mrs. Nosy, calm down. I'm just joking. I know you take a risk on the Internet, but there are all kinds of legitimate dating services available now."

"You never did tell me how you and Marcus met, so how'd you two meet?"

"Carmen and I attended a dinner, he was there, I noticed him, he noticed me, Carmen noticed us noticing each other, and as they say, the rest is history."

Summer laughed; her sister had a way of getting to the point without a lot of embellishment. "You mean my Carmen? My shrink set you two up?"

"Noooo…a friend of mine introduced us, by way of a blind date. It was not a setup for either one of us. And why is she all of a sudden your Carmen?" April was pleased to hear that Summer was continuing her sessions with Carmen as she stopped and looked at a dress in the window and could almost picture herself in it. She tried to see the price tag tucked in the sleeve but couldn't. "Let's go in and check out that dress."

"Fixed up, set up, hooked up, acquainted, introduced, it's all good. So, tell me more about Marcus. I really do like him. I like the way he looks at you." Summer took a look at the dress and immediately knew April would look fabulous in it. "You don't have to try it on, that's you, honey. Let's see if they have your size."

"Are you sure? Forget that, you have the best fashion sense of anyone I know." April and Summer turned into the small shop. April didn't miss a beat. After she found the dress in her size, she turned to Summer and said, "Well, you saw how fine he is from the party. He is soooo…special, in a good way. He's articulate, witty, great sense of humor and above all a wonderful listener. He gets me…" April paused and thought about how to best explain her feelings for Marcus. "I mean, he understands what I'm trying to do with my neighborhood organization and he supports me. He gives me space."

Summer pulled out her wallet. "This purchase is on me. You've earned it. And I won't take no for an answer." Summer turned to the clerk and said, "Can you gift wrap this? It's for a special lady, and she's trying to impress a special man."

The clerk smiled and looked at April. "You bet I can, this is going to look wonderful on you."

The sisters left the store and continued to stroll along, occasionally stopping to window-shop. "I've never had a man who supports what I do, let alone one who understands my need to be me." April said it softly, indicating it was something she had given much thought to, which caused Summer to turn and looked at her sister. April told her sister how Marcus had written a letter to the local paper about the efforts of the community-based organization just before he left on his business trip. The letter was published and brought such a favorable response that two companies had donated money to the organization without a solicitation. "That's real support from a man of action. He understands me, probably better than I understand myself."

"You deserve that and more, I think everyone does. I'm so happy for you."

Summer looked at her sister and for the first time realized that April was in love. "Do you think he's someone you could love?"

April's entire expression changed, which delighted her sister. Her eyes lit up and a slight smile graced her face. "I must admit it, yes. Definitely." Summer let out a joyful shriek that brought curious glances from the other shoppers. She hugged her sister tightly.

"I'm so happy for you!" Summer's smile was broad and contagious as April returned the smile.

"Have you told him yet?"

"And risk overwhelming him and running him away? No way. We're taking things nice and slow. He's being patient. It would be so easy for me to rip his clothes off and do what comes naturally, but I want this man to know me and for me to know him before we do that. We've put the book idea on hold for now so that we can concentrate on us. But eventually we'd like to coauthor the book, publish the book ourselves and use most of the proceeds to benefit the organization."

She looked seriously at her sister for a minute and added, "Besides, I don't know if he feels the same way. I think he does, he shows me that he does, but I'm still holding out for that certain something to convince me. We've made future plans, which tells me that he's thought about us being together. There are times when I look at him, look into his eyes, and can tell that he wants us."

Summer stopped in her tracks with a surprised expression on her face. "I could tell the way you two were looking all soulful at each other at the party that something was going on. I mean, the way he looked at you even from a distance made me blush. You didn't see him and Joshua looking at you at the party. I would have loved to have been a fly on the wall to hear that conversation." Summer let out a small snicker as they continued window-shopping.

"I love the fact that he's not arrogant like most doctors." The way she said 'doctors' made Summer laugh. She said it almost with sarcasm.

Summer tried to appear surprised. "Excuse me, Dr. April, but seems to me I was there when you graduated from University Of Missouri-Columbia with a DVM."

April waved her hand. "Please, I'm a vet, we don't get arrogant. Hey, let's go to that little Mexican restaurant." April pointed toward the restaurant. "I feel spicy." She did a saucy little step as she said the words. It always amazed Summer how her sister seemed to take her own success for granted. Considering their scarred childhood, she was very proud they both managed to complete high school, let alone excel in college and get advanced degrees. It was a struggle, and they both faced insurmountable obstacles constantly along the way.

The hostess seated them, gave them their menus and afterwards brought water. "Your waiter will be with you shortly, we're just a little busy." The two sisters smiled and thanked the hostess. They picked up their menus and began reading the selections. April set her menu down and thought about how far she had come since college. She always felt left out in college, she didn't have the nice clothes or the extra money to do things that her classmates did. No spring break trips, or shopping sprees, even during the end of the season for drastically reduced clothing. Her scholarships covered tuition and books and her part-time jobs barely yielded enough money for the occasional off-campus meal.

She looked at Summer, who also set her menu down. She raised her eyebrow in anticipation of continuing the conversation where they left off. April laughed, "Please don't give me that look."

"I want to hear more about Dr. Feel Good, you're holding out and I can tell." Summer smirked.

"I just said we had a good time, and he seems like the real deal. Now you're calling him Dr. Feel Good, when we haven't, well, you know, gotten to that stage yet." April blushed and took a drink.

"Although, I must admit I'm ready for something to feel good, if you know what I mean. Come to think of it, probably not. I'm sure you get enough in that department."

"And what department is that?" Summer inquired, knowing full well what April was saying, but wanting her sister to be upfront about it.

"Oh, you know what I'm talking about. The way a man makes you feel when he wraps his arms around you and whispers in your ear. That closeness you feel when he calls you in the middle of the day to let you know he's thinking about you." April put her elbow on the table and rested her chin on the palm of her hand.

Looking like she was daydreaming, she continued, "Making love. If I don't get some soon I'm going to start climbing the walls. You don't know what it is to do without since you're married. I swear I haven't had any in so long I feel like a born-again virgin. I sure hope I remember how to do it."

Both sisters laughed good-naturedly and after a few minutes Summer murmured, while watching the shoppers, "It's like riding a bike, you never forget it."

"That's easy for you to say. I haven't 'ridden a bike' in some time."

April took another drink of her water and watched as the waiter made his way over to them. When he came over she said, "Please bring us two margaritas for starters." She nodded at her sister for approval. "Make them virgins."

"Don't hold back on my account," Summer joked.

"I'm not, you're driving me back to your house. I have to drive home and you know how confused I get out there in suburbia, so neither one of us needs a drink. Anyway, what was I saying?"

"You were talking about not riding a bike for a long time." The two looked at each other and laughed.

The young waiter returned with their drinks and happily replied, "Here you are, two virgins," and winked at April.

When he left, April giggled, "Girl, did you see that baby flirting with us? What's he trying to pull? A bigger tip, no doubt."

"He's not trying to pull anything. He sees a sexy, beautiful, vibrant woman and is trying to flirt."

"Summer, please, he's almost Drew's age. I'm old enough to be his…his aunt."

The two broke out into another fit of laughter. Summer said, "Admit it, girl, you can still draw young cuties, and I'm happy for you." The sisters high-fived each other and April suggested a toast.

"Here's to getting your marriage back on track and to a beautiful, vibrant woman who can still draw young cuties." Summer was laughing so hard other patrons of the restaurant began looking at the two sisters and smiling, as they could tell the sisters were celebrating.

"Are you sure that's a virgin you're drinking?" Summer asked when she was able to stop laughing at her sister.

"Come on, let's go, the movie starts soon."

"I know." April sighed ruefully; she had let her sister talk her into seeing a foreign film with subtitles.

They paid the bill for lunch and were headed out of the restaurant when April heard someone call her name. She turned around but didn't see anyone so she and Summer proceeded out of the restaurant.

They'd only gone a few feet when a lady rushed up to April. "I know you heard me calling you. I just wanted you to know that Marcus and I were together last night." The woman anchored herself and put her hands on her hips, waiting for a reply from April.

April had to do a double take before she recognized the woman. It was Brianna. She was not going to give her the show that she wanted, so she calmly said, "Oh, hello Brianna, I didn't recognize you." April looked her up and down as Brianna had done to her the last time they met. "You look different without *all* that makeup and you're wearing *casual* clothes." The sarcasm in April's voice couldn't be missed. The idea of Marcus being with Brianna jolted her, but she was not going to allow it to show.

"You don't look any different." She gave April a dismissive wave of the hand and said, "Don't think Marcus is the least bit interested in you." Brianna arched her eyebrows up and looked at April in defiance.

April chuckled and looked over at Summer. "Oh, Summer, this is Queen Brianna, I told you Marcus escorted her to the hospital dedication." Summer looked at April and thought back to the conversation.

"Oh, yes, as a favor to her father." Summer smiled sweetly and extended her hand to Brianna. "Nice to meet you."

Brianna looked at her with disdain and then looked at her hand as if it would bite her. "Who are you?" she asked with her lips curled down in a frown.

"This is my sister." April flashed a sickeningly sweet smile that dripped with sarcasm.

"Did you say your name is Summer? And you're April? How totally urban. I think they call it 'ghetto' where you girls are from. What on earth were your parents thinking?" Brianna laughed haughtily and held her head just a little too high. She reminded them both of never having nice enough clothes or any of what the other kids had.

April put a stop to her laughter when she said, "They were thinking that we were naturally beautiful, blessed by nature like an April day and summertime. They thought with such beautiful names they would never have to ask someone to take us out as a *favor*." April squared her shoulders before continuing, "So, if you'll excuse us, we were about to leave." April and Summer turned to leave, giggling loudly.

Summer laughed and said, "That was a good one!"

Brianna watched the two and finally stormed off, but not before she yelled, "Marcus was with me last night, and my father didn't have to ask him." The words spilled out of her mouth fast. She stared to see if they had hit her target. But all she saw was their backs as they had already turned and walked away.

Summer turned to April and said, "Do you think he was with her or do you think she's trying to make you mad?"

"She's lying. Marcus is still in Chicago, but I would like to know why she tried to make me think they were together." April looked at her watch. "Let's go. If we miss the first part of the movie, I know I won't understand it at all."

Later that evening April tried several times to reach Marcus on his cell phone and for the first time since they'd met, he didn't return her phone calls. She refused to allow doubt or insecurity to creep into her thoughts.

Chapter 16

April was feeling melancholy at the meeting. She was there as guest of the chief of police who was awarding her a plaque for her community service. The affair usually was one of her favorites because there were always plenty of dignitaries who were willing to offer some support for her neighborhood group. She'd come to the affair unescorted and found people assumed they could demand more of her time.

She still hadn't heard from Marcus. She no longer wondered why he hadn't returned her call. She assumed Brianna was right. Marcus had lost interest, had probably grown tired of her putting him behind everything and everyone else. She had only herself to blame for losing such a good man. The evening seemed to last forever for her as she tried to network and solicit meetings or some interest from those who could help her attain funding for several neighborhood projects.

The group was trying to get the city to do some upgrades

to one of the parks that had become so run-down and infested with undesirables that none of the parents allowed their children to play there. She thought if the police could patrol the park frequently and the city upgraded the old equipment it could be a safe place for children to play again.

When she left the affair, she had a plaque honoring her along with promises of added police to patrol the park. In her purse, she had checks that had been given as donations from private citizens, who agreed to fund the purchase of new playground equipment. Several representatives of various companies gave her their cards and promised to see what their companies could do to help out the organization. All in all she felt it was an accomplished evening. She looked forward to going home and relaxing, but she missed Marcus. Home didn't hold the same satisfaction for her any longer. She wanted more—she wanted Marcus.

The next day April was talking to Mr. Martin, whose German Shepherd was becoming incapacitated with arthritis. She was carefully explaining how to care for the animal and different methods of treatment when Bridget informed her she had a visitor. "I'll be out in a few minutes. Please ask them to wait."

She could tell from Bridget's voice that she was slightly excited, but she refused to rush her consultation. She made sure Mr. Martin fully understood the animal's condition and tried to ease his pain as she knew there was no cure.

All they could do was make the animal as comfortable as possible and continue with treatment to keep it mobile for as long as possible. The dog was a member of his family and April understood that. He appreciated her compassion. He often teased her about "fixing" her up with his divorced son. An offer she'd gracefully declined, but it made him laugh when she said, "Maybe in a few years when I'm looking again."

They continued to talk for several minutes and Mr. Martin thanked her for all the times she'd taken such an interest in his pet's well-being. He gave April a hug and left with sadness in his eyes.

When April got to the reception area Marcus was sitting casually in a chair. He wore a pair of khakis and a navy polo-style shirt. Despite being upset with him, she had to admit that he made her heart do aerobics whenever she looked at him. No other man had that impact on her. She had mixed feelings as she watched him rise from the chair to greet her. She looked around the room for any patients and turned to Bridget. "What time is my next appointment?"

Bridget could tell from the sound of April's voice that she wasn't happy. She looked over at Marcus and said, "Four-thirty. Do you want me to reschedule?"

"No, this won't take long." Her voice lacked any emotion as did her expression when she looked at Marcus and said, "We can talk privately in my office." She looked over at Bridget and said, "Hold my calls for about ten minutes, and let me know as soon as my next appointment arrives."

"Sure thing, Dr. Nelson." Bridget's tone was not the usual cheerful tone, she was concerned about April and it showed on her face. Samantha had grown close to April in the short time she'd worked for her, and she looked to her cousin for understanding. All Bridget did was click her tongue, and Samantha knew that Dr. Nelson was not pleased with the handsome man standing in front of their appraising eyes.

April immediately recognized that more of her personal life was being told than she wanted. "Thanks, Bridget, you're the best. Don't forget, you two, we've got lunch out this coming Friday, so don't bring anything and start fasting Thursday." She tried to sound lighthearted to stop Bridget and Samantha from worrying. The two just smiled tightly and nodded. As Marcus followed April to her office, she could hear Samantha say, "I'd have to forgive him, he's way too fine!" She could hear them slapping high fives, and laughed to herself. .

April took a deep breath once she and Marcus got to her office. "Please have a seat." She was being formal. Without a word he sat down in the chair she'd pointed to.

"I've missed you and was hoping that we could get together this evening for dinner." He seemed unsure of himself, which was very contradictory to his usual style.

"If you missed me, you would have returned my calls," April said matter-of-factly while she picked up her personal planner. "Besides, I have an engagement this evening."

Marcus's shoulders slumped slightly and he leaned forward. "I've been a fool, April, and I know that. I shouldn't have listened to Donald."

"Donald! What does he have to do with us?" She dropped the planner on her desk and looked at Marcus.

"I guess he didn't tell you." He looked at April for some familiarity, but saw none.

"Tell me what?" she asked sharply.

"I ran into him in Chicago and…"

"What was he doing in Chicago?" April nervously stood up, suddenly aware of the butterflies that had made a home in her stomach.

"Calm down and let me tell you." Marcus leaned over the desk and took her hands. She calmly sat down. "Like I was saying, he came to see me. Told me you and he had, how'd he put it, 'moved forward' in your relationship. Said I should just step aside and let you two be. Said you'd tell me yourself when you were ready. When I got the call from you later that day, I just didn't want to hear it. Couldn't face losing you."

April and Marcus sat looking at each other for what seemed

like an eternity. He didn't realize that he was holding his breath. He wanted so much for it to be untrue, but he did believe it at the time. Donald didn't appear to be the kind of man who'd make up such a thing. Something in April's eyes gave him hope as she'd softened from when he'd first entered the room.

"He told me if I didn't believe it I could see the two of you together at the Millennium Hotel where you would be with him at some function and that you two had reserved a room. Out of curiosity, I called the hotel and yes, they did have a reservation in Donald's name."

That was enough to send April over the edge. "Of all the…" She caught herself and realized Marcus was still holding her hands. "Why would you believe such a thing without talking to me first?" she asked incredulously. "You know how I feel about you." Her eyes danced with his.

"I *thought* I knew how you felt about me and then Brianna told me she saw you and Donald at the mall earlier that day. She said you guys had plans for a romantic getaway. I just… I just knew I'd lost you. Thought maybe there was more to you and Donald than just friendship. You guys had years together." April pulled her hands away from him and walked around the desk.

She sat on the corner of the desk and looked him in the eyes. "You're nowhere near losing me, unless you believe lies someone tells you about me. Didn't you ever think that both Donald and Brianna had something to gain by us not being together?"

Marcus looked at her and suddenly she could tell he was angry. He shot up from the chair, his confidence was back. His lips became thin straight lines as he said, "I'll be damned! I never would have thought anybody could have played me like that. I fell for it, too! If I get my hands on Donald." Almost as a second thought he added, "Or Brianna."

He tried to calm himself as he looked at April and realized

that she had softened even more and was looking inviting with her skirt slightly at midthigh. Her hair framed her face and her lips seemed to beckon him. What a fool he'd been. Even before he knew about the lies Brianna had told him, he didn't want anything further to do with her. He suspected she would do just about anything to get him into her bed, so he'd wisely kept his distance.

"I am so sorry. I was stupid to listen to either of them. You're right, I should have spoken to you. I've never been a coward before, but when I thought I had lost you, I just didn't want to face that." He lowered his voice and it had become almost seductive as he eyed April appreciatively. "I promise that will never happen again." He had missed her so much all he wanted was her forgiveness for being such a dunce. He was angry more at himself for allowing someone to manipulate him in such a manner, something he definitely was not accustomed to.

April smiled at Marcus and asked, "Promise?" He walked around to her, seated at her desk. He knelt down and looked into her eyes.

"Promise," he said and wrapped his arms around her waist, bringing them both to a standing position. He placed an incendiary kiss on her lips that left them both gasping for air afterwards.

"So, what do we do now?" she asked as the two continued to embrace.

Marcus looked at his watch. "Looks like you have an appointment in five minutes, so it's your call."

"It's too late to reschedule, but if you come by this evening I can cook you that nice dinner. Maybe we'll call Donald and Brianna."

Marcus seemed to become annoyed just hearing their names. "Dinner sounds good, but I don't want to talk to either one of them right now. I might do or say something that'll land me in jail." April laughed, but Marcus didn't. She figured she'd wait to tell him what Brianna had said about them being together. He was mad enough. The two kissed again, and he asked, "What time's dinner?"

"Is seven too late?"

"Seven is perfect. I'll see you." They stood holding hands for a few minutes as neither wanted to say goodbye. Bridget buzzed April and informed her that her appointment was waiting.

When Marcus left, Bridget noted the smile on his face and the look of pleasure on her boss's face. "Everything okay, Dr. Nelson?"

April looked at Bridget and said, "Perfect."

Chapter 17

April finally had calmed down enough to call Donald. She wanted to know why he'd been so deceitful. She thought she knew him well enough that such a trick would not be in his nature. She knew there were times when he would let his temper get the best of him. Never in a million years did she ever consider him scandalous enough to deliberately lie to Marcus the way that he had done. She couldn't imagine why he would deliberately sabotage their relationship and her feelings were that Donald was her friend only when he could be the only man in her life. She realized that Donald did not love her like he said, he wanted to possess her. He wanted something entirely different from what she wanted. She never wanted to possess anybody, and surely did not want anyone to possess her.

"Hello, Don." April was in her office at work when she made the call. She sat at her desk and contemplated whether or not she'd make the call. She felt betrayed with a hint of anger mixed in. But mostly she felt a need for closure and an explanation. She made the call.

"April?"

"Yes, it's me. How are you?" She was unbelievably calm, she thought.

"I'm fine, a little surprised is all. I thought you'd call before now." He sounded confident and it annoyed her.

"You mean, you were hoping you'd done enough damage to my relationship with Marcus that I would come crying to you," she countered sarcastically.

"You know they say all is fair in love and war."

"I can't believe you would do something so manipulative, so deceitful and then say you did it for love. You can't possibly love me if you don't want to see me happy. I'm so disappointed in you. Why did you do it?" Her voice suddenly hinted at the sadness of losing a good friend. She turned off her computer and began gathering her keys and purse.

"I don't know if Marcus is the man for you." His voice became lower; maybe he was finally feeling some shame about what he'd done, she thought.

"It doesn't matter, you knew how I feel about him. Why would you deliberately hurt me like that? What you did was not about caring for me, it was about you trying to win at some game or something. I thought you were a better person than that. I'm so disappointed in you." April let out a long sigh, she sat back in her chair and waited for the explanation.

"Well, no more than I am in myself. I'm sorry, April. I should've never listened to Brianna."

"So you two cooked this up together?" April stood up then and listened carefully, she didn't want to miss a word.

"Yes, we did, although she was the one who contacted me with the idea initially. That doesn't absolve me from my wrongdoing. I think I was still holding out hope that you and

I could… I'm so sorry. I do wish you and Marcus the best. Will you tell him that for me?" Donald waited before adding, "I really am sorry, I wish things had worked out differently. Be sure to extend my apologies to Marcus."

April began gathering her briefcase and prepared to leave her office. She felt tired. "Yes, I will. Goodbye, Don, I hope you stay in touch." She felt she should forgive him, there were many times that he had been there for her. Overall he was a good man, maybe one easily persuaded by a pretty face, but a good man just the same.

"After what I've done I'm not sure if Marcus will be as forgiving. You know, you will always be very special to me, April."

"He will eventually forgive you, he does love me." April said it with unfaltering confidence as she set the alarm and headed out the door of her office.

"Goodbye, April." Donald's voice hinted at finality and if that was how he chose to end their relationship she was going to accept that.

When April got home, Marcus was sitting on her porch waiting for her. She knew this man was all she ever thought he was. Not pretentions; he had her best interest at heart.

"Hey, beautiful." He stood and greeted her with a kiss.

"Hey yourself, it's so good to see you." She tried to hide her excitement as she eyed the bags sitting next to him on the swing. She pointed and asked, "What's all that?"

"Dinner. I thought you would rather spend the evening doing something other than cooking, so I ordered from a restaurant that specializes in home-cooked meals." Marcus looked at her with such longing and sincerity it literally took her breath away. He stood and greeted her with a kiss and a hug.

All she could think about the entire day was her commitment to take it slow. Now, looking at him, all she could think about was how good and natural his arms felt around her. How protected he always made her feel. "Let me put the dogs away, when they smell this food and see you, we won't have any peace."

Marcus waited a few minutes on the porch and thought about his budding feelings for April. She returned and the two looked at each other. Without saying a word, he gathered the bags and followed her inside. He set the food on the counter and went to the bathroom to wash up. He could hear water running in the kitchen. Marcus looked around and smiled as he inhaled the familiar scent of April. He could get used to this easily, he thought.

Once back in the kitchen, he helped with warming up the dinner. "This smells delicious." April smiled at him. "You sure know how to greet a girl after a hard day. I love cooking, though."

"I can tell from all the cookbooks and fancy cookware." He pointed to the pot she was holding. April glanced at the cookbooks on the counter and then at the pot in her hand.

April laughed. "It's kind of a passion, especially when I'm upset. I don't cook anything fancy unless it's a special occasion. But I love creating new dishes for me to try."

"Next time maybe you'll create something for us to try." He winked at her and turned to put the covered dish in the microwave. She admired the expanse of his back, she could tell it was muscular. She allowed her eyes to travel down, but turned away. She thought another minute of looking, and he would be dinner, and she was very hungry. She occupied herself by setting the table. She lit candles and dimmed the light. When they were all done, they settled down to a wonderful meal and great conversation.

"You know, we'll never eat all this food. And I'm not going to even ask what that dessert was that you put in the refrigerator. I could smell the calories from here." April lifted her fork to her mouth and smiled at him.

"There's plenty for later, and you don't need to count calories." April shifted under the gaze of Marcus across from her. His eyes and lips were even more inviting by candlelight and her thoughts about taking it slow played in her head again.

After dinner they were cleaning the kitchen when Marcus said, "I saw Brianna's father today, and guess what he told me?" He could barely contain himself and it made April laugh.

"What?" April asked as he handed her a pot to dry.

"He said that she was dating a well-known architect and that she was sure he was going to ask her to move to Seattle with him." Marcus could no longer contain his laughter.

"Are you serious? That didn't take long. He never mentioned that today." April hadn't meant to tell him that she'd talked to Donald so abruptly.

"Why, did he call you?" Marcus wasn't laughing now as his eyes bored into hers. He was still angry at being manipulated and lied to by the devious pair. His anger would be with him a long time, and he was in no mood to try and pretend that everything was forgiven.

"He didn't call me, I called him." She watched him closely as he became tense. His relaxed posture was replaced with a stiffness that she'd never seen in him before.

"It's not what you think, Marcus," April pleaded with him as she reached out to touch him. For the first time, he pulled away.

"It's getting late, time for me to go." He dried his hands and turned to leave. "I've got an early day tomorrow, maybe you can call me whenever you're not busy calling Donald." He didn't mean to say it, but he couldn't always control himself where she was concerned. The thought of her being in contact with Donald after he'd tried to sabotage their relationship angered him. He let his emotions get the best of him.

April became angry and resentful. She couldn't believe how quickly things had turned sour. Marcus had told her that sometimes he allowed his temper to get to him when he was passionate about something. She knew he was jealous because he had misunderstood her reason for calling Donald. She would have jumped to the same conclusion if she had found out he had called that scandalous Brianna.

"Listen, Marcus, you got it all wrong. I called Donald to find out why he lied to you and to tell him goodbye. He's leaving for Seattle." She looked at his retreating back.

Marcus wasn't sure what to think. All he felt was pain that his woman had called a man she'd admittedly had feelings for. It pained him to be so close to her and not touch her.

He stopped and turned to her. "Are you sure it's all over between you and Donald?" he asked quietly.

She looked at him and took his hands in hers. "I've never been more sure of anything else in my life. You're the only man I want in my life."

Marcus felt his heart doing somersaults and he tried to control himself as he heard her repeat in his mind, *Take it slow.* It took a lot of restraint. Her piercing eyes and seductive lips were making it incredibly hard for him to take it slow. He knew if he stayed any longer he would have to have her naked and on the couch, floor, bed, anywhere....

"I...I...I'll call you tomorrow." Marcus had never stuttered in his life but this woman was making him do all kinds of things foreign to his nature. She was telling him she wanted him in her life, but they had to take things slow. He was full of passion and wasn't sure if he was able to control himself any longer. He hurriedly left. He understood why she called Donald, and maybe he would explain it to her tomorrow, but for tonight he had to leave. If he stayed any longer he couldn't take it slow, he would have to make love to her. His self-control was all gone as he lost himself in her gaze.

April was devastated. She'd told him how she felt and he'd

rushed off. Who was running from whom? she wondered as she prepared for bed. She knew Marcus was still angry about what Donald and Brianna had done. She was still angry, too, but she was willing to forgive them and move on. April then realized the sense of betrayal Marcus must have felt thinking that he had been cast aside for Donald. She knew how she felt when Brianna had lied to her, how she felt when she thought Marcus had been with Brianna. She then understood his reluctance to let go of the anger. She would have to be patient. How could she ask him to do something she was unwilling to do? She'd be patient. She had a restless night and found herself dead tired the next morning as she prepared for work.

Chapter 18

April sat out on the patio with her sister watching Kenneth grill steaks for dinner. He looked at Summer enjoying the warmth of the afternoon sun and said, "I heard on the radio today that Frankie Beverly and Maze, along with Anita Baker, are coming to the UMB Center for a concert. I know how you love Frankie Beverly—think you may want to go? I promise not to get jealous when you're looking at him all glassy-eyed."

"Man, please, when have you known me to get glassy-eyed at a concert?" Summer clicked her tongue, pretending to be insulted. She knew what he was talking about and it made her smile in spite of herself.

"I seem to recall back in the day when we went to see the previously mentioned group with your friend." Snapping his finger as if trying to recall the name, she smiled at him. "You remember, the one the security guard had to carry back to her seat because she was trying to get at Frankie. You were swooning and screaming all over the place. I think you even forgot I was there."

"Man, you can distort the truth better than anyone I know. You should have been a lawyer. First of all, you should remember her name because you kept sneaking peeks at her huge chest."

They both began laughing at the memory of that night. "Her name was Tamara, and she was not trying to get at Frankie. He bent down to shake her hand and a rush of women ran up. Now, I know you remember this part, cause when she returned, the gauze top she had on was soaked with sweat and you along with every man in the place, were taking in the sight of her naturalness. That girl was completely shameless. Never wore a bra, betcha her boobs are down to her ankles about now." The two of them laughed easily together, something they hadn't done very much of lately.

April suppressed a laugh as she watched the exchange between the two. She understood what it meant to love someone for so long, to give yourself to someone. "Also, Mr. Man, I don't swoon and I don't scream at strangers, whether they're performers or not."

Summer looked again at him with amusement before continuing, "It was our three-month dating anniversary so it was impossible to forget you were there. Especially as good as you were looking that night. I'd nicknamed you Dark Gable, because I swore you were finer than anything I'd ever seen. I wanted to just rip your clothes off. You surprised me with those tickets and dinner at that Mexican restaurant. It was wonderful."

"Yeah, the one where the waiter tried to flirt with you and the girl with the see-through blouse and no bra. It was a night. I thought me and my boy were going to have to fight our way out the joint. Every man in there was making eyes at you two."

"I know I was a sight with all the Chaka Khan, wild-looking hair." The two shared another laugh. Kenneth kissed her softly on her lips. April quietly watched the loving exchange.

"Yeah, but it wasn't the hair they were looking at, it was that beautiful smile and those come-get-me-baby eyes of yours." The reverie was fun and the relaxed look on Summer's face was as good as gold to Kenneth.

"You remember the other significance of that night?" she asked him curiously.

Kenneth stared at her and smiled; she was testing him.

"What, you thought I'd forget the first time we made love? Woman, you made me see fireworks, and it was nowhere near the fourth of July. I knew then we'd be together forever." When he smiled and his dimples deepened, Summer felt as compelled to rip his clothes off as she had done that night so long ago.

"Well, that's more than I wanted to hear, I'm going inside." Kenneth and Summer laughed as April sprung from her chair.

"Sorry, sister-in-law, I kind of forgot you were over there. Didn't mean to get so graphic," Kenneth teased.

Summer looked over at April. "Drew is really excited about being accepted into Morehouse. He's going to be sorry he missed you."

"I know, but I really can't stay long, I've got neighborhood patrol tonight."

"That sounds so dangerous."

Before Summer could launch her protest, April said, "Don't worry, there will be others with me. We have radios, and the police patrol the area. It's more for show than anything else. We don't want the gangbangers to think they can take over the neighborhood."

"Don't forget we're going out for dinner to celebrate Drew's acceptance into Morehouse. You said you would join us. You can invite Marcus if you want." Summer couldn't help

but smile. She knew that April was truly happy with a man
for the first time in her life. She had found someone special,
Summer was sure of it.

April smiled at the familiar figure as Marcus came around
the corner. He was also on neighborhood watch. He had been
walking with another group and was glad he was finally able
to see April. He'd missed her, and knew he'd made a fool of
himself. He had no reason to doubt her. He'd called and apologized that morning, but felt it was inadequate. She understood, and told him she was under the same pressure. She
wanted him, too, but didn't want their desire for each other
to get in the way of their getting to know each other. They had
made amends, but the sexual tension was as thick as ever, no
matter how they tried to ignore or deny it.

"Everything looks in order," one of the volunteers said,
looking around. "I guess we can call it a night." The group
bid their farewells, and Marcus walked April home. His car
was parked in front of her house.

"Want a decaf?" April asked.

Marcus took her hand in his. "Sounds good." They walked
up the stairs and when they got to the porch, he turned her
around.

Looking into her eyes he brought her close to him and
with one swift move he claimed her mouth with his in a hot-
blooded kiss that took her breath away. She could feel her
lower body respond to the heat. Her thighs began to tremble
and she arched her back to nestle closer to him. Another
kiss, and the two seem to become one. Although it had
been a long time, April recognized the warm feeling of
heat pooling between her legs. She could tell that Marcus
felt the same. There was no mistaking the rock-hard
presence that met her center. The two slowly separated.

Breathing hard and fast Marcus gently dabbed at the beads of perspiration that had collected on April's face. She wanted him, and the thought made him smile. "I have something for you." He turned and walked to his car. She watched as he opened the passenger side and took out a small bundle.

"I hope it's something to cool me down," she crooned to herself softly, and fanned herself.

When he returned, he kissed her warm cheek. "I have an early day tomorrow and so do you. I wanted you to have this though." He handed her the gift-wrapped bundle and waited while she opened it.

April sat down on the bench and slowly unwrapped the gift. Her eyes widened and heart leaped when she saw the gift. "You didn't have to buy this for me." She brought the doll to her chest. "Thank you." Tears pooled in her eyes and she couldn't hold them back.

"I wanted you to have it. You seem to always do for others, and I just wanted you to know there's someone who wants to do for you."

April looked at Marcus and then at the doll. "It reminds me of my mother. I don't have a lot of pleasant memories, but I remember the day she gave me a doll that looked just like this. She was actually warm and loving that day. It's one of the few times I can recall my mother actually kissing me."

Marcus sat on the bench next to her. He couldn't imagine growing up without kisses and hugs from his mother. Because he was an only child, he received an abundance of hugs and kisses. He took April and held her close. They sat for a while and enjoyed the night breeze and the warmth of each other.

Three days later, Kenneth, Andrew, April and Summer all went to her favorite Italian restaurant for dinner to celebrate

Drew's acceptance into Morehouse. April explained that Marcus was working late and couldn't join them. One of the doctors at the hospital had a family emergency and Marcus was covering for him. There was lots of laughter and talk during dinner.

Kenneth teased April about her new love. "My son told me how he had interrupted your date when you two first started dating. I told him with the dry spell you'd just ended you need every date you can get." He looked over at his wife, who tried to suppress a laugh. Knowing his sister-in-law would have an equally entertaining response, he waited.

Even Andrew had to laugh at his father. "Oh, man, Pops, that was cold." Andrew couldn't stop laughing. Kenneth was usually more subdued, but he was having a good time teasing his sister-in-law and enjoyed seeing his wife laugh.

"Well, for your information, I'm leaving in a few minutes so I can meet him at my place for a—" looking over at Andrew, April cleared her throat and continued "—little dessert." She took a sip of water because her throat was so dry, the group started laughing again.

"That's the first time I've ever seen you search for words, Auntie." It was Andrew's turn now to tease his aunt.

Summer got in the act when she said, "Yeah, he must be somebody special because I swear you are glowing, and I haven't seen a smile on your face that broad in a long, long time."

Once they left the restaurant and were in the parking lot, April whispered to her sister, "I didn't want to say anything in front of Drew or Kenneth, but tonight's the night. And girl, it's been a long, long time, for real." It took a few minutes for Summer to catch the drift, but when she did, she chuckled.

Patting her sister on the back, Summer replied, "Listen, love, try not to hurt the man." The sisters bowled over with laughter as Kenneth and Andrew looked at them and continued getting into the car. Summer couldn't stop laughing, but finally she managed to say, "Call me tomorrow and tell me all about it."

April whispered, "Something tells me you'll have plenty to tell me, the way Kenneth has been looking at you tonight. I saw how he couldn't keep his hands off of you. I don't know what I was thinking, talking about the passion's gone, it may have been on hiatus or something, but it looks like it's returned and brought more with it."

"You're too much, go home to your man. And I do want to hear about it tomorrow," Summer said, causing her sister to grin.

April hugged her sister and waved at her nephew and brother-in-law, "Good night, everybody. Kenneth, take your crazy wife home."

"Good night, Auntie, love you." Andrew waved at his aunt from the rear car window.

"I'm so full, all I want is my bed." Andrew yawned as he headed upstairs to his room. Stopping midway, he turned to his mother. "Good night, Mom, and it's good to see you laugh again. I love you."

Summer felt wonderful. She was a good mother. Her son was proof of that. Somewhere along the way, despite not having a role model, she got it right. Turning to her husband to speak, she was immediately quieted by a soft but gentle, passionate kiss on her lips. When the kiss was over she looked into Kenneth's eyes. He responded by sweeping her off her feet and into his arms, carrying her upstairs. She spontaneously put her arms around his neck. "What are you doing?"

"What does it look like I'm doing? I'm carrying my wife to our room." Summer placed her head delicately on his chest and closed her eyes. She enjoyed the feel of his chest and could hear his heart beating. "Do you know how much I love you?" she inquired softly, unsure if he even heard it. It had become their standard love pat.

Once in the bedroom, Kenneth laid her on the bed. In a low whisper, he said, "Yes, I do, and I love you even more." The moonlight filtering into the bedroom highlighted the passion in his eyes. "Come on, let's take a bath together." He was smiling and looking so sexy Summer had to catch her breath. Her hand instinctively went to her throat as she wasn't sure what was going to come out.

"Baby, that sounds nice, I'll get…"

"You just lie there for a minute, I'll get the water started." Removing his shirt slowly, he walked toward the bathroom, all the time Summer's eyes never leaving him. *He's one fine man. Did he always walk like that?* she thought. His walk made her throat dry as a soft moan escaped her throat. No doubt, the seduction was on.

When Kenneth returned from the bathroom, Summer had fallen asleep. He lit a few candles and looked at her in the glow of candlelight. He put his hand over his heart as he felt like the first time he saw her. He was falling in love with her all over again. He wondered how that was possible because he loved her so much already. Smiling, he sat on the bed softly and moved a strand of curly hair from her face. He gently stroked her face and leaned over to kiss her.

Summer lazily opened her eyes as he began unbuttoning her blouse. His kiss was so sweet and seductive she just wanted to savor it. She enjoyed his familiar touch and unique scent as he undressed her, planting small tender kisses along the way. Then he finally led her to the bathroom where he had a bubble bath ready for them. Will Downing's soothing voice and music was barely audible in the room and the glow of candles seduced them both.

Unbuttoning his pants and removing his belt, she could feel the strain of his Calvin Kleins as he was obviously ready for her. She wondered if they would make it to the tub when she finally removed his pants. She wanted him more than ever before as their eyes did the lovers' dance. No words were spoken, no words needed to be spoken as they slowly descended into the tub, hand in hand.

Their lovemaking that night could only be described the next day to her sister as magical.

Chapter 19

When April returned home that night there were policemen and fire trucks blocking the street. She put her car in Park and ran over to one of the policemen she recognized and asked what was going on.

"There was a small fire at your neighbor's. Mrs. Anderson fell asleep while cooking and there was a small kitchen fire."

"What's her condition? Where's her husband?"

The policeman knew April was concerned and gave her the information as efficiently as possible. "She was able to get out but suffered some smoke inhalation. Paramedics said she'd be okay—they just took her to the hospital overnight. We don't know where her husband is, haven't been able to locate him." He hunched his shoulders. "You have any idea where he might be?"

April looked at her watch to note the time. "What hospital did they take her to?"

"Barnes Jewish."

April thanked the officer and drove to the Masonic Lodge where she thought Mr. Anderson would be. He usually attended monthly meetings there and that was the only place he ever went without his wife.

She tried calling Marcus on his cell phone but was unable to reach him and left a message. She was concerned about how Mr. Anderson would react, and didn't want him to come home and find his home damaged and a note from the police about his wife.

When she reached the facility, the meeting was still going on and April scanned the room for Mr. Anderson. She finally spied him up front and quietly made her way to him. He was startled by her appearance and immediately asked, "What's wrong? Did something happen to my wife?" He knew that April would never come for him without having good reason to. He was visibly upset as he begun to shake. His face became flushed and April knew she would have to calm him down.

April smiled and calmly whispered, "She'll be fine. Let's go outside so I can explain." She took his arm and gently ushered him outside where she explained what happened. She then drove him to the hospital to be with his wife. Mr. Anderson was relieved when he finally was able to see his wife and know that she was okay. They constantly thanked April and were not short on hugs or kisses to her forehead. "You treat us better than our kids. We couldn't ask for a better neighbor, friend. Hell, you're like our daughter." Mrs. Anderson's eyes flooded with tears as she thanked April again.

After being at the hospital for some time and making sure that the two were fine, Mr. and Mrs. Anderson insisted that April leave. He and his wife could not spend a night apart. He would spend the night there at the hospital in a bed next to his wife. April had arranged it with the night supervisor. Seeing the two so in love brought a smile and hope to her heart.

"Mr. Anderson, I'll pick you up tomorrow. Just call me at my office when you're ready."

"Thank you so much for looking out for us, April, I don't know what I would have done if I'd come home and heard my wife had been in a fire." Mr. Anderson's eyes moistened slightly and he turned to look at his wife, who was smiling at him. "She's all I got in the world."

April patted his hand and smiled at the couple. "I'll see you both tomorrow. And you should know that there are lots of neighbors who were concerned about you two. I think you should get lots of rest here because when you get home, there will be a flood of visitors. My phone has been ringing all night, I've checked my messages and they are all about you two. I left a voice mail message to update everyone. So I would venture to say that you have others that care about you, as well."

Mr. Anderson couldn't help but give April a smile so full of gratitude her heart melted. Her eyes became misty, too. She turned and left. When she reached the door she gave one more look at the couple and it made her feel worthy to know she was a good friend, neighbor, sister, daughter and aunt. She knew that she could never be bitter. She loved life, people and nature too much. There was a lot to living and she planned to savor it all, with or without a man. She loved all that she did even if it left little time for other things.

Her body and mind were tired as she noted the clock on the wall of the nurses' station. It read one-thirty. She said good night to the nurse on duty and pushed the button for the elevator. She heard the ding of the elevator and slowly began to step inside.

"April." She recognized Marcus's voice and looked up.

"What…" He embraced her and she immediately felt a blanket of comfort envelop her.

"I got your message. I went to your house and waited but when you didn't show up I figured you'd be at the hospital.

One of your police friends told me what hospital they'd taken Mrs. Anderson to. You okay? What about your neighbors, are they okay?" He was studying her intently.

April smiled wearily. "They're fine. I'm fine and so are you. But you should be home in bed."

"You're fine, but you're tired. Always taking care of everybody else. Let me take you home. I am right where I should be, here with you. Sorry it took me so long to get here." She looked at his handsome face and realized she was hopelessly in love for the first time.

Concern etched his face and the comfort of his arms around her made her comply. They walked out into the late night to his car, arm in arm, her head resting on his shoulder. She'd never felt so well cared for. April fell asleep as soon as she got home. Her dreams were about Marcus and his comforting smile and welcoming arms. He'd tucked her into bed, fed her dogs and stroked Midnight. Even the birds chirped for him.

He left her reluctantly in bed alone while he slept on the couch. He would be there when she woke in the morning to take her to work and later to pick up her car. He checked on her during the night to find her sleeping. He couldn't help but stroke her face as she lay sleeping. He watched her for a few minutes and returned to the sofa.

Her sleep was peaceful and the morning found them chatting and making plans for later in the day. "I can't believe you stayed all night with me, that was so thoughtful."

Marcus laughed, "Why? That's what a man does for his woman."

April laughed, "You like calling me that, don't you?"

"Hell, yeah, but you know you're even more than that, right? I just use that to keep from scaring you away. Taking it slow, right?" Marcus took a big gulp of orange juice and finished by saying, "After dropping you off at work, it's home for me. I'll shower, take a quick nap and pick you up for lunch.

We can then pick up your car and the Andersons. Sound okay to you?" Marcus was eating the last forkful of eggs that April had cooked for him.

"Sounds like a good plan to me." She tried hard not to imagine doing this every morning, but her imagination just would not cooperate. She loved it, and judging from the big grin on Marcus's face, so did he.

April had faxed an outline of ideas about the book to Marcus and they'd met for lunch to discuss them. They'd decided to pursue the idea once again. Their time together was always an exchange, they enjoyed sharing ideas and their conversations were lively.

Marcus had gotten them tickets to tour some of the historic homes in the area, which included lunch, and even complimentary wine. The two walked hand in hand during the tour. They enjoyed the tour, but did not limit their conversation to the tour, or the book. They were often mistaken by others as a married couple, which made them smile. They had become very comfortable with each other and enjoyed being together, even if it was not nearly as much as they wanted, or needed. Their time together was special and they made the most of it.

During the drive back to her house, April said, "I think that was the most unique date I've ever been on. It was romantic, fun and enlightening. I've learned so much about this neighborhood since we've been together. I love being with you." She looked over at him to gauge his reaction.

"I love being with you, and I love you." Marcus glanced over while driving, but no return was made by April. He understood, though, and took her hand in his. This was hard for her, but he knew how she felt. That was the necessary element about truly discovering a person mentally before the physical part. He knew how she felt even when she never said a word. He knew about her struggles with her family, herself, and more importantly he knew she loved him even if she had not said it. He looked forward to the day when she would say it to him. He smiled at the thought, and April, who had looked over at him, also smiled.

April was excited about finally getting to spend some extended time with Marcus. It was Saturday and they were going to see *The Lion King*.

The two spent many late nights talking on the phone, giggling and flirting like love-struck teenagers. When time permitted, they met for a quick lunch and seemed reluctant to leave each other but their many obligations kept them both busy. A small emergency at work caused her to get a late start on getting ready, but once she got home she flew through her routine and was ready when Marcus arrived to pick her up.

April had decided on an understated elegant look that suited her. She wore a turquoise and dark blue caftan set. The dress was dark blue with a scroll pattern in shimmering strokes of bronze tones. The dark blue fringed caftan had a hint of the same scroll pattern at the bottom and draped beautifully over her shoulders. She wore bronze sandals with an ornate medallion in the center that contained the same turquoise color as was on the dress. Her look could only be described as stunning.

Marcus stood speechless at the door when she greeted him. "Come on in." April couldn't recall him being speechless before and wasn't sure what to think of it so she inquired, "Is it too much?"

Marcus reached and lightly stroked her face. "You look exquisite. Absolutely exquisite." He continued to stare at her and when he followed her into the living room he noticed the slight flecks of light in her hair. "What did you do to your hair? It's shimmering."

"Oh, just a little secret my sister, the beauty aficionado,

gave me." She laughed jokingly and picked up her purse. She looked around and said, "Well, I guess I'm ready."

Marcus was staring steadfastly and when she looked closely at him she became warm all over. Longing was as clear on his face as his eyes, lips, nose and mouth. He longed for her and she felt it. Her throat became dry and the urge to forgo *The Lion King* dominated her.

"You certainly look handsome," were the only words that seemed to free themselves from her lips. He wore an elegant black silk shirt tucked neatly inside a pair of black pants. The simple ensemble looked elegant on his tall, solidly built frame. April tried not to stare but found it difficult to look away.

"Thank you." Marcus had noticed the change from her usually rich and vibrant voice. He hoped his obvious thoughts of lust were encouraging and not scaring her away. He couldn't help himself. From the moment she'd opened the door all he could think of was them lying in bed with their bodies drenched from love sweat, legs and bodies slightly entangled with each other. It had been so long and he knew April was as much a part of his future as she was his present. He did all he could each time they were together not to move too fast in the relationship. She'd made it clear she wanted to take it slow and now it was slowly driving him crazy. He had fallen in love and was ready to move to the next level with her.

Marcus knew to listen to April and to respect her wishes. He'd never taken the time to get to fully know a woman before they'd let lust overtake them. He'd paid the price because now he couldn't think of one meaningful relationship he'd had with a woman, not even his wife. They'd not taken the proper time to get to know each other and their marriage ended shortly in divorce.

He tried blaming his schedule, which was partly responsible, but the real truth he discovered was his desire for instant gratification. Everything that was ever worth anything to him had taken time. He'd learned that lesson and refused to follow any other pattern so he was going to take his time with April because he wanted them to last.

He'd being seeing April now for months and knew more about her than he knew about any other woman he'd ever dated. They'd taken the time to get to know each other, and he had fallen in love with her. The revelation hit him when he walked in on the thugs that were trying to threaten her. He called a friend who worked as a detective in the police department and reported the incident. His friend had assured him that they'd keep a close eye on the individuals in question. The surveillance paid off and it didn't take long for the thugs to get caught during some illegal activities.

He tried to think about his life without April and his heart sank. He knew when he held her in his arms that night that he'd fallen in love with her. His only concern was when and how he would tell her and what her feelings were for Donald.

Looking at her now only made his heart and other parts of his anatomy long for her more. She looked so alluring and he swore her smile was driving him to distraction. He thought back to once when she had planted one of her incendiary kisses on his lips and chest, and found out just how aroused he was. "You know I'm not ready for that now," she barely mumbled in a low voice. He was not fooled; she was as ready as he was.

"Yeah, baby I hear you, but that doesn't make me want you any less," was all he could say and the two ended up enjoying their evening, but beads of sweat were popping off each of them the entire time. Both were forced to retire to a cold shower, and lots of thinking about what could have been, at their respective homes.

He wanted to start planning for his vacation and intended to ask April to join him on a trip. He had no idea where they would go, but as long as they were together it really didn't matter. The thought of her on a beach with him intrigued him. He planned to ask her as soon as the opportunity presented itself.

After the musical the two heaped praise on the cast, the costumes and everything else they could think of as they left the fabulous Fox Theatre on the way to the car. Marcus had made reservations at a nearby Cajun restaurant. The drive was short and they were seated within minutes of their arrival.

"This place is wonderful." April smiled at Marcus and he returned the smile.

"You mentioned that you wanted to come here." He picked up his menu to avoid looking at April. He thought if she looked at him again with her sweet brown eyes that he wouldn't be able to control himself. The menu provided a distraction and he began reading the choices. Everything sounded delicious to him including her, but as he snuck a peep at her he couldn't imagine anything being more delicious than her.

April crossed her legs and tried to remember the conversation they'd had when she mentioned wanting to try the restaurant. *Damn, this man so gets me*, she thought to herself. She liked that about Marcus—he listened and he wasn't ostentatious in his pursuit of her. He understood she liked understated things, not big productions. He would never send her a roomful of roses.

He had sent her one rare and exquisite flower two weeks earlier. She'd barely gotten home when the doorbell rang. The delivery man stood with a grin on his face as wide as the Grand Canyon when he announced the delivery. "You must really be special. I've never even heard of a white lotus before, had to have it shipped in." He handed her the flower adorned in a beautiful container, with directions on its care. Marcus had attached a note that simply read, "One can't find such rare beauty in quantities. That's why it's important to nourish and love it. Marcus."

She smiled at the remembrance and looked over her menu

at Marcus. He genuinely understood her pursuit of a safer neighborhood. He didn't challenge her on her interest, instead he joined her, encouraged her. They had many shared interests and she felt comfortable with him. He understood her better than any man ever could, she thought. Looking over at him, all she could think about was being in his arms and feeling his lips on hers. She ached to have his body pressed close to hers. The overwhelming desire to feel his heart beat against her bosom as she gave herself completely to him caused her to look at him longingly.

"Have you decided yet?" he asked.

"Yes." Her voice teased as she stared at him in a covetous gaze. Marcus knew immediately she wasn't talking about food and he put his menu on the table.

"What have you decided?" His voice mirrored her teasing.

"That it's time," she uttered.

Marcus looked at her with a sense of anticipation and asked, "Time for what?"

"Time for us to be together." She said it with righteous conviction and Marcus knew it was time for them to consummate the relationship.

"Can we get dinner to go?" Marcus asked, as he had to have her at that moment or his body would surely combust. He hoped she agreed that dinner could wait.

"I think we could do that." She smiled coyly.

"Your place or mine?" The timbre of his voice raced down her spine and back up again, her legs automatically uncrossed. He was getting to her and she was about two months past ready for this night.

"Yours," she replied with a hoarseness that surprised her. Marcus stood up and walked around to April's chair and pulled it out for her. She stood and the two went to the front where they ordered their food to go.

April hadn't been to his home before and was amazed when

she stepped into the foyer. She'd spent a lot of time and money rehabbing her house because that was what South siders were known to do. It was like a hobby to them; they spent the weekend working on their old, historic homes to preserve the neighborhood and increase property values. The old homes in the area had "good bones," meaning they were well-built and could be purchased at a moderate price, but sold at much higher prices once rehabbed. But Marcus's home looked like a palace. It was brightly lit and the man had exquisite taste, she thought as she looked at the Tiffany lamps that graced the living room tables.

"Your home is magnificent," she said in a breathless voice that sounded more like an invitation than an declarative sentence.

"Thanks, but let me show you around. I'll put this food in the kitchen."

She followed him into the kitchen and was amazed at its huge size. It looked like something from a magazine. It was well-equipped and very functional, designed in exquisite taste.

The two-story home had previously been a two-family flat, he explained to April. The house had undergone extensive renovations for almost four years and he was proud of the results. Much of the original wood and tile had been restored and he'd taken time to research the period in which the house was built. He had found light fixtures, doors, handles and knobs that were true to the period and had had them installed to give the home a period look.

When he showed her the den she was most impressed. It had floor-to-ceiling bookcases filled with books that lined one complete wall. She looked at him. "You said you love to read, but you have thousands of books here. Have you read them all?"

He proudly smiled. "Yes, I have. I don't put them on the shelf until I've read them. That way if people want to borrow one, or ask for a recommendation, I've already read it." Nothing pretentious about him, she thought.

She'd always loved a man who took time to read. She

walked over and fingered the books. "You have any favorites?" Her smile and her eyes weakened him, causing him to draw a blank.

"Yes, I do, but I can't remember them now while I'm looking at you. Sorry, but you distract me." April had to laugh at the coincidence of his thinking she was a distraction. He'd been a distraction for her since the first time their eyes met at the fund-raiser. The two walked hand in hand from the den into the foyer where she admired the ornate wood.

"That's what I love about our neighborhood. Each house has so much potential. From the outside you think it's just another old brick house. But when you go inside they're all so special and beautiful. They don't build new houses like this." April ran her hand across the mahogany wood of the staircase. "So much character."

Marcus smiled and softly murmured, "They sure don't." He was standing behind April with his arms around her waist. He removed one hand from her waist and pushed her hair up. He gently kissed the back of her neck. She let out a little whimper as his tongue slowly traveled to the side of her neck. He walked around to face her and teased her lips with more tender kisses. He kissed her face and the corners of her mouth. He held her face gently with his hands. April wanted him badly and she could feel that warm pool forming between her legs again.

He removed her caftan, allowing it fall to the floor as he kissed her bare shoulders. His kisses trailed down to her cleavage where he took in the slight scent of jasmine and kissed the swell of her breast. She gasped again from excitement. It has been too long, April thought.

Marcus prayed that he would be able to control himself now that she had acquiesced to their making love. He'd been wanting and waiting for what seemed like a lifetime even though in actuality it had only been a few months.

April's hands began to travel the length of his body and she pulled him closer to her. She felt unashamed as she grabbed his bottom and brought her pelvis to meet him. She could feel his excitement, and his moist breath on her breast caused her to moan louder this time.

Marcus took a remote from the table and turned on the CD player. To their amazement the song "At Last" by Etta James filled the room. Marcus smiled at her and she returned the smile. It was an appropriate song for them and continued to ignite the passion they both felt.

Marcus swept her up and carried her to the bedroom. The room was dark except for a sparse flicker of moonlight that shone through the half-closed blinds. The speakers in the bedroom surprised her as the song replayed. "At last, my love has come along. My lonely days are over. And life is like a song." She could feel his sense of urgency as he gently laid her on the bed and began exploring her body with his hands and tongue. His touch was certain but gentle, urgent but soothing.

Her mind floated as he slowly caressed her, exploring her body with his. He unhooked her lavender bra and slid the straps down while he rained kisses on her shoulder and arm. She couldn't help but moan in delight. His touch and lips sent her into overdrive as her breathing became deep.

She closed her eyes and enjoyed how he slowly removed her clothes. Finally, the only article of clothing left were her lavender lace panties. He fingered the lace softly and traced the outline along her skin. She let out a moan and arched her back. He allowed his tongue to trace the outline until she couldn't stand it any longer. His mouth seemed to burn every part of her body that it touched, igniting her with passion.

She pulled him to her and claimed his mouth with her fiery tongue. She traced her fingers along his chest and slowly caressed his left nipple. A soft moan escaped his mouth and he managed to slowly pull away. He removed her panties and pulled her to him. She was completely nude and fully aroused. He pulled away again and stood back, admiring her perfectly feminine body. She allowed him to take in her beauty for a time and then she began removing his clothes. She unbuttoned the silk shirt and it fell to the floor. His fully exposed chest caused her head to swim with passion. He had just the right amount of hair and a trim waist that invited her to remove his belt. She slowly unzipped his pants and caressed him. She could feel the pulsated heat from his male member. Like everything about him, it was more than she could have hoped for.

He was more than enough man for her, she thought with delight. She finally removed the pants. She set her sights on the slight patch of hair just below the top of his briefs. Her mouth was dry, but the rest of her was drenched. They embraced again and this time neither was willing to let the other go. They allowed their bodies to feel the other's until they were writhing in passion. April pulled away and removed his briefs. The sight of his naked body sent uncontrollable waves of desire throughout her body. She enjoyed looking at the muscular arms that had brought her so much comfort before. They now brought her passion as they held her waist, as they brought her to him. Everything about his body caused her to heat up.

His muscular thighs were perfect, and she wanted to feel them on top of hers. She wanted to feel them beneath hers. She just wanted to feel them. The two lay in bed nude while they stroked, tickled, teased, soothed, savored, licked and discovered each other's bodies.

Their bodies danced a duet that seemed as natural as breathing. Marcus reached over into the nightstand and took out a condom. Without a word she took the package from him and opened it. Gently she slid the condom on his full erection, causing him to moan in delight. "I've found a dream that I could speak to, a dream I could call my own," Etta continued, and April found herself melting. Her hands softly beckoned him. She lay back and let him take them to Nirvana.

Marcus had shared her many passions, they had laughed together, he listened and held her at the right times. He had become her confidant, someone she shared secrets with and now, she shared her body. When he slowed entered her body for the first time, April moaned his name. She closed her eyes and wrapped her legs around him. He thrust slowly at first, and with each thrust, she moaned louder. He could no longer control himself and his thrust became deeper and faster. Her pelvis rose to meet his and the demanding rhythm caused her to erupt in a river of passion as she called out his name. He whispered her name and kissed her again. He watched as she closed her eyes again and felt the flutter of her body as it submitted to passion. He kissed her closed eyelids and then her lips. He wrapped his arms around her and allowed himself to submit as she had done.

Drenched in sweat, they became one that night and they both knew that this was truly their time. It was beyond what either had hoped it would be. They couldn't get enough of each other.

Afterwards, they showered together, which allowed them to explore each other's bodies more. They barely made it out of the shower before they were locked in an embrace, followed by more lovemaking.

Later, as they drifted off to a fulfilled, deep sleep, Etta could still be heard singing soulfully, "For you are mine at last." With their bodies entwined, meshed into one, and contented smiles on their faces was how they slept the entire night.

Sunday morning April awoke to find Marcus staring at her while she lay in his arms.

"Good morning," she said once her eyes focused. Her body was stiff and she felt the effects from the night before. It had been too long, but well worth the wait, she thought. To say she was satisfied was an understatement—she had never experienced such a passionate night. Her body ached in a good way.

"Good morning, beautiful." It was melodious to hear his voice first thing in the morning, she thought, and when she looked at his face her heart sang, *at last*. A smile automatically graced her face. She still remembered the tender kisses. His arms around her felt magnificent and she nestled in closer.

"I find it hard to believe you think I'm beautiful before I've had a chance to wash my face or brush my teeth," she said sheepishly.

Marcus brushed her hair from her face and said, "I absolutely find you beautiful this morning and tomorrow morning, the next morning and the one after that if you'll have me."

April had to think for a minute before asking him, "What are you saying?"

"What I'm saying, evidently not as eloquently as I should, is that I'm madly in love with you and want to spend every morning from here on out waking up with you in my arms. I want to marry you." Marcus's directness startled her momentarily, causing her to rise up on both her elbows.

"Are you serious?"

"Very."

Moments passed before either said a word but their eyes remained locked in a quiet conversation. April finally admitted, "I love you, too, very much, and want to marry you. I want my days and nights filled with you. I can't tell you what you've meant to me these past months. You have been more than a friend, lover, more than I ever thought I would find. I have loved you without even realizing it because you make it so easy to love you." She leaned over and met his eager lips with hers.

"I thought you wanted to take things slow. Are you sure this is what you want? You want to make the kind of commitment a marriage requires?" Marcus didn't want to pressure her but he prayed she was ready and he had to ask her the question that made his heart stop. He wanted them to start their life together.

"I did want to take it slow and, and… and we did. Well, sometimes love just happens. You can't deny your heart no matter how you try. Besides, it's been long enough. It was torturous not being in your arms." April looked into his eyes for agreement.

He had to smile because he felt the same way. "Will you make time for us?" he asked and planted a tiny kiss on her neck.

The feel of the kiss lingered and April enjoyed it before replying, "Yes."

"Promise?"

"Promise," she returned, and they sealed their vow with another kiss filled with promise.

Marcus took her left hand. She was amazed when she looked at it. There was a large, sparkling diamond on it.

"Oh my goodness, how did you manage this? You wonderful, wonderful man! I can't wait to tell Summer."

Marcus smiled and confessed, "She already knows, she helped me pick it out and told me your size."

April reached over and pulled him to her. She held him tightly for several minutes. Their lips met and the two made love again. It was the most precious time of either of their lives, well worth the wait, they both agreed.

The two spent the day talking, planning, making love, talking and making love. It was indeed their time, a time both shared enthusiastically.

Her tall, handsome, wonderful distraction had somehow become a permanent fixture in her heart. The two each swore to give the other support and to always find time for one another, even with their busy schedules.

one. The therapy sessions with Carmen were helping her work through some of the childhood hurts that she'd unconsciously clung to. She hated to admit it, but April was right, as usual. The ringing phone interrupted her thoughts.

Kenneth had barely made it to his office when his phone rang. He knew it was the call he was waiting for. After hearing the news he sat and tried to absorb all that he could and wondered what was the best way to fit all the pieces together for his wife. He thought about calling April and decided against it. Maybe he would go and see the man himself, first, or maybe he'd call and explain who he was. There were too many maybes, so he decided the element of surprise would be best. He had to be certain it was the man he was looking for.

At three o'clock, Kenneth shut off his computer and left work early. He was on a mission that would change the dynamics of his and Summer's relationship. He wasn't sure if it was something he should do, but his wife needed some closure on the issue and it was up to him to find out if it was possible.

Summer was still very guarded anytime issues about her father came up. Despite her unwillingness or inability to discuss her father, Kenneth knew deep down her many unanswered questions about her father were the source of much unhappiness. If he could provide her with some kind of answers, even if they weren't the ones she wanted, at least she would know something about why their father left.

April had provided him with very little information to help him locate their father. They had spoken about it several times and agreed it would help both April and Summer to understand why their father left them. April had encouraged him but he hadn't told her about finding the most current address for their father. He wanted to be sure.

After the thirty-minute drive, Kenneth sat across the street from a ranch-style white frame house with a modest front yard that boasted yellow and red roses, a mixture of yellow and red carnations and several green shrubs. The house looked well maintained, and the yard showed the pride of the owners. Two chairs, a small table and potted plants sat on the front porch, while a welcome mat graced the front door entrance.

Kenneth looked at the address on the left of the front door and compared it to the address on the sheet of paper he held in his hand. He hadn't noticed that his hands were shaking until that moment. Looking to his right, he gathered the papers that he had copied from the library, social security office, Recorder of Deeds and various other places that held public records. Taking a deep breath he gathered his thoughts and opened the car door.

He straightened his tie and did a quick inventory of his clothes before crossing the street. "I look like an insurance salesman," he mumbled to himself. He removed the tie, put it in his pocket. He then rolled his neck to relieve the stiffness in it before knocking on the door to meet his father-in-law for the first time.

"Hello, sir, are you Mr. Bernie Marshall Nelson?"

"Yes, sir, I am. What can I do for you?" This man was obviously proud, not at all the withered old man Kenneth was expecting. The years had been good to him. He wore pressed khaki slacks, with a short-sleeve knit shirt tucked neatly in the waist. His face appeared more youthful than expected and the silver frames of his glasses seemed to accent his gray hair. The man looked like he'd been well taken care of and was in good shape. He seemed mature without looking old, Kenneth thought.

"Mr. Nelson, my name is Kenneth Hughes and I'd like to talk to you about a rather personal and sensitive situation."

"You ain't selling no insurance are you, boy, trying to trick me?" Peering at him though the screen door, he smiled and

Kenneth instantly knew this man in fact was his father-in-law—he had his wife's smile, or she had his smile. The thought caused him to return the smile.

"No sir, but I do believe we have a mutual interest in a young woman named Summer." He didn't have to wait long for a reaction as Mr. Nelson's eyes lit up and he grabbed his chest.

"Have mercy, what did you say? Who are you? What do you know about my baby?" His eyes had begun to mist as he spoke rapidly, gesturing with his hands.

"Please, Mr. Nelson, just calm down. I'm Summer's husband and I've come here without her knowledge or consent. I wanted to be sure you were in fact her father."

Mr. Nelson opened the door. "Come in, please, come in, what did you say your name was, boy?"

"Kenneth Hughes, sir. I'm married to your daughter and I thought it was about time we met." He extended his hand, which was enthusiastically taken by the older man as they shook hands, which ended up in a hug.

"I can't believe what you're telling me. How did you find me? I searched all over the city of St. Louis for my family for years, and couldn't find them." The mist was now tears as the older man welcomed Kenneth into his home and offered him a seat. "Please, sit down and tell me everything. I can't believe my daughters are still here, I thought their mother had taken them and run away to Lord knows where. After the last time I found them, she told me I would never see them again, and I thought until this day that I would go to my grave thinking I'd never see my daughters again." Kenneth thought about Autumn, and didn't have the heart to tell the man that he wouldn't see her again.

"Can I get you a cup of coffee or something, Mr. Hughes?"

"Oh, no sir."

"Well, I need something, I'll be right back. You sure you don't need any water or anything?"

"No sir, I'm fine."

Kenneth waited patiently for his father-in-law to return and began telling him the story of how his search began.

"Well, sir, my wife and sister-in-laws are the reason I'm here. They have struggled for years trying to figure out why you left them. Summer has had a particularly difficult year and after years of not knowing why you left them, I thought it might help them to know something about their father and why he left."

Kenneth began to wish he'd taken advantage of the man's offer and had accepted a glass of water. His mouth suddenly felt dry and his throat felt like it was about to close. The older man put his head down and cradled it in his hands while resting his elbows on his knees. It was obviously too much for him.

"Can I get something for you, Mr. Nelson?"

"No, son, I think you've brought me the greatest gift I'll ever receive. Let me just thank God for this blessing." The man began to pray and thank God for sending his children back to him. He prayed out loud, with his eyes shut tightly and his head bowed as Kenneth sat with his head bowed and listened.

When he was done, Mr. Nelson opened his eyes and asked Kenneth if he had any grandchildren. Kenneth proudly told him about Andrew, but stopped short of discussing his sister-in-laws. He asked Mr. Nelson to be patient, that all of it would be told, but he needed to know what had caused him to leave his family in the first place.

"Sir, I don't mean any disrespect, but my wife has suffered many years thinking that you just up and left without any thought or consideration to them. That you didn't love them enough to even want to try to see them again."

Removing his glasses and taking a deep sigh, it was obvious that the man was in pain himself. "Well, the truth be told, son, I didn't just walk away from my daughters. My ex-wife was more than a handful, she could be downright evil once you got on her wrong side. Somewhere along the line, that's just what I did, got on her wrong side. Don't even ask me what it was, but she made it impossible for me to live with her. She cut up my clothes and set them out at the curb like garbage. She wouldn't talk to me and wouldn't let me see the girls. Threatened to have me locked up if I tried seeing them at school."

His eyes began to tear and he removed a handkerchief from his pocket. Dabbing at them lightly, he continued. "She picked up and moved, didn't tell anybody, and finally when I found her, she moved again. Every time I tried to see my girls, she threatened me with violence and moved on. The last time she had me arrested, claimed I was threatening her. I spent two days in jail for something I didn't do. She filed a restraining order against me." Mr. Nelson sat silently for a few minutes as though remembering the time. "Mildred was a very cold woman, she was about as mean as a woman could be. She wasn't like that when we first met. She was good at hiding things, but when she set her mind to something, there was no way you could change it. I couldn't find them after that."

Dabbing at his eyes again, he took a sip of water. "Only she knows what she told them. Black folks in St. Louis weren't spread out like they are now, and there were only a few neighborhoods we occupied back then and I searched for them. I never found them, thought they probably moved out of the area."

Although he'd seemed to have drifted off mentally, he returned quickly with his eyes bright and alert. "That didn't mean I just gave up, or didn't want them anymore. My resources were limited. I just prayed that they were all right and that they knew I still loved them. Time went on and I met someone else, the lady I'm married to now. I filed for a divorce, and since I didn't know where my wife lived, they just ran some kind of ad in the paper, and after a few months it was over. Next thing I knew, folks was saying I ran off from my wife and kids for some other woman. I didn't run off to be with another woman. Mildred *put* me out, and anybody that knows that woman knows out is *out*. I didn't meet my current wife until years later."

Kenneth lowered his head and tried to think what it would take for his wife to understand what it was like to be a black man all those years ago, not having the education or legal means to fight for the right to see your children. He believed Mr. Nelson could have tried harder, but maybe the man did all he knew how to do. He wasn't there to judge, but to learn and try to understand. His wife wouldn't be easily convinced, but somehow he'd have to make her visit her father. He'd have to make her understand, or at least hear Mr. Nelson's side of the story.

"Mr. Nelson, I do believe you and your daughters should meet, but I'm not the one to say that this will happen. I will try to do all I can to get all of you together. She doesn't think she needs a father at this point in time, nor does she admit to wanting one."

Kenneth could see the hurt in the old man's eyes and his slumped shoulders as he continued, "But either way, I would like for you to meet our son and perhaps be a part of his life if you want."

Kenneth felt it was all he could offer the man, and he'd have to fight his wife tooth and nail for that. Although nothing like her mother, Summer could be stubborn, and if so inclined, unmovable. When she took a stand, it was a stand till the end. It could be an endearing quality, but every once in a while it could be aggravating. He'd always admired her strength, and if it occasionally made him angry, that was okay, at least he always knew where she stood. But Summer could never be cruel, she'd never deny their son the right to meet and spend time with his grandfather. She was as loving as she was tough.

"Whatever you can do, Mr. Hughes, would be appreciated. I felt I had grandchildren, but always thought I had more than one. Don't April or Autumn have any children?"

Kenneth stood quickly, ready to leave, handing his father-in-law a business card, and a gentleman's handshake. "No, sir, they don't, but that's best left for another time. My home telephone number is on the back, along with my cell number, and sir, please call me Kenneth. I'll be in touch, I have your number. Thanks for your time, Mr. Nelson. Hopefully we can get you reunited with your family."

His mind had begun to ask questions he hadn't allowed it to ask prior to knocking on the door of the modest white-frame house. But he knew if he'd allowed his mind to ask these questions prior to coming, he may not have had the courage to come. It was always easier to take the road of least resistance, he could have kept his newfound knowledge to himself. But something inside of him wouldn't allow that to happen; love for his wife, and her finally knowing the truth. It wouldn't be any easy task, but it was a necessary task.

April had sought his help in finding their father. She had long suspected that their father hadn't just left but could never convince Summer of it. April and Kenneth knew it was time to mend Summer's broken heart in a way that neither of them could. Kenneth thought of the best way to tell his wife the news during his drive home. He thought about calling April to have her join them for dinner but nixed the idea, thinking maybe she and Marcus had plans. It was a situation he was going to discuss with his wife first.

* * *

April set out early in the morning, preparing to spend the day in Columbia, Missouri, at her graduate school alma mater. She had been invited as a guest speaker and presenter for a scholarship to a worthy student. It was indeed an exciting honor for her to have been asked and she had accepted it with enthusiasm. The day was full of activities, starting with a tour of the Veterinary Medical Teaching Hospital, which included a small-animal clinic. The school now had extensive specialty services for small animals which included oncology, cardiology, nutrition, referral medicine and community practice along with various other services for the care of small animals.

Growing up in the inner-city, April had always been exposed to smaller animals, so it was a natural specialty for her to pursue. She knew from her experience that pet owners wanted to give their pets the same quality of health care they themselves received. After all, most people felt that their pets were a part of their family. The faculty greeted April with open arms, despite the fact that only a few had been on faculty during her graduate years.

The campus had changed over the years, but memories of her studies at the university were fun. She'd worked hard, and struggled, but it was the first time she had lived totally on her own. Looking back, she thought about how serious she was about studying and pursuing her advanced degree. April swelled with pride at the thoughts. Although just a few hours from St. Louis, she'd felt independent for the first time, and didn't have anyone to lean on, not even her sisters. Now, she had been invited back to offer encouragement and a scholarship to a deserving student. She reminisced on how she felt the day she was notified of her scholarship.

Her speech and presentation were a success. The director of the Veterinary Medical Teaching Hospital approached her about a faculty position. Even though she juggled enough with her practice and wouldn't consider the position, it was an honor being approached and asked.

At the end of the day when she got to her car she gripped the steering wheel and looked in her rearview mirror. "Damn, I've been a nervous wreck all day, what's wrong with me?" She realized then that it wasn't the revisit to the campus, or the memories that had her nervous. She had completed her day on campus, but she couldn't explain the uneasy feeling which plagued her, like bad news was coming her way.

April felt she had a sixth sense for such things. She'd taught herself long ago to listen to that voice which warned of bad news. It took years, but she finally learned to listen and to calm herself for the anticipated bad news. She'd felt it the day her sister died. She'd felt it the day her father left. She always felt it when her mother was around.

She drove home slowly on autopilot, not remembering when she got on or off the highway. She sat tensely inside her car, looking at her house. Never having had the feeling before when coming home, she prayed that her pets were all fine. She was relived once inside when they all ran to greet her, even Midnight. The birds were fine. She spent time with all of them and finally she kicked off her shoes and walked into her office.

She began playing one of three messages she had on her answering machine. "Hey, baby, welcome home, call me when you can." Marcus's voice sounded from the recorder when she played her messages. A brief smile graced her face and the nervous feeling subsided temporarily. She played the next message and it was from the private investigator she had hired to find her aunt and uncle. "Ms. Nelson, I have an update for you. Call me…." He left his cell phone number and his office number. April jotted them both down and sat back in the chair waiting for the third message. It was a hang-up and she finally exhaled the breath she was holding. She looked at the phone number from the private investigator. "An update…" sounded rather official and she dared to hope it was something positive. His agency had come highly recommended. April looked at her watch and decided the call could wait.

Her mind then wondered again. If something was wrong with Summer, she would have been called, so she dismissed that idea. She decided a walk in the park with her dogs would help, so she went to her bedroom, took a quick shower and put on a warm-up suit. She tied her hair back and grabbed the leashes. When the dogs heard the noise the leashes made, they all came running. She laughed and that relaxed her; it was a successful, but temporary diversion.

The sky was in that in-between stage, turning into night, but not quite dark when she pulled up in front of her house after spending time in the park. Marcus should be home by now, she thought, and she was planning to call him as soon as she got inside.

His voice mail picked up, and she called his cell phone. It automatically went to voice mail. Usually that indicated he was unable to answer the phone. "Probably with a patient," she said out loud, and began making preparations for dinner. She'd make enough for both of them and the thought caused her to become more relaxed, but she still couldn't shake the feeling that something was about to happen.

She walked over to the kitchen phone and called her sister. She sat casually in the chair and laughed when Summer answered cheerily, "Hey, you, how'd it go today?"

April laughed because she knew her sister looked at caller ID before ever answering a call. "Excellent, I enjoyed being back on campus. Had an opportunity to talk to the recipient of the scholarship, and she's wonderful. How about you, how are things on your end?"

"Couldn't be better. I'm taking some of my vacation time. I'm off for the next two weeks, and still have plenty of time left. We scheduled a visit to Morehouse to tour the campus, so we're all excited about that. Everything's good." She could hear contentment in Summer's voice.

"Where are the boys?"

"Out back, playing basketball," Summer chuckled. "Can't you hear them? I've got the window and patio door open. They are so loud."

"I just called to check in. I'm tired, I'll talk to you tomorrow."

April thought she could dismiss the ominous feeling that had plagued her all day, but after hanging up with her sister, it remained.

She picked up the phone to call her mother. The phone rang and rang, until a man answered. "Who is this?" she demanded immediately.

"This is Officer Johnson of the St. Louis Police Department." April jolted from her chair, almost knocking it backward. Her dogs came running, and she calmed herself.

"This is her daughter, Dr. April Nelson. Has something happened to my mother?" She rarely used her title, but knew she could get more information and cooperation from the officer if she did.

Officer Johnson knew Dr. April Nelson. While he was not in her precinct, her reputation was well-known. He'd met her at several award dinners, and wasted no time documenting who she was. "Mrs. Nelson is being taken to Barnes Jewish Hospital. We don't know what her condition is yet." He gave April his badge number and took her telephone number for his report.

"Is she conscious?"

"Yes, she is. She should be there in about ten minutes."

Her first concern being her mother's condition, and her second being Summer's condition when she heard the news, she thought it best to talk to Kenneth to make sure he and Drew were there for Summer.

April used her cell phone to call Kenneth's cell phone, knowing that Summer would probably answer their house phone. Kenneth's voice mail picked up, as she thought it would, and she left him a message. He was to call her on her cell, it was an emergency. Determined to be at the hospital when the ambulance arrived, she grabbed her keys and purse and left.

She had just parked her car at the hospital when her cell phone rang. "What's wrong?" Kenneth wasted no time. He knew his sister-in-law, and if she said it was emergency, something was definitely wrong.

"They just brought Mother to Barnes Jewish, I don't know what her condition is, but you guys need to get here pronto."

"We'll be there in a few minutes." He was slightly out of breath, but he explained to his son what had happened. They went through the garage door to avoid Summer, and he had Andrew follow him to his home office, where he quickly wrote a note and said, "Call this number and say just what I have written, I'll explain later."

Kenneth went to the kitchen where Summer was taking food from the oven. He waited until she'd finished and he walked over, turned her around and brought her to him. He released her and then said, "Summer, your mother has been rushed to the hospital. April just called me. She doesn't know her condition yet, but we need to leave now."

Summer wasn't sure what to think or do; she looked up at her husband and the tears began.

He dabbed at the tears with his hand and then slowly walked over to the sink, got a glass of water, and returned to Summer. "Here, drink this."

While drinking, she stared at him. She grabbed his hand and kissed it. "I love you so much."

"And I love you more." The sound of his voice calmed her. "Let's go to the hospital."

Summer turned around, looking for her son. "What about Drew?"

"He knows, we'll talk to him later."

The sounds and smell of the hospital made Summer immediately nauseous. All her experiences with hospitals had been unpleasant ones. She'd gone to a hospital to view her sister's body. She remembered how she and April clung to each other afterwards, while people walked around and continued their activities as though nothing had happened. It was like Autumn had never existed in the world. Summer would never forget April's words. "I don't know how the world just keeps on going without mourning for a lovely young woman killed at the hands of man who claimed to have loved her." She felt no comfort in going to a hospital.

Kenneth took her by the hand as they headed for the front desk where he identified them and inquired about his mother-in-law. The stern nurse, in clinical, typical hospital format directed them to the waiting area where the doctor would come to discuss their mother's condition shortly. That was another thing about hospitals; how they made you sit and wait for wretched news, Summer thought.

April saw them coming and immediately leaped from her chair. "Has the doctor been in yet?" Summer asked.

"No, not yet. She was conscious, though. I saw her for a few minutes when they transported her to the room. She knew who I was, which is a good sign."

"How do you know that?"

"I saw a glimpse of recognition in her eyes. She definitely knew who I was."

April looked at Summer and wanted to burst into tears. Her

sister had been through so much the past year. Her appearance showed it; she'd lost at least ten pounds from her slender frame. April wrapped her arm around her sister. "It's all going to be all right." Summer smiled weakly at her sister, and found some comfort in her words and touch.

They all made their way to chairs in the waiting room and sat down heavily, knowing the stay would be long.

The trio sat and waited thirty minutes for the doctor before Kenneth announced, "I'm going to go find out what's taking him so long. You two going to be all right?"

They both replied, "Yes." Then they looked at each other and smiled as if little girls again, holding hands. Kenneth smiled briefly and left in pursuit of the doctor. He knew his wife was in good hands with April.

Sitting quietly in the room, the two heard footsteps and sat up attentively. Drew walked into the room. "Where's Dad?"

"He went to find the doctor. What are you doing here? I thought you were going to stay home until we called you."

"Uh…no. Dad wanted me to do something before I came here." The two sisters looked from Drew to each other.

"What?" Once again as if on cue, and each let out a slight chuckle as they looked at each other again. They'd always been so close it was scary. They knew when the other was in pain, needed help, was afraid or needed to be just held.

"I think you two need to sit down, I'll let Dad tell you about it." Before he could continue, they heard more footsteps and conversation. They both walked to the doorway and looked down the hall to see Kenneth walking with an older man and a young woman. They each looked at each other and turned back to the trio.

As they got closer, April murmured, "Oh, my God, oh, my God. It's Daddy." She walked rapidly to the older man and hugged him with all her might. Kenneth was pleased to see her reaction, but watched as Summer stood completely still in the doorway.

April finally loosened up her hug. "Daddy, it's you, it's really you. I knew you were still alive. I felt it." She hadn't looked at the young woman or Kenneth. "My God, how did he find you...how, who..."

Kenneth took over then. "Let's all go to the waiting area, I'll explain." He looked cautiously at his wife as she opened her mouth to speak, but no words came out. She looked to her father and the young woman who was with him and instantly knew who she was. Her resemblance to Autumn was remarkable.

She felt her heart beating rapidly in her chest. Quietly they all took seats in the waiting room, all eyes on Kenneth, waiting for an explanation.

"Yes, April, it's your father." Pointing to the young woman, he continued, "And this is your half-sister, June."

April immediately said, "Daddy, you're the one who named us! I always thought it was Mama who gave us our names." She looked over at Summer, who was perfectly still and quiet.

The room became so quiet a mouse crying on cotton would have made more noise. They all turned their attention away from Mr. Nelson and looked at the sister, whose eerie resemblance to Autumn amazed yet endeared them.

"No, sweet daughter, I named all three of you." Looking over at June, he said, "I mean, all four of you."

Kenneth began telling the story about his and April's quest to find their father. He told them how he'd gone to see Mr. Nelson, and then later June called him and introduced herself. His story was compelling as the group listened. He was near the end of telling about his research and how he actually found their father when the doctor entered the waiting room.

The group all stood up at once as if cued and looked at the

doctor. They waited for the news on Mildred's condition with held breaths.

"Mrs. Nelson suffered a mild heart attack which has left her weak. She has done some damage to her liver and kidneys with alcohol, but for now she is stabilized. Maybe you two can talk her into taking better care of herself. We are still running tests, so we don't know the full extent of the damage." He scratched his head. "She's quite feisty. Her recovery will be slow depending on the extent of the damage and how well she takes care of herself." He looked at the group and for the first time since coming into the room released what appeared to be a tiny smile. He looked directly at the two sisters and said, "Summer and April, your mother's asking for you." Mildred evidently had described and asked for them, which put their minds somewhat at ease.

They all knew the doctor was being nice by calling her "feisty." Even if she was in a weakened state they knew Mildred could still raise plenty of hell with whoever. It was silently acknowledged that Mildred had probably behaved rather caustically, as it was in her character to do so.

Kenneth shook the doctor's hand and thanked him. You could almost hear the collective deep breath the group took, as if they'd all been holding their breath since the doctor had entered the room.

Summer took her father's hand. "It's good to see you, Daddy. It's going to take me some time. I have lots of questions, but right now I want to see my mother."

Mr. Nelson gently nodded and kissed his daughter's hand which brought so much joy to her heart she felt as though it would burst.

She knew from the tender way he held her hand that whatever happened between her mother and father all those years ago had nothing to do with her. She knew her father loved her and had always loved her. She felt it in his touch, saw it in his eyes and felt it in her heart. April and Summer hugged their father together, a hug filled with love and understanding.

Once they stood apart both Summer and April hugged June with the same kind of love and understanding. The three began smiling and the others stood by and allowed them their time. Once they'd gathered their composure, Summer acknowledged, "We've got a lot of catching up and getting to know each other to do."

She looked at Drew, who had remained uncharacteristically quiet the entire time, and walked over and kissed him on the cheek. "Looks like you've got another aunt, son." Andrew smiled broadly because it felt good to see his mother with so much joy on her face rather than the anguish he'd seen for the past year.

It wasn't until the two had left that Mr. Nelson gathered himself enough to realize his third daughter wasn't there and asked, "Kenneth, where's Autumn?" It would be difficult for Kenneth to break the news to Mr. Nelson, but he believed his wife and sister-in-law had enough on their hearts without having to tell their father his daughter was deceased. He wasn't sure what Summer's condition would be once she had spent time with her mother. So he delicately took Mr. Nelson by the arm, searching in his heart for the words that could possibly relay to him what had happened to Autumn.

April and Summer entered their mother's room quietly, unsure if she was awake until they heard her weak voice. "Damn, I could've died before you two got here, what took y'all so long? I need some cigarettes, and they won't give me none. I guess a beer would be just way too much for them." Mildred hadn't lost her bark or her bite.

"Mom, you're in a hospital, of course they're not going to give you cigarettes. In case you missed the report, you had what they believe is a mild heart attack. No more smoking for you." April had gotten closer to her mother's bed while Summer stayed comfortably back.

"Hell, when it's my time, it's my time, and when it's my time, I'm going with a cigarette in one hand and a beer in the other. To hell with the doctors and you, too, if you ain't gon' brang my cigarettes. Why you think I ast to see you two?" April recoiled as if she'd been bitten by a rattlesnake.

"Well, it's good to know your brush with death hasn't changed or softened you. You're still a bitter old woman. You know, Mama, if I was as close to meeting my maker as you are, I'd start at least thinking about some kind of redemption." April, who'd remained in contact with her mother, had managed to overlook the bitterness and tried her hardest to remain civil even in the most difficult times. Mildred never made it easy for her, but that didn't stop April from making sure that her mother had what she needed. April had never spoken to her mother in such a manner, even when her mother was at her most difficult.

April thought back to a few weeks ago when she confronted her mother about putting her out of the house because she was late returning home from work years ago. She'd known the conversation wouldn't be easy, but she wanted answers. When she'd approached the subject, Mildred was beyond her usual caustic self. "Mother, I just wanted to know why you would do such a thing. It was late, a bad neighborhood, anything could have happened to me."

"I followed you until you hailed that cab! You were too damn stubborn to apologize!"

"Me, apologize? For what, for missing the bus, or for the bus breaking down? You were the one who didn't want to listen to why I was late. All you wanted was to beat me senseless, take your frustrations out on me and I just wasn't having it that night. It was too much. Yes, I was wrong for hitting you back, but I was tired of the abuse."

"I said I followed you until you got in that cab, or are you so busy still blaming me that you ain't heard that part."

"No, I heard you, but the point is you put your daughter out of the house late at night, even if you did see me finally hail down the cab. You don't have any shame about that?"

"Anytime a woman think she can fight me in my house, I ain't got no shame about what happens to her."

"Not a woman, your young daughter, who until that time gave you all the respect in the world. Who never gave you a minute of trouble, who got good grades in school, a scholarship, and worked two part-time jobs to help out at home. Yes, you should have plenty of shame about the way you treated all your daughters." April sat and stared defiantly at her mother, who stared back equally defiantly.

"It don't really matter what you think. 'Cause thinking and knowing are two different thangs. You think you know how to raise three daughters in the city with no help? Your trifling daddy ran off with that woman…"

April interrupted her mother. "Please stop blaming Daddy for every bad thing you ever did to us. Take some responsibility for your actions."

Mildred sat up, fist balled, and her voice boomed, "What did you say? You must have forgotten how I knocked you on your ass that night. You ain't too big for me to beat, girl, you better show some respect."

"Mama, please, you aren't in any shape to threaten anybody, I'm not a little girl anymore. This conversation is over. I'm leaving. I'll call you in a few days." April stood up and gave her mother a kiss and a hug. It didn't soften Mildred, who maintained her defiant stance.

The thought of her mother getting riled up and threatening to knock her down was a little funny to April. It did make her smile, and at least her mother admitted to following her.

Now she was standing beside her mother in the hospital praying that she would recover fully. Clearing her throat April spoke with directness as she held her head high and stiff.

"I was going to save this for later, but now's as good a time as any. I've found Aunt May and Uncle Henry and they're coming to St. Louis for a visit. They were overjoyed to hear from me. I didn't tell them about the heart attack yet, and I wouldn't want you to run them off again, so if you want them to visit you, just let me know. Otherwise, they can visit with the rest of the family, including Daddy."

"What, who dug that fool up?" Mildred's voice was so laced with resentment both daughters decided to completely ignore her questions. They only looked at her and shook their heads.

April said, "I'll call you later, Mama, and if you want anything other than cigarettes and beer let me know. I'll be back tomorrow, so let me know if you want me to go by and bring anything from home to make your stay more comfortable." Mildred looked sheepishly at her daughter, and for the first time a trace of remorse may have been on her face. April smiled ever so briefly and kissed her mother's forehead. "I love you, Mama."

Looking at her mother's frail, alcohol-consumed body, Summer's heart softened. The alcohol had clearly ravished her once smooth café-au-lait skin, the skin under her eyes was dark, and her eyes looked too big for her face. Mildred Nelson had been a beautiful woman in her day; men fell at her feet and women constantly sneered at her because she was one of those women who knew she was beautiful and let you know she knew. But as she walked closer to the bed in silence, Summer wondered how she got into such a state. She knew at that instant she would never touch another drink of alcohol again. The loss was too great.

Mildred was being all that she knew to be, bitter and terminally, irrevocably mordant. Not even the love of a good man, children, a grandchild or the threat of death would soften or change her, she was what she was. Summer was convinced it was because of alcoholism.

Summer walked over to the bedside and took her mother's hand. "I'm sorry for whatever happened that made you so bitter, Mom. I love you, but I can't be around you when you act like this. I'll be back to see you."

Mildred softened and patted her daughter's hand. "Will you at least let me see my only grandbaby? I hear he's a good boy."

Summer was pleased. "Of course you can see him, you always could. I would never keep him from you. Andrew is here now if you'd like to spend some time with him. And if you'd like to spend more time with him, you may want to at least think about what the doctor said. I love you, too. Get some rest." Tears had pooled in Summer's eyes.

Mildred just nodded. "Good, I'd like to get to know him."

Summer slowly retreated and left the room, her eyes so full of tears by then she couldn't see, but some things were clearer in her mind than ever before. If her mother could treat her own children with such indifference one could only imagine what their father must have endured with such a bitter woman.

Despite the request to see her only grandchild, Summer knew that her mother could run hot and cold almost at will. She wanted her mother to know Andrew, but she remained skeptical. She would bring him tomorrow when she visited and pray that her mother would recover. The thought of seeing her Aunt May and Uncle Henry again brought much joy to her. She wiped away her tears, squared her shoulders and straightened her back, and, with a smile, headed toward the waiting room where she knew love awaited her.

Upon returning to the waiting room, Summer looked at her family, all lovingly in a huddle, chatting nonstop. Andrew had gotten a Coke and candy bar from the vending machines, which he knew was forbidden in her eyes, but she could find no fault with her son at that moment.

All she could find was love. He was listening intently to his grandfather with all the wonder a child should have for a grandparent. Suddenly in her mind she didn't care what LaFlair Cosmetics did. It didn't matter if she would start her own business or find a new job, it didn't matter that her mother was a bitter woman who probably never loved anyone, she didn't care that her father had left them so long ago, it didn't matter that she struggled through college with bologna sandwiches as her main dietary staple.

She finally knew in her heart that the only person responsible for her sister's death was the man who killed her. She and April had done all they could do to extricate Autumn from the man who would finally murder her in a drug-induced rage.

April looked at her sister as she returned, and knew that her pain and suffering was not without life-learned lessons. Lessons she would pass on to her son. Summer had finally shared her struggle of growing up in a household like the one she did with her son. April thought of her college years and the first time she heard the aphorism, "It doesn't matter where you start, it's where you finish that's important." She thought about the wonderful gifts she and Kenneth had given her sister. She felt herself becoming filled and complete with love. She may have been her mother's daughter, but she wasn't her mother. She was very capable of love.

* * *

Summer looked up and saw Marcus walking toward the group, then turned to look at her sister April. April's face lit up and Summer swore she could almost see the love on her sister's face. April and Marcus met with an embrace, said a few words and kissed passionately.

The group stopped their chattering and turned to look at the two. After noticing the silence, April turned toward the group with her hand holding on to his hand. The man smiled broadly as he enjoyed the feel of his hand in hers. Summer smiled as April beamed. "Everybody, I'd like for you all to meet Marcus Davis. Actually, it's Dr. Marcus Davis."

She suddenly had a confused look on her face as she turned to look at Marcus, who smiled and gave her a warm kiss on the cheek which encouraged her to continue. "Marcus and I are, are, well…we're…dating." She looked at Marcus and added, "Seriously dating." Marcus and April had more than dating on their minds as they looked deeply into each other's eyes and completely ignored everyone else. They finally broke their staring and looked at her family all gathered around, and they both blushed.

Almost as if on cue, the group began welcoming him. One by one April introduced everyone. The comfortable way in which he placed his arm around her waist, the look in his eyes when he looked at April made Summer know. He exchanged glances with Summer as if he knew what she was thinking. The man was truly in love with her sister—he wore it like a badge of honor. Summer saw it in his eyes. She smiled and thought, *The eyes always give you away.*

The two smiled, looking deeply into each other's eyes as though no one else was in the room. One would have had to be totally blind not to see the love in their eyes.

"One more thing." April looked at the group before

continuing and then turned her attention back to Marcus. "I said we were dating, however now we're planning a December wedding."

The group all sighed and happily congratulated the couple. The love and warmth in the room couldn't be denied. Summer wore a natural, radiant smile as she truly had what she needed and deserved, a loving family, and faith, and that was all she'd ever need. She deserved it as did everyone. Summer's time was now, her heart was filled with love and happiness as she lovingly stepped into the family huddle, hugging her father and half-sister. Looking at her husband she smiled, puckered her lips and blew him a kiss, then mouthed, "Do you know how much I love you?"

His eyes gleamed and he answered her with confidence, as only a longtime lover can, "Yes, I do."

During the quiet drive home Marcus looked over at April. "You know, we're going to have to stop meeting at hospitals." The two shared a quiet laugh.

"I think we should both take a vacation day tomorrow and spend time with each other." April knew that she had to make time for this incredibly wonderful man that she'd found at last.

Marcus pulled up to her house and turned off the ignition. "Are you sure?" His eyes beamed with anticipation, he was obviously enjoying the idea already.

"Yes, very sure." She smiled at his euphoria.

"We can spend the day doing whatever you want," he said to her, and smoothed her hair away from her face. He leaned over and gently kissed her lips.

When they parted she said breathlessly, "I want to stay in bed with you and listen to Etta singing, 'At Last.'" Her enigmatic smile was his undoing.

"Do we have to wait until tomorrow to do that?" He was caressing her arm with his hand and pleading with his eyes all at the same time.

"No. I think we should start tonight." Her voice was so low and seductive all he could do was open the car door and rush around to open her door. The sooner they got inside, the sooner they could get their night alone started.

He was eager to bury himself deep inside of her. Once inside, he turned to her and murmured, "At last."

Marcus popped the trunk and took out a briefcase and another bag.

"What's in there?" April pointed to the second bag.

"Wishfully thinking, I packed an overnight bag."

April laughed and leaned into him with a big-hearted kiss. She really had gone too long without this man, she thought.

April put the dogs in the basement, and when she returned upstairs Marcus was in the shower. She undressed and joined him. "Feel like company?"

He could almost feel himself salivate when he looked at her joining him. He took her and held her close, kissing her passionately.

"I take that as a yes," she said when they finally parted. She turned to begin showering, but he was too aroused to just watch. He caressed her back and began to plant tiny kisses on the side of her neck. They were both drenched by the time he turned her around to him. With ease, he picked her up and she wrapped her legs around him. He backed her against the shower wall and was fully aroused when he entered her. She moaned in delight with each thrust as she held him tightly.

Between marathon lovemaking sessions, April managed to call a retired veterinarian who occasionally covered for her when she needed. She apologized for the late hour, and he only laughed, "I'm retired, girl, I have nothing but time on my hands. I'll be there tomorrow." She invited him for dinner the following week and he accepted with enthusiasm.

She had met him years ago at a conference and despite their age difference they became friends. When he retired, he called and asked if she needed any part-time help. At the time her practice was just getting off the ground but she knew there would be times when she would need some help, so they came to an agreement.

He showed up at her house late one night. He told her he needed a huge favor, and from behind his back he brought a kitten. "I thought my dog would take a shine to him, but he's way too ornery. I'm afraid he's going to kill the poor thing." One look at Midnight, and April was taken.

Her next call was to Bridget to inform her as well. She told her that her mother had been hospitalized. True to form, Bridget assured her that she and Samantha would make sure everything ran smoothly. "Thanks, Bridget, I knew I can count on you and Sam."

"I hope your mother gets better."

"She will, even if I have to make her." April smiled and knew it was a tough order. She was sitting on the sofa when she heard Marcus walk up behind her.

He kissed the top of her head. "You okay?"

She smiled at him. "Couldn't be better."

He walked around, joined her on the sofa and wrapped his arm around her. She whispered, "Feel like some more Etta James?"

"I promise I'll always feel that way with you."

"Promise?"

"Promise." The two headed for the bedroom hand in hand.

* * *

The next morning April awoke to the smell of food. She looked over and saw that Marcus had gotten up. She got up to go to the bathroom, where she washed her face and brushed her hair. Marcus came in and said, "Back to bed, you. You're getting breakfast in bed."

"Really?"

"Yes." He took her by the hand and led her back to bed. He took the tray from the dresser and set it over her. She marveled at the meticulous way he served her. The food looked delicious and he had fresh daisies from her yard. They stood cheerfully in a vase.

She was quite touched by the gesture, and she put her hand over her heart. "I've never had breakfast in bed in my entire life."

"Well, get used to it, because it will be a weekly ritual for us." Marcus smiled broadly. His heart had melted at her reaction and he knew it was something she not only deserved, but something he needed to provide. He thought of the credit card commercial and said, "The cost of breakfast in bed, nominal. The smile on your face and the look in your eyes, priceless." He lifted her fork, speared a piece of fruit and brought it to her mouth.

After she chewed it she asked, "You're not going to feed me, too, are you?"

"No, but I just wanted to look at those luscious lips of yours working with that piece of fruit."

They both laughed. She took the fork and began eating.

Marcus went with April to the hospital to meet her mother. When April entered the room with him, Mildred sat up with her arms folded across her chest. "Who's that?"

"Hello, Mother. I'm fine—how are you feeling?"

Mildred ignored her as she continued to stare at Marcus.

"Mother, this is Marcus and he and I are engaged. We're planning a December wedding."

"Well, well, you finally caught one, a good-looking one, too." Mildred smiled as Marcus took her hand. "It's very nice to meet you, Mrs. Nelson."

Mildred's old self returned briefly. "I need to talk to you in private, April."

April only smiled and looked at her mother and then at Marcus. "Mom, he's going to be my husband, anything you want to say, you can say in front of him. We have no secrets."

Mildred looked at Marcus again. Marcus walked to the other side of the room and sat in a chair while April sat at the side of the bed next to her mother. April took her mother's hand. "What is it?"

"This ain't easy, but I want you to know that a long time ago, I was madly in love with your Uncle Henry. I met him my second year in high school, and we went together for several months. I made the mistake of bringing May along on one of our dates, and well, evidently he fell madly in love with her. They were older, and seemed to have more in common, but I thought since he was my boyfriend, it didn't matter. Of course, I was the last to know. They snuck around behind my back for months, and when he finally fessed up, he told me they were getting married."

April gasped. She never suspected anything. She rubbed her mother's hand. "I'm so sorry. I can only imagine how painful that must have been for you."

Mildred took April's hand in hers for the first time in years. "Trust me when I say you can't really imagine. I secretly carried around hatred for both of them for years. I started drinking right after that. I dropped out of school, married your father on the rebound. I never really loved him. I thought in time I would grow to love him because he was a good man, but that just didn't happen. I never loved a man like I did Henry. Whenever I looked at you girls, all I ever saw was your father and wondered what could have been if I'd married the man I wanted. Years of drinking just made me more bitter. I know I wasn't much of a mother to you. I was very young and very stupid."

April released a breath that she didn't realize she was holding. Finally, some honesty from her mother.

"Thanks for sharing that with me. I know how incredibly difficult that must have been for you."

Mildred looked over at Marcus. "Young man, I saw the way you looked at my daughter, I know you'll be good for her. I've had enough bad men in my life to know a good one when I see one."

Marcus walked over and kissed her on the forehead. "I'll be better than good to her."

Mildred smiled at April, who returned the smile. "Do you mind telling that to Summer? I know she won't ever forgive me, but I'd like for her to know. She's too much like me, always being secretive. She's stubborn, like me."

"Mother, I think that's something you should tell her yourself. She told me she was coming to see you today with Andrew. This family doesn't need any more secrets."

Mildred could only nod in agreement. "So, tell me, Marcus, what do you do for a living?"

Chapter 21

On a crisp December Saturday morning, the small church was packed with family and friends. The stepmother and natural mother sat side-by-side, and much to everyone's delight, Mildred was civil. She held her grandson's hand and a small smile made its way to her face.

The crowd began to mumble when the pianist began to play "At Last," instead of the traditional bridal song. Only Summer knew the true significance of the song for the soon-to-be husband and wife. The others knew April wasn't much of a traditionalist, so the mumbles quieted and the wedding party made its way down the aisle. June was a member of the party. She had grown to love them as they spent time talking and shopping. She had secretly dreamed of the day when she could spend time with them. They were more loving than she could have imagined. She was embraced by the family, and even though Mildred was surprised by her the first time they met, she gave her a tiny hug.

The wedding party was dressed in silk chiffon and silk

charmeuse dresses with empire waists. The bride entered with
her proud father; she was dressed in a beautiful off-white silk
crepe gown. The gown was designed especially for her by one
of the residents of her South side neighborhood, who owned
a vintage wedding store.

Collective sighs were heard when she began her walk down
the aisle. April had never looked more beautiful.

April looked to her right and saw Donald and Brianna,
sitting arm in arm. Both looked at her and offered a smile.
Donald mouthed, "Thank you."

The newlyweds had in some form or fashion touched the
lives of everyone in attendance.

Marcus stood tall and proud as he watched her make her
way to him. Her father gave him her hand, and he took it. Their
eyes told each other they'd love one another an eternity. They
had written their own vows, and by the end of the ceremony,
everyone there knew this was truly a union of bliss. As they
left the church, Bridget caught the beautiful wedding bouquet
of pink amaryllis with white and soft pink varieties of roses,
and was ecstatic. She was in attendance with a man that she
had sworn to April was "The One."

The reception was packed with friends and family. April
loved her in-laws immediately when she met them. They were
warm and loving parents, and embraced their new daughter-
in-law. April was happier than she could have ever imagined.
Whenever she looked at Marcus her heart would pound.

Uncle Henry and Aunt May had flown in from Cleveland
and had gotten to spend time with Mildred. Although the
initial meeting was cool, as the evening progressed the three
of them could be seen and heard laughing and sharing
memories of old times.

April was excited when Nia came over to her while talking
with Marcus and his parents. "Look who wants to see you,"

she purred as she handed April the baby. She was a precious bundle that April took without reservation. "Isn't she adorable?" her mother-in-law offered.

"Yes, she is," April replied. The group watched as she rocked and sang a soft lullaby, cradling the baby in her arms. Marcus knew of April's concern about being a mother, but he also knew that she was full of love and was going to be a wonderful mother. He watched as she returned the infant to her mother.

The couple was congratulated and offered good wishes by family and friends throughout the evening. Marcus and April occasionally stole away for a few minutes to be alone. They enjoyed a quick, intimate kiss and embrace but returned. As they neared the ending of the reception, they were more than eager to start their wedding night.

Mildred walked to the bandstand after several guests had wished the couple well toward the end of the reception. Summer was the first to see her ask for the microphone and she immediately became nervous. Mildred had not had a drink all evening, and had been civil to everyone, so Summer made no attempts to stop her mother.

Mildred tapped the mike and began speaking once she was satisfied she could be heard. "I would just like to say, that despite all that has occurred between me and my daughters, I am so proud to be their mother. I can't say I was much of a mother to them when they were younger, and I have to make amends for that. Despite it all, they have turned into fine, brilliant young women. I'm sorry I can't take any of the credit for it, which makes the fact that they turned out the way they did even more amazing to me and to anyone who knows them and their story. God will bless each of you for the support you've shown my daughters, and to my two son-in-laws, God will bless you most of all. God will bless you for having the courage and strength to hold their hands in their darkest hours when I'm sure it was not easy for them to be girlfriends, wives, aunts, lovers and mothers without any help or guidance from me."

With tears flowing freely from her face, Mildred softly dabbed at them and continued. "I love you both and I plan to spend what little time I may have left making up what I missed as a mother and grandmother."

There were plenty of tears and applause as the attendees were moved. They understood how difficult it must have been for Mildred, even though most had never met her before today.

April blinked as she watched her mother, thankful for this amazing transformation. She looked over and saw Carmen standing proudly with her hands clasped together as if she were praying. Her eyes were on Mildred and April knew that somehow it was her doing.

Carmen was there and smiled at the progress she had made. She didn't tell anyone about the conversations she'd had with Mildred. Carmen began the quest to try and put her friend's fractured family together a piece at a time. She made contact with Mildred by visiting her at home, explaining who she was and why she was there. Mildred was her usual caustic and cynical self at first, but soon became relaxed and began enjoying the visits. She wasn't judged, she was allowed to talk when she wanted, and didn't say a word when she didn't. She grew to look forward to the visits, and the first step she took was to join Alcoholics Anonymous. Carmen went with her to the first three meetings, and then Mildred found a sponsor. It was not an easy road, but she had begun. Today she was happy; she was there to see her daughter get married and was even happier to spend time being a grandmother. She realized she had missed so much, and hoped that she could make some of it up by being a good grandmother.

* * *

Marcus was standing beside April and pulled her closer to him. "I think your family's on the mend." Looking at her, he saw the tears starting to swell in her eyes. He watched in agony as they began to fall, then gently wiped them away. "I know they're happy tears, but it hurts me to see you cry."

April allowed him to wipe them away, and then shook her head, grabbed his hand and led him onto the dance floor. "Oh, come on, I think you still owe me a dance."

"There will be plenty of time for dancing, go talk to your mother."

"Do I gotta?" She playfully pouted, but was proud to have a man that knew how to unselfishly give to others.

"Yeah, you gotta. I'll come over in a minute. Let you two have some alone time first." He kissed her lips, and she smiled.

"Hmm, I want more of that."

"Don't worry, there's plenty for you."

There were no words spoken as April and Summer joined their mother near the bandstand. They all embraced for the first time in memory, and there were happy tears flowing freely. Finally Mildred spoke. "All I can say is that I'm so sorry for what I've done. I'm sorry and ashamed." April and Summer continued to hug their mother.

April and Marcus spent the night in the honeymoon suite at the B and B before leaving for their honeymoon in Tahiti. He waited patiently for April to come out of the bathroom, and he was delighted when he saw her. She had splurged on a beautiful peach silk negligee that clung to her and revealed all the curves he loved. He smelled the soft scent of jasmine and motioned for her to join him on the bed.

He sat eagerly in a pair of black silk pajama pants. She was amazed at the sculpted perfection of his body. His chest called out to her, and she thought about the times she'd simply rested her head on it. He was truly built for loving, she thought...her loving.

Once she was in his embrace, he claimed her lush, waiting mouth with his. He held her face with both hands as he kissed her face, her nose, cheeks, eyes and her lips again. He gently carried the trail of kisses down her throat, eliciting a low deep moan from her.

He fingered the silk shoulder straps as he made his way down to the swell of her breasts and began to unbutton the tiny pearl buttons. He took his time, and she waited breathlessly. When his mouth claimed her left breast, she clung to him and called his name. He answered, but continued as he moved to her right breast. He teased her nipple with his lips before fully claiming it and she drew him closer to her. He continued down her stomach, kissing and teasing along the way. She moaned again and then reached and pulled him back to her face, where she whispered to him, "At last."

Dear Reader:

I sincerely enjoyed bringing you *At Last* and I look forward to bringing you more romance and exciting reading in my next novel. If you'd like to share your thoughts or comments, you may contact me at carolynj@nothnbut.net. Thanks to the many wonderful readers who contacted me after reading my last novel.

Peace and blessings,

Carolyn Neal